Saving Fable

TALESPINNERS

Saving Fable

SCOTT REINTGEN

Crown Books for Young Readers
New York

Text copyright © 2019 by Scott Reintgen
Jacket art copyright © 2019 by Maike Plenzke

All rights reserved. Published in the United States by Crown Books for Young Readers, an imprint of Random House Children's Books, a division of Penguin Random House LLC, New York.

Crown and the colophon are registered trademarks of Penguin Random House LLC.

Visit us on the Web! rhcbooks.com

Educators and librarians, for a variety of teaching tools, visit us at RHTeachersLibrarians.com

Library of Congress Cataloging-in-Publication Data
Names: Reintgen, Scott, author.
Title: Talespinners: Saving Fable / Scott Reintgen.
Description: First edition. | New York: Crown Books for Young Readers, [2019] |
Summary: Indira Story grew up in Origin, yearning to be the hero of her own story, but after finally being chosen to attend Protagonist Preparatory, she learns that side characters can be heroes, too.
Identifiers: LCCN 2018057026 | ISBN 978-0-525-64668-6 (hc) |
ISBN 978-0-525-64669-3 (glb) | ISBN 978-0-525-64670-9 (epub)
Subjects: | CYAC: Books and reading—Fiction. | Adventure and adventurers—Fiction. | Heroes—Fiction. | Fantasy.
Classification: LCC PZ7.1.R4554 Tal 2019 | DDC [Fic]—dc23

Printed in the United States of America
10 9 8 7 6 5 4 3 2 1
First Edition

To all the heroes
who started out thinking
they were side characters

Contents

When in Fable,
do as the Fablefolk do.
—St. Imaginate

1

The Last Chance

Once a week, Indira Story woke up *early*.

Like before-the-sunrise early. Stars-still-in-the-sky early. I'm sure you know the feeling, my dear reader. The bed is warm. The floor is cold. Even the moon watches you, one eyebrow raised, a little unsure why anyone would get up at that hour. If you know the feeling, then you know exactly how Indira felt as she got ready that morning.

She lit a single candle in the corner of her shack and started getting dressed. It was one of the few times that having just one outfit to her name came in handy. Even in the semidark, she never ended up putting on mismatched clothes, because these were her *only* clothes. She slid instinctually into a pink homespun shirt. The tunic was cinched at the waist by a well-worn leather belt, from which a silver hammer hung.

She packed her bag with the two biscuits she'd saved from the day before. Her stomach growled a little because of the skipped meal, but she knew from experience that it was worth it. All packed up, she snuffed her candle and slipped quietly outside. The stars twinkled overhead.

Indira walked beneath their gentle glow, moving past a row of identical shacks. All the other characters-in-waiting were asleep at this hour. She might catch an early riser or two practicing monologues, but most of them were dreaming of other worlds.

She made her way down to the village proper. There were always a few people huddled by the docks. At this point, the morning crew recognized her. She received a few tired hat tips or mumbled greetings as a boat drifted toward them. Indira nodded in return before waiting her turn to climb aboard.

It was a short trip. The boat ferried travelers from Origin—her hometown—to the neighboring town of Quiver. If you were out at sea, looking at the two towns side by side, it would be hard to tell which was which. Both cities had hunched buildings, their roofs decorated with green stones that looked almost like fish scales. Even the docks looked identical.

But Indira had learned to recognize the differences. Origin was a hopeful place. It was full of characters who could still be chosen, who were still waiting to be invited to Fable to be trained at Protagonist Preparatory. Quiver, on the other hand, was populated by characters who *hadn't* been chosen. Characters like her brother.

Indira disembarked with the other travelers. Quiver's streets felt particularly abandoned and sad this morning. Indira always shivered a little as she navigated through the alleys, following the familiar turns to reach her brother's apartment. The door looked more like the entrance to a cupboard than an apartment, but Indira kept that thought to herself.

She knocked twice. "Pizza delivery service!"

Inside, there was rustling. It took another second of fiddling for her brother to work the stubborn lock open. The door gave a ghostly groan. David looked out at her sleepily. The two of them were *clearly* related. Both boasted the same amber-brown skin, dark hair that never behaved, and wide cheeks that—unfortunately—old ladies always wanted to pinch.

"Pizza?" David asked skeptically. "You don't really have pizza, do you?"

Indira grinned before sliding past him and into the cramped apartment.

"We can pretend it's pizza," Indira said. "Just like we can *pretend* your door isn't haunted by a ghost that was obviously murdered here and now seeks vengeance."

David closed the door, and it offered another ghoulish groan.

"I thought we agreed the ghost was cursed by a witch," he said.

Indira removed the biscuits she'd saved from the day before and set them on the table. A quick glance showed that David had not taken her advice from their last visit. The whole place was a mess. She gestured for him to take a seat. "Eat up before the ghost takes your biscuit."

As he took a seat, she set to work on the apartment. She picked up clothes that looked relatively clean and folded them in a stack in one corner. She ushered stray wrappers into an overflowing trash can. She even found an abandoned plate wedged under the mattress. Behind her, David let out a satisfied noise as he took his first bite of the delivered biscuit.

"I miss the food over there," he said with a full mouth.

She finished tidying up and took the seat across from him. His eyes closed as he took a second bite. She noticed the way his shoulders hunched. He also had a few bruises running down one arm. David was only a few years older than her, but he looked so very tired.

"How's everything going, D?"

He finished chewing. "Long hours, but it's fine. I got promoted this week."

She raised an eyebrow. "Promoted? That's great."

He nodded. "Going deeper into the mine now. I have my own team and everything. We get assigned to some of the trickier story nuggets buried in there. You know the routine. We excavate the nugget. Another team refines the story idea. And then it's straight to the Authors!" He smiled a little. "Without us, there'd barely be any stories at all!"

Indira nodded along. She had heard David talk about all of this before. It was a good thing, she realized, that he had such a positive attitude. David liked to think of their world as one big system. Indira knew that his bosses preached about it all the time. Stories were a team effort. Everyone had an important part to play in creating them. But she also remembered how badly David had wanted to be an *actual* character in a story. Her brother was living proof that not everyone was chosen.

"Anyways," he was saying, "what about you? Training hard?"

Instead of answering, Indira dug through her backpack. There was a little slip of paper buried at the bottom. She unfolded it and passed it across the table to David.

His eyes went wide. "Oh, Indira! I'm so sorry."

It was the same eviction notice that David had been given a few years before. If a character-in-waiting lived in Origin for too long without being chosen, room had to be made for other characters. Indira hadn't realized just how long she'd spent in Origin until she'd opened her little mailbox one morning and found the slip waiting with her breakfast biscuit.

"I'm only going to get one more chance now, D. If I'm not chosen this time around . . ."

She couldn't bring herself to look him in the eye. If she wasn't chosen this time, she'd end up in Quiver like him. Working a hard job. A part of the system, sure, but not training to be a character in an *actual* story. She'd spent

5

so long dreaming of that future that she wasn't sure how she'd bring herself to accept anything else. David walked around the table. He went down on one knee so that she couldn't avoid looking at him. There was a fierceness in the look he gave her.

"You've *got* this. I'm not sure why it's taken so long, Indira. But you *will* be chosen. Look, I'm cut out for this kind of work. I like it just fine. But you? You're supposed to be a hero. I can feel it in my bones, baby sister. You're meant for more than this."

His words cut through her fears. Indira allowed herself a smile, and David swept in for a quick kiss on the cheek. "I don't know when the next selection round will be," he said. "But fight for it. I—I don't want you to come back here. No more visits. I'm doing fine. I want you focused. Train until your bones ache, yeah? Put your nose to the grindstone. Got me?"

"David. I'm not just going to *abandon* you."

He smiled back at her. "You're not welcome here! Get lost!"

She couldn't help grinning. David always seemed to know the right thing to say. She watched as he unwrapped the other biscuit and handed it to her. He lifted his own in the air to offer up a proper toast. "To our last biscuit together! And to Indira Story, a hero in the making."

The two of them bumped biscuits. Indira did her best to smile and laugh, but as David got ready to go to work, she felt a little thread of fear snaking back through her.

She couldn't stand the idea of leaving her brother behind, but beneath that fear was a deeper one. What if she wasn't chosen? What if she had to join her brother in Quiver forever?

She gave David a hug and found it hard to let go. He finally pulled away and winked at her like it wasn't a big deal, like this might not be the last time they'd ever see each other. She watched him join the growing stream of workers heading out for the morning. He waved back at her once and flexed an arm. It was a reminder. *Be strong. Fight.* She almost started crying as she nodded back, and then he vanished around a corner, lost in the crowd.

Indira walked back toward the docks. At first, she convinced herself that she was going to ignore David's request not to return. Of course she'd come back and visit her brother. But as she looked out over the dawn-lit ocean, she realized David was right. She needed to focus.

This was her last chance.

"I'll be back," she whispered. "But only when I find a story big enough for *both* of us."

And with that, she made her way back home.

2

The Author Borealis

Peeve Meadows was playing the guitar. Again.

Indira curled beneath a blanket, one house over, trying her best to not allow the strangled music to steal her precious sleep. Life in Origin offered very little comfort. Each of the characters-in-waiting assigned to the coastal town enjoyed the following: a private room, a comfortable bed, and a view of the sea. And right now, Peeve Meadows was ruining Indira's favorite of the three.

Indira rolled out of bed with a groan. She did the same thing she did *every* morning that she wasn't visiting David, the same thing that every character in Origin would do as soon as they woke up: she looked out the window.

Her shack offered a porthole view of the sea. Great crashing waves, a rocky shoreline, and the town's rustic harbor. But Indira looked out past those things. They were just background noise. Every character set their eyes on the distant sky, hoping beyond hope to see the arrival of the Author Borealis.

"Just clouds," Indira said, rubbing her window with a sleeve. "Almost always clouds."

She sighed before heading outside, eager for breakfast. Her door opened on rusting hinges. She let it swing hard into the side of her shack, hoping the noise would give Peeve an idea of just how loud *she* was being. Indira walked out to the mailbox that was assigned to her decrepit shack. She popped the back of it with a fist, and the broken front came snapping open. Inside, she found a wrapped biscuit smothered in honey.

A glance showed Peeve Meadows striding over from her identical shack with a smile on her face. Indira thought it was a little early in the day for smiling.

"Good morning!" Peeve said. "Trying out a new song. I think I'm getting the hang of it."

Indira took another bite. "They say practice makes perfect."

"Exactly," Peeve said, smiling again. "I thought it would make me a more rounded character, you know? If I don't know how to play an instrument, I'm automatically disqualified from any stories about music. The teachers are always telling us to broaden our horizons!"

That was the standard instruction. The same advice Indira had heard every day she'd lived in Origin. Local teachers taught the characters-in-waiting to broaden their horizons. Become more well-rounded individuals. Develop interests and quirks. Anything to catch the eye of a potential Author. *All it takes is one detail! One little thing to set off your beacon and earn your way to Protagonist Preparatory!*

"Good idea," Indira said, trying not to sound *too* sarcastic. "Maybe I should take up the piccolo."

She took a final bite of her biscuit before stuffing the wrapping back inside her mailbox. A single road led past all the identical shacks, curving ever so slightly out of view. Indira stretched her tired limbs and started off at a jog.

"Where are you going?" Peeve called.

"For a run," Indira answered. "Broadening my horizons."

The characters that called Origin home had thousands of strategies and rituals and myths for getting noticed by the Authors. But Indira had been in Origin for years, and none of them seemed to work. Peeve was her newest neighbor. Indira shook her head, remembering that the Author Borealis had chosen the person living in that particular house *four* times now. She hadn't even really bothered getting to know Peeve. It seemed unfair, but before long, one of them would be gone. Really, Indira was leaving either way.

She just hoped her destination would be Fable.

When the most recent borealis had come and gone, Indira had decided to take matters into her own hands. Why wait for magical lights to choose her? She would train. She would outwork everyone else. She'd scrape and claw to become the character she knew she had always had the potential to be. Her talk with David had given her one more reason to fight.

Indira's run took her past shack after identical shack. At this point, she could close her eyes and *still* see the squat little buildings. Each home had a white door, always built into the left side of the structure. Every single roof slanted the same way, with the end above the door frame higher by just a few feet. Each building was only big enough for a bed, a small desk, and an even smaller bathing area.

But the most important feature extended from the roof of the building: a rusted circle of metal, no bigger than a basketball. Unlit, the beacons didn't look like much. Indira jogged by, noting cobwebs and discolorations on each of them. Every single character who lived in Origin knew that a lit beacon was their ticket out. When the Author Borealis came, a handful of characters were chosen. If the beacon above their shack glowed green, it was a sign that they had potential, that there might be a story brewing in the mind of an Author with room for a character like them.

It wasn't a guarantee they'd get into a story, but it was an invitation to the city where every great character eventually made their way—the city of Fable.

Indira rounded the corner of their village and began a tough, uphill stretch. She enjoyed losing herself in the winding hills and trails. She tugged down the collar of her pink homespun shirt as she ran. Her one-handed war hammer bounced against her hip. She always ran with the weapon hanging from her belt loop, just in case she needed it.

She reached the high point of their coastal valley—an empty hillside that offered her favorite view of Origin. It wasn't much, but it was all she had ever known. She wiped sweat from her forehead and looked out over the scene.

Waves crashed along the shore. Characters stood in front of their shacks—some she recognized and others she didn't. It was almost impossible to make friends in Origin. Too much coming and going. By the time you knew someone's name, they were heading somewhere else. About half the kids who came through ended up in Fable eventually. The rest were shipped out to working towns like the one David lived in.

It took a few seconds to notice that the normal chaos of the town was absent this morning. Indira squinted. All the characters were standing at attention. That could only mean . . .

Indira's eyes flicked up to the distant sky.

The gray clouds had given way to something bright, something far more hopeful. She saw the color blue first, spiraling out over the sea, followed by sapphire and periwinkle and fuchsia. The brightest, most impossible colors she'd ever seen: the Author Borealis had come.

Indira's chest heaved as bells started to ring. "No," she said. "No, no, no . . ."

It wasn't possible. The borealis had come—it did that,

sneaking into the sky as if it had always been there—but how had an emissary from Fable *already* arrived? That wasn't possible!

She started sprinting, desperate not to miss her chance. The bells continued ringing. The distant borealis crept over the ocean, making its way over the land. The colorful tendrils danced above the coastal shacks, draping the sky with the loveliest infusions of color.

She nearly fell twice, taking steep corners far too quickly, but managed to reach the main row without more than a few bruises and scrapes. Other characters went wide-eyed as she came vaulting past them.

In the distance, she saw a figure walking up the street. Like all the emissaries who had ever visited their town, the man looked as if he'd just come from a business meeting. A neat suit, a fine briefcase, a striped tie. He made his careful way down the rows as Indira sprinted, trying to get back to her shack in time. There were flashes of bright green on her left and right.

Beacons were lit. Characters had been chosen!

Ahead, the emissary had paused right in front of *her* shack. He removed a clipboard and was noting something to himself. Hearing Indira's approaching footsteps, he looked up.

Indira was too breathless to say anything. From all her frantic running, but also because of the sight of the little beacon *glowing* above her shack. She had actually been chosen this time. David's prediction had come true. She was going to Fable. She stared at it, mouth hanging open, for several seconds.

Until another surprise knocked the breath from her lungs.

Peeve Meadows was standing in front of Indira's shack as if *she* lived there.

3

The Lying Beacon

That was where Indira should have been standing.

There was a brief and terrible moment where Indira thought she'd simply gotten the count wrong. In all the confusion, maybe she'd mistaken Peeve's house for her own. But a glance over Peeve's shoulder showed Indira a familiar unmade bed, all the books she'd borrowed from the library. It was definitely her shack. Peeve was trying to steal her chance.

"What do you think you're doing?" she asked.

Peeve avoided eye contact, shifting the weight of her packed guitar to the opposite shoulder as she stared instead at Fable's emissary.

Indira shook her head. "Seriously? Peeve, you know this is my shack."

The emissary finally looked up and took in the scene.

"Hello there. Dexter DuBrow, emissary of Fable. I'm sorry, but what's going on here?"

Indira's fingers itched for her hammer. Instead she pointed. "Peeve is standing in front of *my* shack. She must have seen the beacon light up. She's trying to steal my invitation."

Dexter considered both of them. "Is that true?"

Peeve shrugged. "No, sir, I'm not sure what she's talking about."

"No?" Indira asked angrily. "How many houses are you from the end of the row?"

Peeve started to glance to her left, but Indira snapped her fingers.

"Without looking, Peeve. Go ahead. If this were *really* your home, you'd know."

Indira felt a moment of guilt as Peeve's cheeks turned bright red. The girl glanced down at her feet, no doubt trying to remember the houses she'd never bothered to count, because Peeve had only lived there for a few months. She hadn't been there for years as Indira had . . .

"You'd know it's number seventeen from this end." Indira pointed east. "And you'd know it's number two hundred eighty-nine from that end. I know that because it's my house, Peeve. I've lived here long enough, waited long enough, to be chosen to go to Fable. You won't steal that from me."

Peeve withered, hearing that. The girl pulled the strap of her guitar over one shoulder and skulked back to her own shack. A thousand knots in Indira's stomach loosened as she took her rightful place in front of the lit beacon.

"Good monologue," Dexter said. "I'm noting that. Your name?"

"Indira," she said. "My name is Indira Story."

He nodded. "Okay, I've got you noted for that little speech, but I've also noted that you were absent from your post. A potentially unreliable narrator? If you had been on time, after all, wouldn't we have avoided this whole scene?"

Indira stared. "I mean . . . I was just going for a run. . . ."

He wrote that down too. "I have to finish my head count. When the bells stop ringing, meet me at the center of town. We've arranged travel for all the chosen characters."

Indira watched him walk away, and even her anger at Peeve couldn't steal the joy of that moment. The Author Borealis had *finally* chosen her. Somewhere out there, an Author was writing a story that had room for a character like her in it.

She was *actually* going to Fable.

Grinning from ear to ear, she rushed back inside to pack her things.

4

The Chosen Characters

Indira closed the door to her little shack. She set a hand on the frame, picking one more time at the peeling paint, before steadying herself and walking through the ranks of other characters-in-waiting. What was her title now? If all went to plan, she supposed she was about to become a character-in-*training*. The thought had her heart beating faster than ever.

Most of the characters who hadn't been chosen were back at their everyday activities: trading breakfast rations or arguing about the best ways to get noticed by an Author. Indira saw Peeve sitting on her front stoop looking frustrated. She felt just a little guilty before remembering she wasn't the one who had tried to *lie* her way into Fable.

As she walked, Indira tried to look the other unchosen characters in the eye and nod encouragement to each of them. She knew from experience, though: it always hurt to watch another character head off for the place you were dreaming of going.

The shacks grew fewer and fewer as she made her way to the town center. Origin's "downtown" was just a gathering of hunchbacked old buildings, their frames distorted, once-bright colors faded.

A pair of characters waited on one corner, standing in awkward silence. There was a pale redheaded boy wearing threadbare wizard robes. In front of him stood a rather tall girl with dark brown skin. She fluttered long lashes in Indira's direction before pretending not to have looked.

Indira walked over and took her place at the back of the group. It should have been exciting enough to be chosen, but Indira couldn't help comparing herself to the other two chosen characters. The tall girl was *really* pretty. And the red-haired boy seemed so *mysterious*. She'd been chosen, sure, but how could she make it in a story with competition like this?

Indira forced herself to take a deep, steadying breath. *I was chosen,* she reminded herself, *I belong here just as much as they do.*

A few minutes passed as they waited for the emissary — Dexter DuBrow — to join them. The girl with the long eyelashes looked back a few times but always turned away, tapping an impatient foot. Indira noticed the redheaded boy sneaking a glance back too. Even though his bangs covered his forehead, they weren't so low that Indira couldn't see his eyes. She hadn't noticed before, but now she couldn't stop noticing. His irises smoldered with actual flames.

For some reason, Indira liked him immediately.

She reached out and tapped his shoulder. "Hey, what's your name?" she asked.

The floodgates opened.

"I'm Phoenix. Like the bird. The fire bird. With fire."

He thumbed the sleeve of his robe nervously. She smiled a little and guessed that maybe he hadn't talked with other characters very often. "Just Phoenix?"

He shrugged. "Got nervous. Forgot to ask for a last name. What about you?"

"Indira Story."

The girl swung around at that. "I *love* that name. Say it again."

Indira gave her a funny look. "Indira Story."

"I could just melt," the girl announced, batting her long eyelashes. "I really could. *Indira*. That name sounds like a fashion statement. If you were a style, I'd wear you. Not even kidding."

Indira stared back, unsure how she should respond. Phoenix came to her rescue.

"And, you—what, uh—what's your name?" he asked the other girl.

"Maxine Maydragon," she answered, all confidence. "But my friends call me Maxi."

"Friends?" Indira asked.

"Well, that's *obvi*. You two!"

Maxi slid one arm around Phoenix's shoulder. He looked profoundly uncomfortable in her grasp, but the pose didn't last long. Maxi let out a little gasp and released him.

"You're like hot lava!"

He held out one hand, and an actual flame flickered into his palm.

"That's kind of what I do."

Maxi thought that was just the *coolest* thing in the world. Indira was about to say that she thought it was really cool too, but a gasp of dust came shooting out of the nearest alleyway. Peeve Meadows sprinted around the corner. "Wait! I've been chosen too! Wait!"

Indira watched as the poor girl's foot caught on the uneven cobblestones. It all happened in slow motion. Peeve sprawled through the air, golden hair flying out, a faceplant inevitable. Indira's instincts took over.

In less than a breath, she dove forward. Her path intercepted Peeve's. She wrapped her hands around the girl and at the same time began twisting, angled so that her back struck the cobblestones. Peeve's weight came slinging around on top of her. As the dust settled, Indira knew the worst had been avoided. She was a little out of breath and would probably have a bruise, but neither of them had been hurt badly. Peeve rolled to one side.

And that was when Maxi exploded with excitement. She thought it was just, like, the coolest thing she'd ever seen. Phoenix raised a single, curious eyebrow that had Indira blushing.

"Thanks," Peeve muttered. "That was a close one."

"No problem," Indira said. "I'm not sure how I did that. Good instincts, I guess."

"Good instincts indeed," a voice said. The crew looked up as Dexter DuBrow rounded a corner. He was still scribbling busily away in his notebook. "I'll note those as well!"

The group shuffled together, trying to form a more organized line. Indira saw Dexter look up long enough to assess the group. He nodded at each of them, glancing back at his notes, before his eyes fixed on Peeve. He frowned. "You again? I thought we discussed this. . . ."

Peeve's nostrils flared in frustration. She pointed a stubborn finger back to the cliffs above them. Indira traced the distant houses, no bigger than dots from below, and saw two glowing beacons where she knew her little shack stood.

"I don't know why it was late," Peeve said. "But I'm coming to Fable too."

Dexter glanced at his notes. "That's not . . . the only reason . . . Let me check something."

They all waited as he flipped through his satchel. It seemed to hold an endless amount of half-crumpled documents. Indira glanced at Peeve and felt bad for her. The girl was sweating nervously. Even if she had tried to cheat Indira, it wasn't hard to imagine the heartbreak of being *chosen* only to be rejected on a technicality. What if Dexter didn't let her come?

"Ah!" Dexter held up a finger. "Very well. It seems you *are* coming, by a different road. Very rare, but I'll explain all that later. Well, that's settled. We have four departures prepared."

Peeve let out a massive sigh of relief. Indira watched the emissary dig through his bag again. He pulled out a square tile of flawless glass—and Indira couldn't help noting that it was *far* too large to fit inside the satchel. Dexter set the glass down carefully on the flattest surface he could find. When he had it positioned just so, he politely knocked on it. Indira thought that was a really strange thing to do, until a knock answered back. The clear glass filled with color—a gorgeous turquoise.

"What *is* that?" Maxi asked.

"Dragoneye," Dexter replied. "As I mentioned before, my name is Dexter DuBrow. The official welcoming party. Congratulations on being chosen by the Authors. Fable welcomes you with open arms. All of you will be meeting up with your mentors before visiting the city. The dragoneye is the fastest way to your various destinations."

A dark slit opened in the square's center. Indira thought she heard a distant rumble as the bright blue parted like a curtain. *No*, she realized, *like an eyelid*. A great marble of an eye was staring out from the tile. Patterns of gold wove like bright rivers through a backdrop of forest green. A voice spoke from somewhere deeper than stones or bones.

"Come now," it boomed. "I haven't all day."

Dexter clapped his hands together. "It's very simple. Step onto the glass and answer the question. You'll be whisked away to your proper location straightaway. Phoenix is first."

Indira watched her new friend situate himself carefully atop the glass. He took a steadying breath and nodded over at the emissary. The deep and booming voice sounded again.

"Why are you sweating?"

Phoenix glanced back, eyes locking briefly on Indira. "I'm nervous, I guess."

Indira's stomach did a backflip. The answer was as surprising as Phoenix's sudden absence. The great eye winked shut, and her new friend vanished.

"What the *what*?" Maxi cried.

"He just teleported!" Peeve shouted. "This is amazing!"

Dexter gestured for Maxi to come forward next. The girl looked like a queen, her chin tilted as if she owned the world. The great blue eye opened beneath her feet.

Indira was so excited by the prospect of teleporting to some other place that she missed the question the dragon asked. One second Maxi was there; the next second she was gone.

At Dexter's signal, Indira stepped onto the square. Excitement raced through her. She was *really* going to Fable. A quick image of David leaped into her mind. She thought he would be proud of her. It felt strange to leave him behind, but deep down she knew she wasn't really leaving him. She was going to start a new life. She'd find a story big enough for both of them.

Indira looked down as the great dragon eye opened for a third time.

"If you could be any animal, what would you be?"

Indira shrugged. "Anything that flies."

—

Now we must pause, dear reader.

I must ask you a rather demanding favor. I would like for you to hold your breath. Go ahead. The story won't vanish. Indira will be right where you left—well, not quite where you left her, but that's a minor detail. So hold your breath and count to fifteen. I'll wait. . . .

. . . All right. Did you feel your heart start to pump and your lungs start to burn and your brain start to protest? Well, that's *exactly* how Indira felt as the dragoneye sucked her right up. She heard the quietest whisper, saw a flash of blue, and felt a gentle, chest-centered tug.

And just like that she was *elsewhere*.

5

Deus

*E*very cage has a key.

Those were the first words she heard. Indira's eyes opened to cradle-blue sky. She felt soft and new. Everything looked a little too bright, every sound a little too sharp. The words echoed in her head and stretched across the sky as chalk-white clouds. Indira started to read the cumulous letters aloud:

"Every cage . . ."

Indira couldn't finish the sentence. It felt as though her lungs hadn't managed to fill up with enough air yet. She took a few seconds just to *breathe*. After a minute, Indira pushed to her feet. She brushed dirt off her shirt.

Hidden birds chirped on her right. A stash of trees and paths were working up the courage to call themselves a forest. On her left, a massive canyon was marked by a wooden signpost. It took a few seconds of squinting for her to realize that directions were etched into the wood.

The sign read: INDIRA STORY—ADVENTURE THIS WAY.

An arrow pointed toward the sprawling canyon. Indira frowned. Why would the sign be pointing to the edge of the cliff? The safest way was clearly in the other direction. A trail led through the trees. For the first time, she noticed the great domes of whitewashed buildings. The sight stirred excitement in her chest. Fable. That was actually *Fable* in the distance.

She glanced back at the sign. "Adventure this way? Why *that* way?"

"I believe I can explain."

A man's voice cut crisply across the quiet. Indira flinched. She hated being snuck up on. She turned to find a perfectly average man striding forward. How he had arrived or how long he had been there, Indira didn't know. His features were plain. Not the kind of person one would notice in a crowd. The only thing that *did* catch Indira's attention was his fingers. They danced and drummed and snapped. He looked as if he were rolling an invisible coin across his knuckles.

"The pleasure is all mine," he said. A business card appeared in his hands like magic. She took it, eyeing silver letters that looked on the verge of vanishing:

Deus Ex Machina
Provider of Convenient Solutions

"So you're Deus?"

He winced. "That blasted Percy Jackson. Everyone always thinks my name rhymes with Zeus now. The pronunciation is actually 'day,' as in 'What a fine day it is outside,' followed by 'us,' as in 'You and I are about to go on an adventure.' Day. Us. Deus. Savvy?"

"Got it," she said. "Provider of convenient solutions?"

He smiled wider. "That would be me."

"But what does that even mean?"

He chanted, "When they don't know what to say, and have completely given up on the play, reach over and press the right button, and a convenient solution will come running."

Indira raised an eyebrow. "That doesn't make any sense."

"Let's try it in simpler terms," Deus said, gesturing across the canyon. "Imagine two henchmen have cornered you. There's no chance of escape. But, at the last second, you remember there are magical birds beneath the cliffs that will fly you to safety."

Indira glanced at the canyon. "Magical birds."

"Why not? If you're going to be rescued, you might as well be rescued in style."

He stepped past her, eyeing the canyon, feeling the weight of the air with one hand. She watched him snap his fingers twice, firm and loud, before turning around.

"Ready, Indie?"

"For what?" she asked.

"I'm your mentor. I'll be escorting you to Fable, of course!"

She pointed to the ADVENTURE THIS WAY sign.

"We have to climb across a canyon?"

Deus laughed. "Do I look like someone who *climbs*? Life affords so many other more interesting possibilities." He removed a pair of goggles and positioned them over his eyes. "Do as I do and not as I say . . . or something like that."

Indira gasped as Deus turned and *leaped* over the edge. Her eyes went even wider as wind rushed up from below and a pair of dark wings unfolded. Deus had landed on the shoulders of a massive black bird. The creature beat its wings twice, hovering over the edge of the canyon.

Deus shouted, "Your turn!"

She cocked her chin. "I just jump?"

"Only if you want to fly."

Something about the way Deus said that made him look *anything* but average.

Most people would have hesitated. Made their cautious way to the edge and looked for some sign that the majestic bird really *was* below, ready to sweep up and save them. Indira wasn't most people. She let out a wild yawp that echoed over the canyon and threw herself into the empty air.

A second black bird curled into existence beneath her.

Indira's jaw shook with the impact. She slid dangerously down the bird's bony back, but not before seizing a handful of feathers to pull herself back up. Adrenaline thundered through her. She didn't take a breath until the dark wings swept out like blank canvases. An eager wind carried them higher, and Deus shouted in wild celebration as both birds soared upward.

Indira caught a final glimpse of the forest before the clouds swallowed the sight. Her bird broke through the white and gave her a view that left her even more breathless.

The whole world spread out below them, full of unknown. Mountains loomed to the south like great iron footprints. A glittering ocean framed the shoreline. She wondered if that was where she had come from, if all the boys and girls back in Origin were somewhere in that bright distance. A curtain of green covered everything else. She eyed the winding hills and forests until her eyes landed once more on the majestic city of Fable.

White buildings gleamed like seashells uncovered by retreating tides.

Deus whistled. She looked over in time to see him urge his bird into a dive. Indira clenched her knees, flattened against her mount's back, and dove after him. The force of the wind ripped the air from her lungs. The two of them plunged into a blur of green and blue and white, and Indira could feel the word *adventure* pounding through her head like a promise.

Wings swept out, and both birds landed gracefully. Indira leaped from her bird, landing with a little roll. Deus gave a nonchalant clap of approval. The great birds ruffled their feathers, and smoke gasped out. Sunlight scattered the dark mists into nothing. Indira might have been amazed by the flight, or the strange creatures, but the city gates towered before her.

The city of Fable was already casting its spell.

6

Fable

Now, dear reader, I must pause once more. It is one thing to describe Fable, and quite another thing to explain the way a character *feels* when they first reach the city's outer walls.

So take a deep breath and think about the last time you visited the beach. Stumble down that familiar boardwalk. Dig your toes into the sand. Look out at the vast ocean. Watch the waves give just to take. When you have the image set in your head, think about how small you really are. An ocean is deep. An ocean is wide. Every night it slow-dances with the moon. You are small by comparison, and there's nothing wrong with that.

That's how Indira felt as she followed Deus into Fable. She knew at once that she was *very* small and that the rest of the world was so *very* large. She also felt, down in her bones, that she belonged in Fable. Of course this was where she had been heading all along. Origin had been a short stop, a brief pause, before her life *really* began. As she looked up at Fable, she knew that no matter how strange or small or new she was, the city counted her and was delighted to have her.

Spiraling buildings surrounded them like great conch shells. To her eyes, they all looked connected and carved from a single stone. Bright tapestries colored windows and doorways.

The buildings looked majestic, of course, but *the people*... She found herself surrounded by a tall race of humans with slender necks and skinny little hips. All of them wore identical bronze watches on their willowy wrists. They sported tight-fitting clothes, and Indira caught snatches of their conversations.

"Walked into the room and shot an arrow at the Game-makers! The nerve of this girl!"

"Just happy to have moved on. I've been stuck outside that castle for an eternity."

"Well, he's a dog. But he's also a man. And he fights crime? You just have to read it. . . ."

Their senseless chatter filled the streets like music. She had never seen so many people, and every one of them *engaged* in conversation with someone else.

"Who are they, Deus?" Indira asked.

He gave the closest circle a perfunctory glance. "The Marks? Our loyal citizens. One of the native races of

Fable. They're flighty creatures, but they've been around since the very beginning of the world of Imagination."

Indira wanted to ask why they were called Marks, but a commotion stumbled out into the street. A slender woman barreled right into Deus, bounced off him, and shot after a fleeing dog. "Stop him!" the woman shouted. "He's got my watch!"

The dog in question bounded up a set of ivory stairs. It turned back, prize dangling from its jaws. Indira thought it looked playful, with one muddy ear standing straight up and the other flopped decisively down. It knelt forward on its front paws, rump still in the air, and wagged a wild tail. When the woman was halfway up the stairs, it turned on its heel and shot down an alleyway. Indira heard the woman shouting as she disappeared after it.

"I provide convenient solutions," Deus said crisply. "And I think the Authors like to counteract my presence with those *bloody* dog-ears. Pests is all they are."

"Books," Indira said suddenly. Something about the realization made the world look a little clearer. "Marks. The marks are *bookmarks*. And the dogs are dog-eared pages. Right?"

Deus cocked a curious eye her way. "Clever thinking, Indie. That's exactly right. Here, everything that has *anything* to do with imagination and story exists. Ever since there were books, there's been a need for bookmarks. How else to remember how far you've read? How else to pick up where you left off? Just remember not to trust the advice of a Mark. They're notoriously bad about getting the details of the stories right."

She really looked at them now. Tall and skinny so they could fit between the pages. Just so. The comments she had heard before floated back to her. She realized that they must have been snippets of whatever stories the Marks happened to be inside.

"Marks and dog-ears. Makes sense. But what about us? Where are *we* going?"

Deus smiled. "Protagonist Preparatory, of course. If the Marks are the little parts that make up a car, and if I'm the grease that helps it all run, then you, and other characters like you, are the engines. We're heading to the one place that's guaranteed to . . . put you in the right car."

"And that's Protagonist Preparatory?"

"The one and only."

Indira had heard of the school before, but only in vague whispers. When she had lived in Origin, the goal was to get to Fable. Get noticed and get your ticket out. Protagonist Preparatory must have been the point of getting out. Naturally. A school. A place for characters like her to train and grow and become who they were destined to be. Indira followed Deus up a spiraling staircase. The word *protagonist* beat in her head like a drum. It stirred some bone-deep desire. A protagonist. That was what she was born to be.

Fable continued on in an endless series of dream-white arches and platforms. Her eyes had adjusted to the city's swirling chaos. The Marks were everywhere, but they looked so similar that characters were easy to spot. One market square had several. She saw a hulking man with greenish skin and silver bolts in his neck. He held a sign that read:

I AM NOT FRANKENSTEIN.
MISUNDERSTANDING IS THE REAL MONSTER.

Beyond him she spied a massive umbrella. The area below it was roped off, and a line had formed. She caught a glimpse of a caped man with pale skin and a high collar. The fan at the front of the line finished paying and stepped forward to take a picture. Indira couldn't help noticing the caped man's smile. There was something odd about his teeth. . . .

"Who is that?" she asked.

"Dracula," Deus answered. "He sets up in town every few weeks. It's a little absurd if you ask me. People taking pictures with a famous vampire."

Indira shrugged. "Don't people always like to take pictures with famous people?"

"Indeed, but most famous people can actually be photographed. Look."

Several photographs were featured on an artsy-looking

clothesline. Deus was right. All of them featured the customer with their arm reaching out in the air and wrapping around nothing. One even showed a Mark in a dramatic pose, dipping backward, as if the vampire were about to suck his blood. None of the photographs actually captured Dracula himself.

"I guess that is kind of weird," Indira said.

As they continued their tour, Indira also had the sense they were being followed, but every time she looked, there was no one there. Thinking about vampires sent a shiver down her spine. She would have been more suspicious if there weren't so many new things to look at. Deus moved through the packed streets with quiet precision. Gaps in the crowd seemed to open for him at just the right moment, and it took some quick stepping for Indira to keep up.

He explained that *protagonist* was basically another word for *hero,* and that Protagonist Preparatory was the school every character in Fable attended. The school's role was to prepare each of them for the stories that Authors were busily writing.

And of course there were auditions.

Indira didn't like that word. The word made her sweat. It was a word that seemed to be naturally followed by words like *failure* and *pressure* and *embarrassment.* But according to Deus, the auditions were straightforward: Indira would compete with a character who was applying for that dreadful Antagonist Academy in Fester (a point that drew Indira's attention, because she hadn't ever heard about a rival city). To which Deus had simply responded: "Where there is good, there is evil."

Indira nodded at that. She was thinking about fighting bad guys and rescuing people as Deus continued his explanation. Characters, apparently, had several possible tracks to follow. If their auditions went well, they'd be enrolled in the Protagonist track.

"That's the one you'll aim for," he explained. "And with your knack for adventure? You're a natural fit for that role, really."

Every character wanted to be the hero of their story, but Fable knew that a story wasn't a story without side characters and romantic interests and cameo roles. Deus explained that characters who didn't have a successful audition would be enrolled in tracks that featured less of the spotlight. Indira nodded along until Deus said something that she didn't think she had heard right. "Naturally, your auditions are today."

Indira stopped dead in her tracks. "Today?"

7

Protagonist Preparatory

"You could have at least *mentioned* that we were going straight to auditions."

Deus shrugged. "That's just the way it works, Indie."

She could feel little hands tying knots in her stomach. "I'm not ready," she complained. "I haven't prepared or studied or anything. How will I even know what to do?"

"It's called instinct," Deus replied. "You know that thing that helped you fly a bird through the sky today? Instinct. That's what the auditions are designed to measure. They throw you into the moment and see *exactly* what you're made of. What would be the point of allowing people to *study* beforehand?"

Indira still felt herself panicking. "What if I fail?"

Everything Deus had said before about becoming a protagonist came echoing back. It made sense that if she really wanted to be the best, she'd have to get off to a great start during auditions. It wasn't hard to see that being a protagonist was probably the only way to drag David into a story with her. And this one test was going to decide all of that? Great.

Deus just kept smiling. "Remember: you leaped off a cliff today, landed on the back of a majestic bird, and flew above the clouds. I think you're going to do just fine, Indie."

Doubts continued to snap at Indira's heels, though, as they rounded the corner and a new building came into sight. Deus did not have to announce that this was their destination. Indira knew at first glance. It had to be Protagonist Preparatory.

How to describe the school, my dear reader? Fable is the kind of city that *isn't* set in stone, so to speak. Every few months the entire city takes on a new look to give its characters a fresh setting in which they might blossom into the best versions of themselves. But the school building always maintains a few qualities. First, it always looks a little older than the buildings around it. Something in the architecture or the slant of the roof or the shape of the windows. This has the pleasant effect of making it seem worn, but comfortable, like a favorite pair of shoes.

Second, the front doors to the building are *always* thrust wide open. No matter the weather, no matter the time, no matter the century. Even during the Fictional Wars of 783, the school did not close its doors, because Protagonist Preparatory closes its doors to no one.

Indira's first look at the school was just so. A pair of looming gothic doors stood open, allowing the sunlight to color the interior. A massive group of characters stood off to one side, forming a line that was slowly turning into a jumbled mess. She spied Maxi and Phoenix in the swirling ranks, but before she could join them, Deus hooked her by the collar.

"All right. As your benevolent and mischievous benefactor, I would like to leave you with some final guidance before you head into the great unknown that is school." Deus held up one finger. "First, I believe you heard a particular phrase after arriving on the outskirts of Fable. I would guess those words are likely still echoing in your head . . ."

She remembered them. "Every cage —"

Deus made an abrupt shushing noise. Indira fell silent, but that did not stop the phrase from echoing in her mind: *Every cage has a key.*

"Don't tell people your Words," he scolded. "They're yours, and they're private. Every character has First Words. Consider them a promise and a warning. If you do well in school, those words will be the very first words of your *story*. If you don't do well . . ." He trailed off awkwardly. "Let's just say I can't snap my fingers to get you out of that."

Indira felt the weight of his warning. *Every cage has a key.* The words were dancing through her head like a promise. This was why she'd come to Fable in the first place. She was a character, and deep down she burned with desire to exist in a story she could call her own. Deus must have sensed her excitement, because he was grinning at her in his knowing way.

"One final thing." He flashed a hand into his pocket and pulled out a bronze penny. "A parting gift. Give it a spin and I'll come running. It will only work once, savvy?"

She nodded. With a deep breath, she took the penny and shoved it into her pocket. Deus offered her the briefest of hugs. She tried to hold him tight, but he felt thin, as if he had already vanished and appeared somewhere else in the world.

"Sorry to run, Indie. There's a rebellious teen locked in a dungeon somewhere."

"See you when I need you," Indira replied with a wink.

He turned on the spot and vanished. In the distance, beyond where Deus had just been standing, Indira saw a little slash of color, as though someone had just ducked into an alleyway and out of sight. She eyed the spot, frowning, before turning back toward the school.

The next step in her journey was waiting.

8

The Brainstorms

All the new and hopeful characters had gathered in front of Protagonist Preparatory. She could not help feeling like there were quite a lot of them. She'd always thought Origin was the only place with characters-in-waiting, but as she approached, she heard the other characters talking about where they'd traveled from. Towns like Prologue and Wellspring and Inception. One girl had even grown up in a little mountain town called Flashback. Indira frowned.

Were they all really here to audition?

Indira saw three imposing figures in front of the building. They looked as if they were as much a part of the landscape as the stained-glass windows and iron weather vanes. Indira could hardly take her eyes off them as she stumbled over to where Maxi was standing. She bumped shoulders with the girl and nodded into the distance. "Who are they?"

Maxi let out a shriek and wrapped her arms around Indira.

"You're alive!"

"Of course I'm alive. Why wouldn't I be alive?"

Maxi gestured vaguely. "I read this book, where people got taken away through teleports, and they all, like . . . I don't know . . . had *very* different experiences on this, like . . . alien planet."

Indira laughed. "No worries. I wasn't experimented on."

She glanced around. Most of the other characters looked around her age—though there were one or two adults in the crowd—and most of the waiting group looked like they *needed* some training. She was still sizing the others up when Maxi let out another squeal. The ranks of gathered characters parted as Phoenix strode toward them.

"You're alive too!"

Phoenix smiled. "Maxi, we talked like five seconds ago."

"Can't a girl be excited?" she asked. "Live a little, you two!"

Indira and Phoenix exchanged an eye roll. Indira took a second to search the crowd for Peeve. Her ex-neighbor hadn't arrived yet, though. Indira remembered the Author Borealis representative saying something about taking a different route. Whatever route they were taking, it was apparently going to make Peeve late for auditions.

Indira's eyes were drawn once more to the three figures waiting in front of the building. It couldn't be more clear that they weren't characters. "Who are they?" she asked again.

Phoenix answered, "The brainstorms."

In spite of the sunny day, Indira felt the air go very still. It was like the exact moment before a storm roared to life, all that lightning and thunder and rain. She finally realized what was so strange about the brainstorms. Their features looked *too* sharp. They seemed to have more substance than the world around them, more color and presence.

Two of them were women. The first was short and slight with dark brown skin. Everything about her had a crisp and orderly quality to it. Her hair had been cut perfectly at the shoulders. It didn't curl or wave or do anything playful at all. Her lips looked as though they'd been carved from the quiet stone of her face. She wore a business suit with a high, dominating collar.

The second woman had a quieter kind of power. Her skin was light and freckled. Indira saw that her eyes were two *remarkably* different colors. The left hinted at green forests and spring leaves. The right looked like the type of amber that encased prehistoric insects. The woman's jacket was made of little black dragon scales. The perfect attire for dancing *or* sword fighting on a bloody plain.

Of the three of them, the man seemed least intimidating. He was certainly tall, but it almost looked accidental, like he'd been given more height than he knew what to do with. His features were quite striking: dark, slanting eyebrows and a sharp nose that were complemented pleasantly by a charcoal mustache. Indira felt that he looked like someone's uncle.

As she watched, the shorter woman with the high collar stepped forward. She held up a hand for silence. "Good morning," she said in a crisp voice. "I am Brainstorm Underglass."

The man stepped forward. "I am Brainstorm Vesulias."

"And I'm Brainstorm Ketty." The woman with the mismatched eyes waved.

The first woman, Brainstorm Underglass, waited for the half murmurs of the crowd to fully die out before continuing. "We are the brainstorms of Protagonist Preparatory. Over the past few months, each of us has spent time engaging with the Authors. Our explorations of the Real World have given us long lists of upcoming availability in their stories. Each of you will be assigned to one brainstorm. We will monitor your grades and your progress, and determine the best possible matches for you based on our research and your school performance."

Brainstorm Vesulias spoke next. "Today is a chance to demonstrate your *potential*. Auditions are a glimpse of your talents. We've found that this method is rather timeworn and proven. You'll each face an antagonist who's applying to the school in Fester. There will be three scene illusions. The first will favor your opponent, the second will favor you, and the third scene will be neutral ground. After completing the three scenes, we will analyze what track we think best fits your talents based on the results."

Maxi grabbed on to Indira's arm and squeezed excitedly. Indira thought she heard the girl mutter something about *destiny* and *protagonists*. Brainstorm Ketty continued. "I am going to call out a list of names. Please line up in order. Your auditions will begin soon after."

Indira felt her stomach begin to turn nervously as the names were called out. Abner Allenby, Augustus Best, Bertram the Beadle, Bollister Borcreaux, Catherine Daedalus . . . Each name dug its steady way to *I*. She watched the other characters step forward and found she was rather thankful her name wasn't Aardvark or Abigail.

Eventually they did call her name. Her stomach did a few backflips. Maxi wished her luck. Phoenix nodded firmly. She went to stand in line behind a shirtless boy who was covered in tattoos. Behind her, a girl played an instrument that looked more like a snake than a flute. The line stretched from the doorway to the middle of the courtyard. When everyone had found their places, Indira counted at least forty new characters.

How many would be allowed to take the protagonist track that Deus had mentioned? Indira's goal had always been to get to Fable. But now that she was here, she had her eyes on a new prize: to be a hero in her own story.

And if I'm a hero, she thought, *I can bring David into the story with me.*

Looking around, Indira found it impossible to measure herself against the others. She saw characters in wizards' robes, a strange creature with eight arms, and one girl with a ponytail so long it almost reached the nearest alleyway. Indira set a nervous hand on the grip of her hammer. It was hard to know how she stacked up with the others. After all, they could be destined for completely different stories.

She tried to focus on making a plan, but realized that that was just as impossible. She had no idea what to expect. The brainstorm's instructions echoed back to her.

Three illusions.

One that fit her enemy's strengths.

One that fit her strengths.

One to determine the real winner.

She didn't have much time to think, because the line was already beginning to move.

9

Antagonist

"Indira Story."

She walked through the open gothic doors and followed a secretary through bright hallways. Little bulletin boards swirled with activity: the last school year's happenings. Indira could not help slowing down and reading, enchanted by all the possibilities.

One flyer offered tutoring in horseback riding (*undead mounts available upon request*). A second invited members to come out and participate in their favorite imaginary sports (*brooms not provided*). Someone had drawn a mustache on the face of a smiling lion who promised that his evening classes could help characters find the courage to face their greatest fears (*especially helpful if you're afraid of your own tail!*).

The final poster read simply: LEARN JABBERWOCKY. The

explanation below made no sense at all, though. Indira was mouthing words like *gyre* and *gimble* and *slithy* when the waiting secretary cleared her throat.

"Plenty of time to sign up for clubs later," she promised.

Indira followed her excitedly. Their journey ended at the double-door entrance to an auditorium. The secretary smiled at her. "Just wait for your name to be called."

She took a deep breath as the secretary's retreating footsteps faded. She was starting to count off the seconds, tapping out each one with her foot, when a voice boomed from inside.

"Indira Story!"

She pushed through the entryway. Inside, a vast amphitheater waited, its plush seats empty. Between the seats and the stage, a table had been set out and three judges were seated with very official-looking clipboards. Indira walked up and took her place onstage, trying to keep her hands from shaking.

She recognized Brainstorm Vesulias, who sat to the far right. She didn't know who the other judges were. In the middle, a boy with rosy cheeks. He looked surprised to be there. The last judge's appearance was the most startling. Indira couldn't be sure, but he looked like a demon. His diamond skin was as hard and unforgiving as stone. Little veins ran through the crystalline of his arms and legs like streaks of faded lava. His burnished eyes gleamed hungrily.

Indira saw a door at the opposite end of the stage. She

guessed her competition was waiting to walk out through it. Indira had been too nervous to consider her opponent. She had been busy worrying about her own strengths, about how to pull David into a story one day. She hadn't considered that some other character's fate depended on this competition too. She tried to make herself feel better by remembering that the person was from Fester.

That made them a bad guy, didn't it?

She wasn't even sure what an antagonist would look like. She imagined horns or an evil laugh or a sword dripping with blood. Which made the name the judges called out even more surprising: "Peeve Meadows."

Indira's ex-neighbor walked through the door. It was all Indira could do to keep her knees from buckling. Peeve's blond hair was in a tight braid. Her guitar bounced against her back, the strap stretching across her chest. For the first time, Indira noticed the scatter of freckles on either side of the girl's button of a nose. "Characters, shake hands!" called Brainstorm Vesulias.

Peeve held her hand out confidently. Indira shook it with numb fingers. Her mind was spinning. She tried to retrace every conversation and interaction, the months that they had spent as neighbors. Indira hadn't even paid enough attention to notice that the girl had freckles.

But what had Peeve learned about her? The girl had always been eager to talk and engage, even though Indira had never given her much time in return. And now they were about to face off against each other. Indira felt a sinking feeling in her stomach. *Peeve has the advantage. She knows me, but I don't know her at all.*

"I've been watching you," Peeve said, as if she could read Indira's mind. "For months now. I even watched you today as you walked around Fable. I didn't want it to be this way, but you embarrassed me this morning. You made me feel like a fool. Now it's my turn."

Indira stared back at the girl, speechless.

Peeve smiled. "I'm going to *win.*"

10

The Audition—Round One

A clatter sounded backstage, and an old raisin of a man joined them on the stage. He wore an official-looking name tag that read: MERLIN? Indira frowned at the question mark. She supposed that if she was lucky enough to live that long, she wouldn't be too sure about her name, either. Merlin waved a lazy hand and three tables appeared. One stood in front of Indira and another in front of Peeve; another hovered between the two of them. A second wave produced three stones on the middle tabletop. One black, one white, one gray.

Merlin spoke in a steady voice. "The illusions that follow will not allow you to actually come to harm. Thus you need not hesitate out of fear that you will actually hurt the person standing across from you. You need only consider how your actions reflect your ability, personality, and self."

The hunched wizard gave a deep bow and left the stage. Indira's heart continued to beat far too fast. She felt as though her life in Fable depended on what happened next. All three judges stood.

"Any last questions, characters?" asked the demon.

Indira shook her head. She felt a deep and growing desire to beat Peeve. It wasn't *her* fault the girl had lied that morning. Maybe that action had turned Peeve into an antagonist? Indira felt the unfairness of it all beating in her chest.

Brainstorm Vesulias gave a signal. "Are you ready?"

Indira and Peeve turned to face each other as the walls vanished around them. For a long, uncomfortable moment, she could only see a stretching whiteness and Peeve's traitorous face . . .

. . . and then the world echoed. She was in the halls of a school. She had a bathroom pass in her hands. The square tiles were painted unenthusiastic colors. She followed a dull purple line to the bathroom, but stopped short at the sound of laughter.

Cautiously she glanced around the corner. A girl with blond hair stood at the far end of the bathroom. She had taken toilet paper from one of the stalls and stretched it over the entire room. It looped through doorways and over sinks, leaving a spiderweb maze hanging in the air. She recognized the girl now. It was that troublemaker, Peeve Meadows.

Indira dropped the hall pass, and the girl looked up, startled.

"What do you think you're doing?" Indira asked. Peeve started forward, fumbling for an explanation, but Indira retreated a few steps. "I'm telling a teacher."

Before Peeve could stop her, Indira bolted back into the hallway. Room 1612. She found the room around the corner and knocked impatiently. A teacher appeared.

"Ms. Lobasso, there's someone in the girls' bathroom. They're vandalizing it!"

The teacher raised an eyebrow and followed Indira down the hallway. Ms. Lobasso paused at the threshold, eyeing the water that had started leaking from within. She muttered something about new shoes and plunged forward. Indira followed.

Peeve had fled the scene, but she hadn't bothered to cover her tracks. If anything, she had made things even worse. The nearest stall had been kicked from its frame. Water leaked out generously, pooling in the room and trickling toward the hall. Indira was about to explain what she'd seen when a soft moan sounded from inside one of the stalls.

"What was that?" Ms. Lobasso asked.

The teacher hitched up her dress a little and walked over to the third stall. She opened it and let out a gasp. Indira hurried forward. The sight stunned her. An entire roll of toilet paper had been used to mummify Peeve

Meadows. She was wrapped from head to toe. The wooden hall pass Indira had dropped had been set carefully on the plumbing, and someone had written the word *REVENGE* in permanent marker. A great wad of toilet paper had even been used to gag the girl, whose eyes were wide with panic.

"Indira!" Ms. Lobasso rounded on her unexpectedly. "Did you do this?"

Indira's eyes widened. "No! I told you, she was in here! I wasn't—"

"The poor girl looks terrified," Ms. Lobasso said, rushing forward to remove the bindings and gag. "Peeve, what in the world happened to you?"

"It was her!" Peeve cried. "Don't let her get me again, Ms. Lobasso!"

"You're safe, Peeve. Now tell me what happened!"

"I was walking to the bathroom and she grabbed me," Peeve explained. "She says I cut her in line yesterday. I swear, Ms. Lobasso, I don't remember it at all! But she pushed me in here and tied me up and she . . . oh, I don't know if I can even repeat it, Ms. Lobasso!"

"Peeve Meadows. I have to report this to the principal. What did she say?"

Peeve put on a pained face, as if it really was unbearable to go on. Indira felt rage boiling to life inside her. She was clearly lying! Indira hadn't done any of those things.

"Well," Peeve continued, "she said she hoped no one

found me before the water got to me. She wanted to drown me, Ms. Lobasso!"

"You lying sack of good-for-nothing—" Indira was so mad she could barely think straight. It wasn't like she was going to hit Peeve, but she must have looked plenty threatening, because Ms. Lobasso stepped forward, placing herself between the two of them.

"Indira Story," Ms. Lobasso said with a raised voice. "If you so much as move from that tile, I'll make sure you never come back to this school again."

The teacher disappeared back into the bathroom as Indira fumed. It was an ugly trick to play on someone, and she realized that Peeve had *wanted* her to react that way. The angrier she looked, the guiltier she'd seem. Indira was going to be expelled. Peeve had pinned it all on her. A minute later, Ms. Lobasso led Peeve out of the bathroom. Actual tears were rushing down the traitor's cheeks. "I'm feeling dizzy," Peeve confided to Ms. Lobasso.

The furious teacher led her past Indira before turning around sharply. "You will remain *right* where you're standing until I return. We're going to have a good, long talk with the principal. And another one with your mother. You are in a *lot* of trouble, Ms. Story."

Behind the teacher's back, Peeve turned. Her face was still streaked with very real-looking tears, but she was grinning wickedly. She winked once, and Indira knew she'd lost.

The scene vanished. White walls appeared.

Indira had a single moment to remind herself of several things:

I lost the first scene.

I was supposed to lose the first scene. Peeve had the advantage.

I'm supposed to win the next one.

11

The Audition–Round Two

A darkish sky blinked into being. She was running down a narrow city street in pursuit of a fleeing figure: Peeve Meadows. The famous thief had stolen an amulet from the Markesh Library, and Indira was the only one who could get it back.

Hearing Indira's footsteps, Peeve darted to the right. She skidded down an alleyway and into the open square beyond. City folk had parallel parked their dragons alongside the main thoroughfare. Indira's quarry had already climbed atop one of them. With a whispered curse, Peeve forced a golden dragon to spread its shimmering wings.

Bad choice, Indira thought.

Peeve was a talented thief, but no one could fly like Indira could. The freckle-faced girl locked eyes with Indira as the stolen dragon swept her up into the gray-blue sky. Indira didn't hesitate. She leaped aboard the nearest parked dragon.

"Every cage has a key," she whispered.

Fuchsia wings swept wide. The dragon sniffed twice and launched itself into the air. She felt the wind snatch at her hair and cloak. The dragon continued its ascent, and she spotted the golden dragon in the distant gray. Peeve clearly didn't know anything about dragons. She had hopped aboard a Destriant. The breed was built for show and size, not for speed. And they were far too glittery to be lost in the clouds.

Indira's own beast was smaller and sleeker, and its translucent wings beat twice as fast. Before long, the speck of gold grew larger and more distinct. She could see Peeve glancing back nervously. Indira set a hand on the hammer at her hip. If it came to an aerial attack, she wanted to be ready. Ahead, Peeve veered right. Another mistake. Indira's dragon anticipated the move and cut the corner off the thief's flight pattern. With a few more sweeping wingbeats, they were in shouting distance. Peeve leaned over her beast. There was panic in her eyes.

Good, Indira thought. *She knows she's outmatched.*

The dragons crossed over a pair of rivers. Indira closed the gap, and with a great crash her dragon caught hold of the other's flank. Wings snapped out, and both beasts fell with stomach-turning spirals. Indira saw Peeve nearly lose her grip before managing to right her dragon and pull away at the last second. Indira's beast had had a taste of the fight now, though, and they harried the other dragon's flank a second time. Not knowing what else to do, Peeve urged her creature into a descent. Indira could see a town glittering in the forests ahead.

She couldn't let Peeve land, not if the thief had help arranged.

And Peeve *always* arranged help.

It was clear: she'd have to board them in the air.

Indira whispered the command in the ear of her beast and they swept above the golden dragon. Gliding smoothly, she urged her mount alongside and slightly above their quarry. Peeve kept glancing up, but she made no move to turn or dive in a different direction. She seemed set on making it to the little town at any cost. Indira had boarded hundreds of dragons over her career as an investigator. The leap was instinctual for her now.

Her own dragon steadied its beating wings, gliding lower and closer. With a little grunt, Indira pulled out her hammer, set her feet, and leaped. The motion shook her senses. A sudden drop of her stomach. A stretch of soundlessness as she flew through the air. And then rising panic as she saw Peeve *smiling*. The girl twisted her beast into a perfect roll. The golden dragon turned *under* Indira's mount, and Indira was falling.

Her hands scraped against sliding scales. She caught hold of the creature's tail, but the momentum shook her grasp free. She fell. Too fast. Way, way too fast.

The ground rushed up to meet her.

White walls again. The scene vanished. Her thoughts came like lightning strikes:

I lost the second challenge.

Peeve knew I was going to jump.

How did she know?

There was a sinking feeling in her stomach.

I lost my challenge.

12

The Audition—Round Three

Her surroundings fluttered to life a third time. She was on a bleak little island. Her younger sister, Peeve, was struggling with a fire as she hunted through their ship's wreckage for useful supplies. "It's not working," Peeve called.

"Of course it's not working," Indira snapped back. For some reason, she felt very impatient with her little sister. After all, it was her fault they had crashed here. "If you hadn't fallen asleep, we wouldn't be *stuck* on this stupid island."

"It was after my shift!" Peeve looked up angrily from the unlit fire. "I was trying to be nice. I was trying to let you get some extra sleep, Indira."

"Whatever," Indira said. "Just get the fire started."

"You do it," Peeve said impatiently. She tossed the

twigs, but Indira's hands were already full, so they snapped painfully against her neck and arms. Indira dropped her supplies and rushed Peeve, all the anger and frustration of being abandoned on an island boiling over. They rolled in the sand until she had her pinned. She gave her sister's collar a good shaking.

"We're stuck out here, Peeve," she said. "If you don't carry your weight, we'll die out here. Start the fire."

"All right, all right," Peeve shot back. "Get off me."

Indira let her up and took a few steps toward the jungle. How were they possibly going to survive here? Strange sounds echoed out from the darkness. Even the shapes of the trees looked foreign and ominous. She had to *think*. They needed to get help, and they needed it fast.

A soft twang sounded. One note followed by two, on into a rhythm. Indira turned around. Peeve was watching her, playing a song that sounded almost like a lullaby. Indira was about to tell her to quit wasting time, that the noise might attract unwelcome attention, but . . . the words didn't come. She blinked. Her arms felt *heavy* all of a sudden.

Peeve maintained eye contact. The song snaked under Indira's skin, coaxing her muscles to relax until she couldn't even stand up straight.

"You never really *listened* to me, did you?" Peeve's words somehow sounded like a bedtime story. "You never actually saw any of my practice sessions. So you have no idea what I'm capable of with this little guitar."

Indira's head sank down in the sand. She was watching

Peeve's hands move easily from note to note, the guitar pick gliding so effortlessly. It all made her feel so *tired*.

"Feeling sleepy?" Peeve whispered. "Go ahead. Fall asleep. I'm going to use that coin in your pocket. I'll use it to call for help. Your mentor gave it to you, didn't he?"

Indira's eyes were closing. She realized, before falling asleep, that Peeve had followed her through the streets of Fable. The flash of color she'd seen after Deus vanished had been Peeve, watching and waiting, learning all about Indira.

"Go to sleep now," Peeve sang. "Go on to sleep, little bird."

Indira fell asleep . . .

. . . and awoke with a startling jolt. A furious magic had split the sky in two. She saw strange lights that reminded her of the Author Borealis. Dawn? Somehow it was already dawn. Indira saw in the distance that a float-plane had landed off the coast. Indira could just make out Peeve's form as she boarded the plane.

The plane took off, gliding over the surface, before bulleting through the sky.

Peeve was flying away to safety. Without her.

Indira had lost.

She heard a sigh. Looking over, she found a perfectly average man standing by the wreckage of their boat. He was holding a coin in his hand. The fingers of his other hand were dancing. Deus considered the smoky streak of the plane's exhaust in the sky.

"Well, that's inconvenient," he said.

The scene vanished.

Indira's eyes adjusted to the dim lighting of the stage. It was as though she had returned to the world and left her heart behind. She knew that she had failed. This fact was confirmed by the stones that the wizard had set on the middle table before the audition began.

All three had traveled magically over to the table in front of Peeve.

She had won every scene.

Peeve didn't throw her hands up in victory, but she had a satisfied look on her face that gutted Indira. It was hard to focus as the judges recounted the events in the illusions and added their own opinions. Indira didn't look up until Brainstorm Vesulias said her name sharply.

He wanted to make sure he had her attention; he wanted her to understand that she had options. Lastly, and most importantly, he wanted to make sure that she knew that taking the protagonist track *wasn't* one of those options. She could still be considered for the side-character track, and that wasn't so bad, according to him. He thanked Indira for her time, and she felt herself vanishing from existence as she left the auditorium.

13

Brainstorm Ketty

Indira did not remember walking out of the auditorium, or back through the halls, or toward the front of the school. She walked like someone surrounded by fog on all sides.

"Indira?"

The sound brought her back to reality. The same secretary who had escorted her to the auditions was looking at Indira as if she'd grown a third eyeball.

"It is Indira, correct?" the woman asked.

Indira nodded.

The woman thumbed through her files. "You were chosen by Brainstorm Ketty. She's actually trying to get a step ahead on meeting with students. Her office is down this hallway. Just walk past Hearth Hall, and she'll be on your left. Okay?"

Indira trudged off. She didn't bother to glance at the bulletin boards that lined the hallways. Those activities felt distant now, as if she'd lost her invitation and would no longer be permitted to take part in them. She found the office with little trouble, knocked, and was commanded to enter.

Brainstorm Ketty had traded the dragon-scale jacket for a houndstooth frock. Indira found that if she looked too closely at the pattern, the teeth took on a rather sharp and real-looking appearance. The backdrop of the brainstorm's office was a huge black chalkboard. A chaos of slanting letters revealed long lists, random thoughts, and obscure references.

Indira's eyes skipped over the phrases:

Dashed hope? Must define taxonomy before continuing.
Be sure to check the Librarian Hall of Fame for leads!
D. M. writing an Adventure story with a side of Horror!

Before Indira could piece any of it together, the brainstorm pressed a button on her desk. The chaos was replaced by an orderly list of student names. Ketty tapped the board, scrolled down, and settled on Indira's name. Indira could not help noticing a massive golden star there.

Brainstorm Ketty tapped Indira's name. It centered itself on the board, and the rest of the writing vanished. She gestured for Indira to take a seat before offering a motherly smile.

"I've just received your results, Indira. I'm sure you're bound to be disappointed. If there's one lesson I'm learning daily, though, it's that Fable isn't done with me. And I daresay it's not quite done with you, either."

Indira forced herself to nod. "I noticed the gold star by my name."

"Yes. That indicates that you're a new student," Brainstorm Ketty said.

Indira felt a little let down by that. She knew she'd completely ruined her auditions, but she'd been holding out some hope that a gold star would be something *good*.

"Protagonists." Brainstorm Ketty shrugged. "Necessary, but often overrated. In my own reading, I find them to be simple reflections of the Authors who write them. The side characters are often where exploration truly happens. The Author feels a distance, and distance allows experimentation. You've more potential than you know, Indira Story."

Indira mumbled, "Yes, ma'am."

The brainstorm sighed. "All right, I will ask you a series of questions. This will allow me to determine the best route for you to take from here. Your honesty is paramount. Lies will only muddy the waters. Just respond with whatever pops into your head first, all right?"

Indira nodded, eager simply to get on with it. The brainstorm snatched a piece of chalk.

"Would you rather be owed a favor by dolphins or gnomes?"

"Uh . . . dolphins."

"What's your favorite color?"

"Gray."

"What's your favorite hair color?"

Indira blushed a little. "Red."

As they continued, the questions appeared in a column on the left side of the blackboard. Indira's answers floated to life on the right. Columns blossomed with checks or x's according to some system Indira couldn't understand.

"Escape through the roof or down through the sewers?"

"Roof."

"Why are cows such boring creatures?"

"They're pampered."

"What do you think about kissing?"

"Gross."

"What's in the closet?"

"Secrets."

"If you had to broker a deal with fairies, what welcoming gift would you bring?"

"Candy."

"The contents of a mysterious vault or a lifelong supply of shoes?"

"Vault."

"It was once said that man is the only creature that blushes, or needs to. Name at least one other animal that blushes."

"Skeletons."

Brainstorm Ketty leaned back. "Skeletons?" she repeated, amused. "Why skeletons?"

Indira shrugged. "No clothes?"

Ketty let out a little laugh as she stood and surveyed the results. Indira couldn't see any pattern in the questions. The brainstorm used her piece of chalk to make a few extra markings on the blackboard. Dust swirled in one corner, and letters began to print themselves neatly along the borders. Brainstorm Ketty quietly totaled a sum on her fingers before turning around.

"Well, at least your options are clear," the woman said. "You're definitely cut out for an adventure story. Your daring is through the roof, and you have a knack for sticky situations. I'm not sure you expected this, but romantic interest was your second highest category. I'm going to put you in the side-character track for adventure with a minor in romantic curiosity."

A chart appeared on the board. Her answers had earned her marks in a variety of categories. She wanted to protest about the romantic-curiosity part. Sure, Phoenix was easy to have a crush on, but the last thing she felt capable of at the moment was being romantically curious about *anything*.

Ketty leaned over her desk and pulled out a glittering orb. She set a sheet of paper on her desk and rolled the orb across it four times. "Here's your schedule."

She handed the piece of paper to Indira:

NAME: Indira Story		TRACK: Side character		
CLASS	COURSE LISTING	TIME OF MEETING	LOCATION	TEACHER
Love by Page 12	ROM 112	Noon	The Rainy Courtyard	Professor Fitzwilliam Darcy
I Thought You Were Dead	TRAG 104	Too Late to Make a Difference	The Sepulcher	Dr. Romeo Montague
Introduction to Sympathetic Characters	SYMP 101	9:30–10:30 a.m.	Room 1001	Mr. Threepwood
How to Get Captured and Narrowly Escape	ACT 203	Just One Second	Room 3047	Alice
Weaponry	ACT 220	Two Hours of Training (minimum per week)	The Arena	Odysseus

As Indira scanned the contents, she found little to complain about. The names of her professors were distantly familiar. The locations sounded mostly interesting, and the classes themselves weren't so bad. She wasn't certain she'd *ever* want to fall in love by page 12, but it wouldn't hurt to know a few things about romance, would it?

"Weaponry?" Indira asked curiously.

Ketty gestured to her hammer. "Unless that's a toothbrush?"

Indira almost laughed. "I recognize the names of most of the professors, but who is Mr. Threepwood? I've never heard of him."

"He owns the Talespin coffee shop. We hired him two years ago. Our first hiring of an unfinished character. It caused quite a stir until the school council realized the man can *teach*. I think you'll like him. Like you, his story began with misadventure."

Indira frowned at that. She glanced down at her schedule again, enthusiasm all but gone.

"Any other questions?" Ketty asked.

"My escape class meets at 'just one second.' When exactly is that?"

"Well, you know how the quote goes," Ketty replied. "'How long is forever? Sometimes, just one second.'"

Indira frowned. "That's nice and all, but it doesn't help me get to her class."

"Oh, Alice's class? Don't worry about it. Students have a habit of showing up for her class without quite intending to. And time works a little differently here."

Yesterday, Indira might have been curious about what that meant, but that's the unfortunate thing about befores and afters, my dear reader. A single day or hour or second can take the taste right out of things. So instead of asking questions, Indira simply folded her schedule and stood.

"Thank you for your time," she said.

She made it to the door before Ketty called after her. "Just a moment, Ms. Story."

The woman fumbled behind her desk and produced a small knapsack. She held it open so Indira could look inside. "Just a few supplies to get you started. Paper and pencils and all that. The stationery even has your name printed on it!"

Indira accepted the bag, and Brainstorm Ketty reached behind her desk for one more item. Indira was pleasantly surprised to see a brand-new jacket. It had a coat of arms printed on one pocket and was the most divine shade of navy blue. Indira slipped into it and was even more surprised to find that it fit perfectly. For a moment, she forgot to be disappointed by how things had turned out. She fixed her collar and quietly buttoned up.

Ketty gave an approving look. "Wear whatever you like beneath it, but the school jacket is required at all times. It helps us identify students within the school."

Indira didn't mind that rule at all. "Yes, ma'am."

The brainstorm smiled politely, and Indira left. As she closed the door, she looked back and saw that Ketty had rotated the chalkboard back to her list of students. Ketty considered Indira's name for a moment before adding *another* gold star to it. The woman then scribbled a note that Indira couldn't read. Something about that second gold star felt magical, almost. Maybe Brainstorm Ketty really thought she had potential. Indira walked down the hallway in her new jacket, clutching her new knapsack.

It felt like the first step out of a very dark and dreary basement.

14

The Adoption Agency

Indira was still admiring her blue jacket when a throat *cleared*. The same secretary was standing in front of her with the same eager smile on her face. Indira was starting to wonder if the woman could teleport or something.

"Last stop for the day!" The secretary handed her a leaflet. "The Adoption Agency!"

Indira glared. Those were two *not-so-likeable* words. *Agency* felt like a grown-up word. It probably hung out with words like *portfolio* and *punctual. Adoption* set off alarms too. Being adopted meant being wanted, and if something depended on being wanted . . . Well, what if no one wanted her at all?

"Everything all right, dear?" the secretary asked.

"I just . . ." She lowered her eyes. "What if no one chooses me?"

The secretary let out a surprisingly loud laugh. "Oh, no, dear. They don't choose you."

Indira frowned. "They don't?"

"Of course not. You choose them." The secretary pointed to the leaflet. "It's all explained in the brochure. Family units are required to complete an internship before their names can be submitted to the Authors. What better way to gain experience than by raising the characters who come to Fable for school? But of course *you* get to choose. You're the character, for crying out loud! Go ahead and just follow those instructions, okay?"

Indira nodded. The instructions led her outside. She followed the marked path around the corner to a building that looked like a pearl. A great, round door had already yawned its way open. Indira double-checked the instructions before ducking inside.

Everything looked exposed and industrial, as if the occupants were moving either out or in at a moment's notice. The wide hallway led to a clerk sitting at a desk. He glanced up long enough for Indira to recognize that it was Dexter DuBrow.

"Indira," he said, smiling. "A pleasure to see you again."

So much had already changed since then. "You too."

"I'm here to oversee your family assignment. We appoint families according to the Once-Upon-a-Time Act of 1837. As a potential character for a story, you will now exercise your right to choose a host family for your time here in Fable."

Indira barely managed to nod. She would have been more nervous, but the day had already taken such a tailspin. How could it get any worse? Dexter shuffled another paper on his desk and traced a finger over the fine print.

"Let's start by reading the prophecy that was made about you."

Indira frowned at that. She always associated prophecies with palm readings or tarot cards. "When did someone even have the time to make a prophecy about me?"

"You took the dragoneye," Dexter explained. "The dragons took your answer, analyzed your innermost being, and created a prophecy. It's standard procedure." Dexter cleared his throat, and his voice raised to a more booming volume. "'Indira Story. You are a child of chance, the eventual owner of three unfortunate grudges, and the very mistress of misadventure.' Enter and choose!"

It took all of Indira's willpower to make one foot follow the other. She'd already messed up auditions, but according to the dragon's prophecy, she had some grudges coming her way *and* she was the mistress of misadventure. None of it sounded very flattering. Not very flattering at all. She took a deep breath and reminded herself why she was there.

I'm here to pick the right family for me. That's the first step back in the right direction.

"The showroom goes in a circle." Dexter gestured to the right. "Please feel free to interact with the families and ask questions. Do keep in mind that other characters will be touring the showroom. We operate on a first-come, first-served policy. If you see a character talking to a family, please politely keep moving. You're free to circle back around in case the character doesn't end up choosing that family. Also, each room features a family *unit*. Unlike you—and most potential characters—these groups were imagined *together*. We do ask that you adopt the entire family. It's always a little awkward when someone tries to leave behind the annoying brother."

He pointed to an archway. "After you complete the circuit, exit here. Just let me know which family you'd like to adopt. Feel free to take your time, though. Today is about you."

Indira followed the glittering footsteps on the walkway. The walls were tall and curved, cutting the interior into huge, drafty sections. An air-conditioning unit hummed in the darkness overhead, invisible behind hanging fluorescent lights and winding metal pipes.

The next room was a massive, open viewing space. On her left, curtains had been pulled back to reveal the interior of a chaotic living room. Indira gaped at the first family.

She had never seen so many children in such a small space. In one corner, three boys had rigged some kind of pulley mechanism with the curtains. She watched them try to send their little sister up to the loft using the rickety system. More children sat at the kitchen table playing cards. Socks and shoes littered the surface of the table like makeshift gambling chips. She spotted the mother standing by a wooden coatrack, one baby strapped to her front and another scrambling to hold on to her leg as she folded clothes. Up in the loft a disgruntled-looking teen lit matches, tossed them in a half-empty cup, and scowled.

Too much, she thought. *Way, way too much.*

A little wooden plaque stood in front of the display. The family's name had been etched there, but Indira didn't bother reading it. This family looked full. How could they possibly raise another human being? A door burst open as the father and yet *another* teenage girl arrived.

"Honey, I'm home!" he called.

The pulley system crashed, and the father caught his plummeting daughter just as he gave his wife a kiss on the cheek. Unexpectedly, the entire family turned to look at Indira, hopeful expressions on their faces. *It was all a performance,* she realized.

She gave them a polite wave before rushing on to the next room, her terror of the whole adoption experience growing with each step. The second room looked identical to the first. A great tall ceiling, curtains pulled away, and a family on a stage.

This family lacked the chaos of the first one. Instead a certain droning silence dominated the scene. Indira was drawn forward as one is to a car crash or a dental appointment. A vibrant blue light came from a flat screen on one wall. Indira couldn't see what they were watching, but every now and again the light flashed a new series of images.

The parents and children had sunk right into the plush couch. Discarded wrappers littered the armrests and floor like dead soldiers. It might have been a painting, but the smallest child kept trying to work his mouth around a huge triple cheeseburger. Indira watched in awe as the boy succeeded in devouring most of the greasy mess.

"Hello?" Indira asked. She read the sign. "Are you the Masons?"

When none of the Masons replied, Indira slipped beneath the arch and moved along. She thought the third room couldn't be any worse than the first two, but a quiet voice whispered a deeper fear: What if she didn't find a family that fit?

Her eyes anxiously found the next stage. Upholstered couches sat untouched. A spiraling staircase led to an unlit loft. Only the kitchen was occupied. A dark-skinned man sat at one end of the table, and Phoenix sat with him. Indira stood there, trying to think of something clever to call out to her friend, before noticing that the man was crying.

Phoenix nodded as the man sobbed and spoke, sobbed and spoke. Her eyes traced the tidy room and landed on a pair of photographs attached to the refrigerator. In one, a lovely dark-skinned woman with short hair and a radiant smile stared back at her. The sign read THE RANDLES.

Realization swept through Indira. This, of course, was Mr. Randle. And the woman in the photograph had been Mrs. Randle. Her presence in the home was obvious. A blanket with watercolor lilies running around the edges. A clever painting featuring slow-dancing alligators. However, her absence was equally noted in Mr. Randle's poorly matching tie and the dimly lit room. Indira felt a deep sadness gather in her heart as she realized he had lost his lovely wife.

Something told her that Phoenix was *exactly* who Mr. Randle needed.

Quietly, she slipped into the next room.

15

Family

Indira had hardly crossed the fourth threshold when a burst of fire scorched the air. It cast a vibrant warmth against her face. The strangest family yet claimed this stage. Couches had been pushed aside, and the kitchen chairs stacked one on top of another. A reed-thin girl with curly hair stood fifteen feet in the air, balancing on the wobbly tower as she juggled fruit. Her twin sister stood at ground level, preparing to toss yet another banana into the circling mix. A muscular woman waited backstage, calling for the girl to juggle faster.

At stage right, a man with dazzling suspenders signaled for Indira to come closer. "Madam! Do not be afraid! What you are about to see is a trade secret of the All-for-Nots. Prepare to be amazed." He backpedaled and clapped twice, and a pony came strutting out from behind the curtain. It was sleek and well-groomed and had a prancing gait. The man clapped a quick rhythm with his hands, and the pony obediently lowered its head. With a final signal, it wrapped its teeth around the back leg of the bottom chair of the wobbling tower and *yanked*.

Indira gasped as the chair ripped from the pile and the stack plunged downward. The new bottom chair tottered slightly and settled. The curly-haired girl continued to juggle, and Indira found herself clapping along with the rest of the family.

The All-for-Nots led the horse through a series of stunts, pulling one chair out after the next. It rolled, trotted backward, and even fetched one of the chairs for Indira to sit in. She enjoyed the show, and imagined how much fun it would be to live with a circus family. When the final chair was pulled, the little juggler gave a bow, and the whole family gathered around Indira.

"Jacob Fornot, at your service." The father extended a hand.

She shook it. "Indira. It was a pleasure. You're all so talented. And I do *love* your horse."

Jacob introduced his twin daughters and wife before turning a fiery gaze on Indira.

"We'll be straight with you. You'll have fun with us, but we're not very stable."

Indira eyed him. "Meaning what?"

"We move around." He snapped his fingers. The horse returned to the stage, dragging a pair of duffel bags. The twins each unzipped a bag and began removing poles and draping. Jacob went on as they worked: "A traveling troupe goes wherever the crowds gather. You'd always have a place to sleep, but it might be inconvenient for your schooling. If your story is going to be an adventurous one, though, we would certainly provide some great training for you."

Indira glanced over his shoulder at the stage. The twins had already constructed the tents and were now restacking the chairs. Indira felt that her story would be full of adventure, but she didn't know if that adventure would involve juggling or fire-breathing.

"I'll tell you what," Jacob said helpfully. "Go through the rest of the agency. If you find a family more fitting, we encourage you to join them. If you think we're the right ones, come back. I can only promise you that life with the Fornots will be vastly entertaining."

Indira didn't doubt that. She thanked the family for their time and the wonderful show. As she slipped into the next room, she was positively glowing. The show had almost been entertaining enough to make her forget auditions entirely.

The fifth stage was occupied by Maxi. Indira hadn't realized before just how easily her new friend stole the spotlight, how both her height and those dazzling eyelashes made Maxi seem like the very center of the universe.

Indira walked over to the edge of the stage to listen. This room looked similar to those before it, but the couches were a little nicer, and a set of fine bone china had been set out on the table. Indira watched a nanny flutter around the room, dusting off furniture and encouraging a young boy to focus on his homework. The boy's parents stood in front of Maxi.

The pair had gloriously blond hair, not to mention matching tans and scarves. The father was explaining something to Maxi using both hands and a *let's talk about the weather* voice.

"I travel to conferences every weekend, and Sandra runs a nonprofit on the West Coast, but Mrs. Verne will attend to your every need." The nanny looked up and nodded sweetly at Maxi. "You'll have a sizeable allowance, and the view from our downtown flat is divine."

Maxi put both hands on her hips. "What about closet space? I'm a walk-in kind of girl."

Both parents smiled like sharks, and Indira could already see Dexter DuBrow stamping their adoption papers. For the first time, Indira noticed a sign hanging in front of this particular stage: PROTAGONISTS ONLY. Indira swallowed. The family was clearly a fit for Maxi, but would they really have rejected her just for being a side character? Before Maxi could notice her standing there, Indira moved on to the next room.

And she was almost flattened by the smell of cinnamon. A middle-aged woman bustled around the kitchen, armed with oven mitts and an apron. Her auburn hair was pulled up in a neat bun, and Indira could hear her humming a pleasant song. A lamp shone in the loft, revealing a little boy curled into a beanbag chair with a picture book. He had on a pirate outfit that didn't succeed at all in making him look frightening.

The smell of cinnamon and the softly hummed song and the pleasant lighting pulled Indira right up onto the stage. Neither of them noticed her. Indira thought about announcing her presence, but at that exact moment the woman knelt, opened the oven, and whisked out a magazine-perfect apple pie. Steam *actually* floated out of the slits in the center.

Indira felt her mouth begin to water as the woman turned around.

And let out a surprised shriek. The dish bobbled in the woman's hands and crashed to the floor. Glass shattered and hot pie splashed everywhere. The woman had both hands against her heaving chest, as if holding them there was all that kept her heart from bursting through.

Indira started forward, apology on her lips, but another cry sounded behind her. She saw a flash of red as the little pirate child barreled into her. They went sprawling off-stage, and Indira landed on her back with a thud. The boy had her pinned and began thwacking the side of her head with a plastic sword. Indira warded off the blows until the mother plucked him off.

"Patch! We do not attack our guests!" The little boy squirmed in his mother's arms.

Indira sat up and said, "I'm sorry for scaring you. I don't know what I was thinking."

"Not at all. I should have expected it. My name is Mrs. Pennington. And this is Patch."

Unintentionally, Indira glanced over Mrs. Pennington's shoulder at the empty stage. Would Mr. Pennington come through the door as with the first family? Did he have a strange profession like Jacob Fornot the fire-breather? Mrs. Pennington caught the glimpse and let out a sigh. She set her son down and knelt beside him.

"First, my little pirate, I want to thank you for coming to my rescue. As you can see, I'm quite safe with our guest. She's here to find out more about our family. Why don't you read for a little bit and I'll call you down when the next dessert's ready?"

Patch the Pirate eyed Indira warningly before wrapping a little-armed hug around his mother's neck. He went running back toward the stairs, making cannonball noises and calling out very pirate-like commands to himself. A little warmth formed in Indira's chest. Was this how David had always felt about her? Together, Indira and Mrs. Pennington made quick work of the mess. The two of them sat down at the table when everything was back to normal.

"You're wondering where Mr. Pennington went. You've a right to know."

Indira didn't think she had a right to know. She almost told Mrs. Pennington so, but the woman barged on with her story. "He left Patch and myself for, as he called it, 'greener pastures.' I can forgive him for finding someone who interests him more." Mrs. Pennington glanced down at her hands. Using her thumb, she traced the fading white line across her ring finger. "But there's no greener pasture than my little Patch. For that he won't be forgiven. For that, he'll not be allowed to return. So if you join the Penningtons, well, we're not much, but we are family."

"Momma?" a voice called from the stairs. They both turned to see little Patch making his way down the stairs on short legs. He had a book almost as big as he was tucked awkwardly under one arm. "Can we read this one?"

It wasn't playacted at all. Indira saw the genuine desire of a young boy to be with his mother and the reflected desire Mrs. Pennington had to spend time reading with him.

"I will be up in one pirate minute. Which is how many human minutes?" she asked.

Patch concentrated, counting on his little fingers. "Three!" he shouted randomly.

They shared a smile. He started back up the stairs, but Mrs. Pennington called out, "Who has it better than us, little man?"

Patch's flop of hair tossed as he turned back. "Nobody," he called back, as if there were no other possible answer to the question. Indira's heart melted just a little bit.

She turned back to find Mrs. Pennington bustling around the kitchen again. The woman could have been the picture beside the word *bustle* in the dictionary. She pulled out two more pie dishes and began sorting through ingredients, talking as she worked.

"We're probably not the most exciting choice, but we'd love to have you," Mrs. Pennington said. "I understand there are a few more families to see today."

"Of course," Indira said. She knew it would be smart to explore every option. The Penningtons seemed wonderful, but who knew what was waiting in the final three or four rooms? Indira stood and thanked Mrs. Pennington. "I'm sorry again about the pie."

Mrs. Pennington said it was nothing, and Indira moved to the next room, a little ache in her heart as she left. *That's a new feeling,* she thought. *I guess the Penningtons are in first place?*

In the next room, a willowy family sat together on the floor. Or it looked that way at first. Every few seconds they would twist into a new pose, backs arching or necks rolling to one side. Colorful dream catchers hung in the windows, and a bright tie-dyed shawl was draped over the couch. The mother rose from her pose like a praying mantis and gave Indira an interesting bow.

"Namaste," the woman intoned. "Your aura is welcome here. Come. Be."

She led Indira to a vacant spot between her and her son.

"Breathe in," the woman instructed. "Breathe out."

Indira felt uncomfortable, so her breathing came out and in raggedly. The family all seemed to notice. The mother nodded at the son, who went to the kitchen and pulled a mug down from the cupboard. She kept giving instructions: "You're feeling stressed. Pinpoint that stress in your body. Let your aura hover over it. Expel the bad; inhale the good. Be free."

Indira felt a soreness in her butt and an itch on one shoulder blade, but she didn't announce either of those things. She practiced breathing, which she already felt she did pretty well, and changed poses twice before the boy returned with a cup of coffee.

"The coffee is organic," the mother bragged. "We eat vegan; we think vegan; we breathe vegan." She gestured to a cat that had just perched on the couch. "Even Muffins is a vegan."

"Draw close to the world and it will draw close to you," the son added.

All of them glanced at the father, expecting additional wisdom, but he seemed to have fallen asleep in his meditative pose. Indira laughed, which drew an annoyed look from the mother. "Your aura is suffering. Quick, what do you see when you look in the coffee? What does your aura interpret in the ether?"

Indira glanced down. She hadn't noticed it before, but the cream had definitely taken on a swirling pattern atop the coffee.

"You mean in the whipped cream? What do I see in the whipped cream?"

The mother corrected her. "It's not whipped cream. It's steam, and it's a metaphor for what can be known. Go on—what do you see?"

Indira didn't understand, but she glanced at the coffee anyway. The spattered pattern looked unreadable, but as she squinted, a rough outline did form.

She saw a person with a gentle smile.

"You see something." The woman nodded. "What is it? What does your future hold?"

"The Penningtons!" Indira shouted. "It's Mrs. Pennington."

The family looked startled as Indira sprinted back through the archway. Patch sat in the loft, turning the pages of his book excitedly. Mrs. Pennington had another pie in hand, and Indira determined to call out *before* she could turn around with it.

"Mrs. Pennington!" she shouted. "Wait, Mrs. Pennington."

The little lady paused, pie held tightly to her chest. "What is it, dear?"

"I want to be a Pennington. Can I adopt you as my family?"

She didn't scream this time, but the pie dish did slip from her shocked hands. This one wasn't glass, so it just clattered loudly on the floor as Mrs. Pennington rushed forward to give Indira a huge and welcoming hug.

16

New Discoveries

The Pennington home was nestled in a comfortable neighborhood called the Skirts. Just south of some of Fable's finer suburbs, the Skirts featured identical townhomes pressed together like cookies on a baking sheet. The architects had left enough room so they resembled individual houses, but one only had to take a few steps back to see they'd all come from the same batch.

Indira's room was not under the stairs or in a tea cupboard or anywhere as ridiculous as one would normally find in stories. She had a pleasant nook upstairs with a view of the southern forests in all their slate-green splendor. Before we continue, I would ask you, my dear reader, to remember a moment in which you *arrived* home. Perhaps after a day of lengthy shopping, or after spending all day hiking through the woods, or after a long journey away from the places and haunts you know better than your own heart. Imagine finally arriving and feeling that tremendous familiarity of *home*. If Fable had felt a lot like open arms, the Penningtons' home was a bold kiss on both cheeks.

Indira slept soundly that first night, the warmth of her new home enough to briefly wash away the memory of her failure. She dreamed of David. The two of them stood under the sun, looking over cliffs and out at the ocean. They laughed together before leaping out into the breathless deep. . . .

———

Indira stared at the ceiling. Even though she felt quite at home, she'd remained in her room, trying to not make noise and pretending she was still asleep. She had heard Patch and Mrs. Pennington roaming about, but she didn't quite know how to go downstairs and join them.

Some things just take practice.

She took advantage of the morning quiet to write a quick letter to David. She took out one of the pieces of stationery that Brainstorm Ketty had gifted her, admiring the finely curving font her name was in at the top. If she wasn't going to be able to visit him once a week, at least she'd write to him just as often. She kept the letter short and sweet, confirming she'd be attending Protagonist Preparatory but not mentioning how poorly auditions had gone.

It did not help that the memory of the day before was slowly creeping back into place. She saw Peeve Meadows and the three stones and all those failed audition scenes. A part of her felt like pulling up the covers and staying there forever.

Mrs. Pennington's voice interrupted those plans, however.

"Indira," she called from the bottom of the stairs. "Someone is here to see you!"

Someone was here to see her? How did anyone even know where she lived? She wondered if it was Deus, come to remind her of a few new rules now that she had picked her family. Maybe it was someone from the school?

The Pennington home was a lot like a person who wants to fit into a pair of jeans they've grown out of. Everything felt sucked in, and once you were inside, you were a little stuck. The stairs were narrow, the living room was barely big enough for the couch, and the kitchen table doubled as the chef's counter. Indira took the stairs three at a time and barely avoided tripping over Patch's scatter of building blocks. Mrs. Pennington gave her a *slow down, young lady* eyebrow raise. Her disapproval was overshadowed, though, by Maxi rushing forward for a hug.

"How'd you find me?" Indira asked.

"*Please,*" Maxi replied. "It was a piece. I just kind of batted my lashes at Dexter DuBrow in the Adoption Agency and asked for your address. The Evertons gave me their city map, since they both had to catch flights to Amsterdam today."

"There's an airport?" Indira asked curiously.

Maxi waved a dismissive hand. "Doesn't matter." She revealed a foldout map with advertised locations and bold-lettered captions. "We have exactly *one* day to ourselves. One day to explore the city! We're taking a tour of Fable."

With a few motherly reminders from Mrs. Pennington, and a brief art show from Patch (featuring some rather colorful interpretations of what a dog should look like), the two of them were out the door. Indira felt a mixture of nervousness and comfort with Maxi. Her new friend was so breathtakingly beautiful. Indira couldn't help wondering if she should put *her* hair up like that, or if that fashionable vest might come in *her* size.

But there was also the fact that Indira dreaded bringing up auditions. What if Maxi had won all three of her scenes? Indira's failure loomed overhead like a dark, invisible cloud.

For all that, Maxi clearly *enjoyed* her time with Indira. Indira had never had someone talk to her the way that Maxi did. Maxi thought that everything Indira said was just a *riot*. And it wasn't lost on Indira that Maxi had gone through the trouble of finding out where she lived.

She was so focused on her private thoughts that she ran right into Maxi's back. Her friend had stopped in the middle of the street, and Indira nearly bowled her over. She looked up to see what was wrong, and a little gasp escaped her lips.

Overnight, downtown Fable had transformed. Gone were the bleached-white buildings. In their place, a crowd of polite castles stood like city gentlemen in gray overcoats.

The most bizarre thing, however, was the mirror image that floated *above* the city proper. Each looming gray building had a twin hanging over it. She thought it might be an illusion or that she needed glasses, but Maxi stood open-mouthed, and Indira knew they were seeing the same miraculous sight. The mirrored buildings had all been tipped upside down. A layer of earth floated above them like a pointy hat made of tangled roots. She squinted and could just make out the Marks walking through those topsy-turvy streets.

Indira fumbled for Maxi's map. "Did we go the wrong way?"

Neat lines showed the city as it had been the day before. A series of spiraling staircases and conch-shell buildings. But as she held it out for Maxi's inspection, the lines began to reorganize themselves. She watched the drawing shrink in places and grow in others. A bold line appeared at the center of the map, indicating the upper and lower halves of the downtown.

The upper half was labeled: WHERE-THE-TREASURE-IS.

The bottom half was labeled: REACH-FOR-THE-SKY.

She continued to watch as shops on the map cordially traded places with one another before settling into their new locations. Maxi whispered, "Oh they're just adorable."

"Is everything in Fable like this?" Indira asked. "Is everything so . . . magical?"

"I hope so. It makes life more exciting. Come on, first stop is the Talespin coffee shop." Maxi tapped a building that fit snuggly between a cobbler's shop and a scarf store. "I've heard their white mochas are *divine*."

Indira remembered Brainstorm Ketty mentioning something about the Talespin, but she had no idea what a white mocha was. She handed the map back to her friend and followed. Maxi led Indira across an old-timey drawbridge. All the Marks had donned medieval clothing, or maybe Fable had forced the wardrobe change upon them? In the distance, a church bell tolled its good morning. A small part of Indira hoped that the story she'd be in would have knights and catapults and lances. She wouldn't mind a medieval adventure.

A darker thought followed: she could only ever be a side character in that story. She'd be the person destined to fall off the horse, or die for the hero, or whatever. Indira had to set the thought aside before it could steal too much magic from the bright new city.

They wound through a series of courtyards, past stretching stained-glass windows, and into a merchant square. Every now and again, Indira tilted her head back to look at the tops of the buildings dangling above them. It was clever magic, she thought, but she hoped it was also *stable* magic. If the spell malfunctioned, half of Fable would come spiraling down on them. Indira shivered at the thought and focused on the buildings that were right-side up.

All around her, log cabins huddled along the castle walls, as if trying to stay out of the rain. Maxi let out a little squeal and slipped forward through a crowd of Marks.

In that direction, Indira spotted a hanging sign that read simply: TALESPIN.

17

A Talespin

The Talespin didn't smell like Indira expected a coffee shop to smell. If you were to ask its owner, Mr. Threepwood, what scent a character caught as they walked through the front doors, he would tell you it was the scent of buried history combined with a touch of oatmeal-cinnamon and a liberal dash of *what could be*. Indira mostly noticed the oatmeal-cinnamon, though.

The shop was divided into two rooms: an immediate room where coffee and little pastries could be purchased, and off to one side a more spacious area filled with mismatched wooden tables. Espresso machines puffed out steam that made the whole place feel crowded. Indira and Maxi stood in line, waiting to be helped by a man with a gray-brown ponytail. Indira couldn't help searching the crowd for Phoenix, but his toss of red hair was nowhere to be seen.

"I think I just saw one of the Lost Boys from *Peter Pan*. I heard that they totally throw the most epic parties," Maxi whispered. A second later she let out a squeal and slapped an excited hand on Indira's shoulder. "There it is! It's actually right there!"

Their angle to the sitting room now showed a massive mirror, set against the farthest wall. Characters waited their turn to stand before the twisting thing, which was framed in fickle gold. Indira had heard about *this* before: a magic mirror. It always popped up in stories. Usually, the mirror gave bad dating advice or complicated the plot for everyone in the story.

"What's so special about that one?" Indira asked.

"Well, you know about the Authors, right?"

"Sure," Indira said. "They write the stories."

"'They write the stories'?" Maxi repeated incredulously. "More like they decide if we ever get to be *real*. They're the ones who breathe life into us. They can have us killed off or they can let us live happily ever after. Without them, we're nothing."

Indira nodded. She hadn't meant to offend. "And the mirror?"

Maxi's face filled with delight. "It's the only place in Fable that shows us the Authors. I think someone brought the mirror back from the Real World like *ages* ago. It's one of those rare connections between here and there. Pretty cool, right?"

Indira nodded again and stepped aside as Maxi ordered

a white mocha but with the whipped cream at the bottom and extra hot because that was the *only* way to drink it. Before Indira realized she hadn't asked Mrs. Pennington for any money, Maxi had already ordered Indira the same thing, and paid for it too.

"This drink is so good that I *want* other people to like it, you know?"

With their beverages in hand, Indira and Maxi joined the line for the mirror.

"So, that's where the name Talespin comes from. It's the moment an Author and Character connect for the first time," Maxi explained. "Together, we spin a tale into existence. I heard from this guy in the audition line—who, side story, had like the worst foot odor ever—that every time Hamlet came to Talespin, he saw William Shakespeare. Cool, right?"

Indira nodded, trying to ignore the mention of auditions and hoping Maxi wouldn't bring them up again. A few seconds later, the line moved and it was Maxi's turn. She sauntered up to the mirror and stared for a full minute. After an awkward silence, she whipped back around.

"How *boring.*" She pouted. "It was just some old lady looking out of a window and trying to be all dramatic. I didn't even see her write anything."

She stormed over to the nearest table, and Indira stood watching her until one of the characters in line coughed politely. Embarrassed, she set her coffee on the nearest table and rushed forward. Before she could even catch her breath, the mirror's surface began to boil. It looked like melted metal rippling from the splash of a stone. She waited as an image appeared, fuzzy and inconsistent at first. The colors sharpened, and she felt as though she had been transported through worlds.

The Author she saw looked like a man accustomed to hunching. It wasn't a pretty posture, but Indira felt that he must always be leaning *into* life, rather than away from it. She counted that as a positive. A busy world spun all around him. Indira saw a constant stream of people coming and going, but the Author ignored them. His eyebrows pushed together in concentration. He looked as if he had told the rest of the world he'd catch up with them later. Indira took a step closer. Printed in fine letters on the front of the journal were the initials *DM*.

She could not stop from wondering what they stood for. Devin Manatee or Dax Maverick? Before she could puzzle it out, the ground started to shake. She heard a voice echo all around her. It was almost as though someone were shouting down at her from a mountaintop.

"Mine! Mine! Get out! Mine! Get out!"

Indira turned, trying to find the source, but something *powerful* came in from the opposite direction and gave her a shove. Indira felt herself stumbling through time and space, back between worlds. There was a moment where she stumbled to the edge of something, like a railing that overlooked a drop into an endless pit. She almost lost her balance before a hand landed on her shoulder. The grip tightened.

Indira spun and screamed. The world spun with her.

Maxi's hand. It was Maxi's hand on her shoulder.

Indira was back in the Talespin. The voice continued echoing, but the Author was gone, and for some reason she could barely keep her feet. "Indira?" Maxi asked. "Are you okay?"

She stumbled back and almost fainted. There was an intense pressure at her temples. As the room spun, she was thankful to discover Maxi's arm hooked into hers. With surprising strength, her friend led her to the nearest seat and sat her down. Maxi's eyes went conspiratorially wide. "You saw something. You *totally* saw something."

Indira shook herself. What had she seen? Like a dream, the images were quickly growing less and less clear. She remembered the Author and his hunched shoulders. But then there was the voice angrily yelling at her from every direction, the powerful shove out of that world and back into this one. "I saw an Author," Indira said. "But . . . there was this voice . . ."

Maxi raised a curious eyebrow. "Like the Author was *speaking* to you?"

"No," Indira said, trying to remember. "It was someone else. They shouted at me, and then I just kind of got shoved away."

Indira glanced around and noticed that the rest of the

customers were staring at them. She steeled herself, stood, and headed for the entrance. Maxi helped her along, and the effect of the open air was instantaneous. Indira felt the tightness in her chest loosening. That voice haunted her, but at least it was gone now, and they could put the place behind them.

18

Where-the-Treasure-Is

Hoping to recapture the spirit of exploration they'd started the day with, Maxi announced they would be heading to the Librarian Hall of Fame next.

"The map says it's up there." She pointed at the inverted castles. "Are you . . . I mean, do you think you'll be okay? We can *totally* wait for another day."

Indira really just wanted to go home. She wanted to curl up in her nook of a room and get some much-needed rest. She didn't want to think about her failed auditions or the strange voice or anything at all, but she knew Maxi had taken time to plan out a fun day.

"I'm fine, really. How do we get up there?"

"Come on," Maxi said. The two girls linked arms and crossed the busy courtyard. At the mouth of a particularly wide alleyway, they found a square tile that had been painted a familiar color of bright blue. "We just have to take the dragoneye!"

Both girls tilted their heads back. A security guard was walking along the rooftop of one of the upside-down castles. He saw them staring and gave a polite wave. Maxi set both feet on the painted square. Indira saw the eyelid split and the familiar eye appear. The creature considered Maxi unblinkingly. Then the deep voice bellowed: "What is your worst fear?"

Clearing her throat, Maxi said, "Public speaking."

Indira raised an eyebrow as Maxi vanished. She was afraid of *public speaking*? Maxi? The blue square shivered with light. Indira tilted her head back. Sure enough, a smaller and harder-to-see version of her friend had appeared in the dangling city above.

Indira stepped forward, and the same earthen voice asked, "What is your deepest fear?"

"Failure," she said softly. "I don't want to leave David behind."

A flash, a pull, and she found herself staring at a new set of city streets. She looked up and realized, with a turn of her stomach, that she was *actually* looking down. The other half of Fable, the forest, the distant ocean, all gleamed like a too-solid sky. Before her stomach could fully settle, Maxi hooked her arm back into Indira's and led them off once more.

She played the role of dramatic tour guide *very* well. Indira couldn't help noting how much Maxi already knew about the city. Some of the information she read from the margins of the map, but other bits were pulled directly from memory. Indira pointed to a building on their right that was cut off by a moat. The only way across was a very medieval-looking drawbridge.

"What's that one?"

Maxi answered excitedly. "That's the headquarters for the Grammar Police."

Indira frowned. "The Grammar Police?"

"Law and order," Maxi confirmed. "The Grammar Police handle all the small-scale crime in Fable. Missing commas, burglaries, trespassing. The Editors are the ones who tackle the *really* big stuff. Dark plots, global threats, that kind of thing."

"Cool. How do you know so much about them?"

"Oh. I read it. Somewhere." Maxi let out a little squeal. "Look! We're here!"

Great Roman-style columns fronted the vast face of a very official-looking structure, complete with ghostly marble steps. It was the kind of building you had to stand and look at for a while to really appreciate. Maxi was right in the middle of reading an official plaque when a puff of dust shot out of an alleyway on their right. A dog-ear came skidding out with it. Indira heard a woman shouting before she rounded the corner. She realized it was the same pair from the day before, the same Mark who had claimed to have had her watch stolen.

Other characters backed away as the dog-ear came

tearing down the street. Maxi stumbled back too, muttering something about her new shoes. The woman shouted again.

"Stop that *dog-ear*!"

Before she could even think twice, Indira launched forward. The dog-ear adjusted, but not quickly enough, and Indira wrapped both arms around its neck and tangled it into a painful roll. Two rotations later she came to a stop with the dog-ear pinned and squirming beneath her. She held tighter, and it dropped the bronze watch to snap at her. She pulled back her face, and the dog-ear snarled, doubling its efforts to slip her weight.

The Mark arrived, panting. Indira had expected all the Marks to look the same, but surely they didn't all have freckles running down their arms or such distinctive light-brown eyes. Indira held the dog-ear tight as the Mark stooped to snatch her watch from the dusty street.

Prize lost, the dog-ear gave up the struggle and let its head flop playfully back to the ground. It watched them, tongue lolling as though it found the whole thing *very* amusing.

Indira scowled and sat up. The dog-ear scrambled to its feet, trotted a safe distance away, and turned to give Indira a piercing stare. She saw that a thread of her pink shirt had ripped free as they'd rolled around. Now it dangled from the dog's collar like a ribbon. The creature huffed once before shooting out of sight.

"How can I *ever* thank you, darling?"

The Mark spoke with a thick drawl. It wasn't hard for Indira to imagine the woman stuck between the pages of some historical romance with fancy dresses and horse-drawn carriages.

"Some days I just don't have the good sense the Authors gave a rock. I mean, really, taking my watch off in a public square. I was just asking for trouble."

"No worries." Indira smiled politely. "It was kind of fun."

The Mark looked down at her watch. "Look at the time! Quick, honey, what's your name? I clearly owe you a favor."

Indira hesitated. "It really wasn't a—"

"Oh, I insist, sweetie."

She sighed. "My name's Indira Story."

"Oh, I could just eat that up!" the Mark said with a wink. "I'll catch you later."

The slender woman glanced at her watch, smiled, and vanished. Maxi squeezed past the crowd of characters who had gathered as witnesses to Indira's little stunt. She hadn't quite realized just how many people were watching.

"You're *such* a natural," Maxi said. "I can only imagine how your auditions went! The way you just went all instincts on that? I was seriously jealous. I might have made protagonist track or whatever, but it's hard to feel like a *real* hero with someone like you around!"

Indira nodded her thanks, but she didn't know what to say. Should she tell Maxi the truth? She had failed. She wasn't even *allowed* to be a protagonist according to the brainstorms. It was one thing to tackle a fleeing dog, but that was the same instinct that had gotten her in trouble against Peeve. Indira had been too eager to play the hero, so her old neighbor had known exactly what she was going to do.

"Coming?" Maxi asked.

Indira looked up. "Yeah, sorry, I'm coming."

The rest of the day ticked away quickly. They saw the endless statues in the Librarian Hall of Fame. They swung by to catch a movie at the Fan-Fiction Cinemas. All twelve theaters were featuring a different fan-written version of some book called *The Lightning Thief.* Maxi and Indira watched one where the story had been converted into a musical featuring a few too many tap-dancing centaurs for Indira's taste.

Even with all the distractions, Indira couldn't stop thinking about how unfair her auditions had been. Peeve had *watched* her and studied her and used all that information against her. Was Maxi right? Was she *really* a natural? And if she was a natural, why had her auditions gone so miserably?

At the end of the day, the two girls walked silently back home. Maxi made sure to show Indira how to get to Protagonist Preparatory for classes the next day.

"We should *totally* meet up and compare scheds."

When they reached the Skirts, Indira made sure to give Maxi the biggest hug she could.

"See you tomorrow, Maxi."

Maxi clapped her hands together in delight and headed home. Indira watched her friend until she'd rounded a corner and vanished from sight. It had been a long day, but at least she had a friend who was willing to put an arm around her when she needed it. And she had a family waiting for her at home. As she walked back to the Penningtons', she realized she also had determination. She'd come to Fable with a *purpose.*

Get in a story. Be a hero. Bring David with her.

One lousy audition wasn't going to stop her from being the best character she could be.

19

Every Cage

Indira dreamed about dragons with great marble eyes. Every time she spoke, one of the great dragons would unfold its wings. Before long their flight filled the empty sky like poetry. It wasn't until the dream was nearly over that she realized she was one of them. She climbed up, up, up through the clouds before waking in a twist of covers.

There are no fair trades between dreams and the waking world. After all, no one wants to trade flying for morning breath.

Indira stared at the ceiling for a long time but couldn't go back to sleep. Not with the first day of school looming ahead of her. She tried to keep in mind the words she'd heard when she'd arrived on the outskirts of Fable: *Every cage has a key.* She felt as if she were in a cage, and she was having a hard time imagining herself finding a key.

Indira started downstairs but was cut off at the landing by Patch. Her adopted brother was already in his pirate attire, bent over a book of bright colors and funny shapes.

"Morning, kiddo," Indira said, ruffling his hair.

He *aaarrr*ed in response, which was funny enough to untangle one of the five thousand knots in her stomach. A second knot unraveled at the sight of Mrs. Pennington. She had on a delightfully blue apron and dangling earrings. Indira's adopted mother set down hot plates and fluttered forward with open arms. "It's someone's special day!"

Indira smiled shyly. "It's just school."

"*Just* school," Mrs. Pennington repeated. "It's your first day! You'll meet your teachers and new students, and *oh*, it's bound to be so exciting!"

She sat Indira down in front of a full breakfast spread before glancing back into the living room and calling, "Captain! Your breakfast is ready in the main cabin."

Patch abandoned pirate decorum and allowed his mother to put him in a booster seat. He went straight for the apple pancakes. Mrs. Pennington poured him a generous portion of syrup and continued. "Now, from what I've read, you'll have auditions first, right?"

Indira's stomach did a nosedive. "I already had them."

"Oh." Mrs. Pennington assessed the look on Indira's face. "And . . ."

Indira moved her food around with a fork, unable to meet her foster mother's eye.

"They didn't go as planned," Mrs. Pennington guessed. "Not to worry! Because the next part matters *just* as much. Classes and practice and training. That's what really makes a character into someone worthy of a story. It's not as if you're just stuck with your fate. Plenty of characters have carved themselves into something more after a poor audition."

Indira stopped chewing her sausage and said with a full mouth, "They have?"

Patch mimicked Indira, showing them both a mouthful of pancakes before giggling.

"Stop that, Patch," Mrs. Pennington said. "Of course. I've read all about it! How was I supposed to give you good advice without reading about it?"

Indira shrugged. "I just kind of thought I was stuck as a side character."

"For now," Mrs. Pennington answered. "That's just the school's official classification for you, but if you prove yourself, there's no telling what role an Author could have in store for you, Indira. I really think you're going to be great. All you have to do is figure out your strengths."

Indira couldn't help feeling as though Mrs. Pennington's interpretation of things was very . . . motherly. Brainstorm Ketty hadn't mentioned any of this, which had her feeling that it wasn't an actual possibility. She took a little hope from Mrs. Pennington's encouragement, but made sure to stay realistic, too. There was a *lot* of ground to make up after how poorly she'd performed in auditions.

"What if I don't have any strengths?" Indira asked.

"Stars and skies, you're a Pennington! Of course you have strengths."

Indira forked another sausage and nodded tightly. She hadn't realized how much faith Mrs. Pennington had in her. Even if Indira didn't know what her strengths were, at least she had made the right decision at the Adoption Agency. Wasn't that a strength? Good decision making?

Before Indira could ask another question, the telephone rang. Indira fumbled her fork in surprise. She hadn't even known they *had* a telephone. Mrs. Pennington bustled over to the receiver and answered in a cheery voice, "Pennington residence!"

Indira couldn't hear the caller, but she listened as Mrs. Pennington *mm-hmm*ed her way through the conversation. She ended by saying, "Of course. You take care of yourself, doll."

She watched Mrs. Pennington take a deep and steadying breath. "All right, loves. That was Mrs. Stevenson. She's had an emergency and needs me to take her shift at work. Indira, I meant to walk you to school. . . ."

"I already know how to get there," Indira said quickly. "I'll be okay, I promise."

Mrs. Pennington looked grateful, but her eyes settled on Patch next. "Little captain, how would you like it if your sister walked you to the park? The Baker twins wanted to play with you today, remember?"

Patch set down his fake pirate's hook sadly. "You can't walk me?"

"Little pirates have to be brave," Mrs. Pennington answered. "Indira's a part of your crew now too. Don't you think she deserves some attention from the captain?"

Patch accepted this explanation gladly. "Can I at least recite my colors?"

Mrs. Pennington's eyes darted to the hanging clock, but after the briefest hesitation she sat down. "Let's hear red."

Patch sat up a little straighter. "Red is an enemy ship. Or a rose! But I don't like thorns."

Mrs. Pennington smiled. "And green?"

"Green is land ho! Or seasickness."

Mrs. Pennington swept over and pulled him into a hug. "That's my little captain. Keep practicing on the way to the park. Indira will help you with any colors you don't know."

Before Indira could ask where the park was, Mrs. Pennington had sketched out a quick map on a napkin. It was only a bit out of the way, and Mrs. Pennington assured her that she had plenty of time before school. She apologized for the inconvenience as she gathered papers and work identification. Mrs. Pennington was set to walk out the door, but Indira stopped her so that she could fix a twist at the back of Mrs. Pennington's collar.

"Don't worry about us," Indira said. In the background, Patch was making cannonball noises. "Thanks for the pep talk. I really needed that today."

"Did I do all right?" Mrs. Pennington asked. "I'm trying to do it the right way."

"You were great," Indira whispered.

Mrs. Pennington gave a wide smile before swinging open the door. She turned back and asked, "Who has it better than us?"

"Nobody!" Patch and Indira answered together.

With that, Mrs. Pennington headed to work and left the two of them home alone. Indira sat Patch down with a book and went upstairs to get ready. Exactly two minutes later she realized there *was* no getting ready. She had no notes to read through, no clothes to change into, no possessions to gather. All she had was her new uniform and the knapsack of supplies Brainstorm Ketty had given her. She slid the gorgeous navy-blue jacket over her normal shirt, tightened her belt, and hung her hammer from the belt loop.

She pulled her dark hair into a ponytail. There, she was as ready as she'd ever be.

Patch followed her out of the house, a favorite toy clutched against his shoulder. As they walked to the end of the street, he pointed out colors from his book in the bright Fable morning.

"Sidewalk is slate," he announced proudly. "Trees are olive. And that's a cerulean jay!"

A blue bird fluttered by. Indira ruffled his hair again as they reached the end of the street. She looked left and right, but there was no sign of any foot traffic. She started leading Patch across the road, but he stopped unexpectedly on the sidewalk.

"What's wrong, little man?"

He held out a stubby-fingered hand. "Can't cross without a friend."

Indira laughed, walking back to take his hand and lead him across the street. They made it to the park, and before she could even say goodbye, Patch had commandeered the Baker twins and was planning a mutiny that involved two rocking horses and mounds of "mustard" gold.

Mrs. Baker took over, and Indira left, eager to get to school as soon as possible. Maybe Mrs. Pennington was right. Maybe there was still a way to improve her standing. Either way, it wouldn't hurt to arrive early. She set out for her first day of school with the tiniest sliver of hope walking along beside her.

20

Three Unfortunate Grudges

Indira arrived at Protagonist Preparatory quite early.

A little *too* early. The secretary's desk was empty. Indira considered the passages that curled out in every direction and remembered walking by a massive hall the day before.

Not knowing where else to go, Indira headed back down that corridor and found the room she was looking for. Great stone columns lined both sides of the hall. Between each set of columns, a fireplace flickered and beckoned.

She walked to the center of the room and counted nine fires in all. Four on her left, four on her right, and the largest of all the hearths at the end of the room. Chairs of varying comfort waited in front of each fireplace. Oddly, not every fire cast a red glow into the room. She saw two that were blue and one that was a fickle silver color. Indira plunked down before the most normal-looking fire she could find in the most comfortable chair available.

It took her about two seconds to fall asleep.

For nearly forty-three minutes, all of Indira's worries drifted away. She awoke to a polite tap on one shoulder. The slender girl hovering beside her chair had thick, square-framed glasses. A curtain of brown hair slanted across her face, and she looked rather indistinct if you didn't count the large birthmark on her neck. Indira thought it looked just like a pineapple.

"I'm sorry," the girl said. "I thought you might have to be somewhere. You were sound asleep when I came in almost thirty minutes ago."

Indira sat up with a yawn. "Yeah. I have a class with Mr. Threepwood."

"So do I. But did you know that you were in front of the Rest Hearth?"

Indira's eyes flicked over to the fire she had chosen. "The rest what?"

"Rest Hearth." The girl gestured to the stones above the fireplace. Sure enough, the word REST had been carved there in very Roman-looking letters. "Each fire does something different." She pointed at them in succession. "Health, Luck, Comfort, and Wit." And then to the side that they were sitting on. "Caution, Rest, Energy, and Courage."

120

Indira eyed the hearths appreciatively. "Do they really work?"

The girl gave a timid smile. "You *were* sleeping rather soundly."

Indira shrugged. "Right. And which hearth did you sit in front of?"

"Courage," she replied quietly. "I think it's working. I don't normally speak to people. But I'm not sure how long the courage lasts. I might be using it all up on you."

Indira smiled. "Well, what do you say we get to class and stop wasting it?"

This seemed like a good first step. Making friends. That was important, right? They walked back to the entrance, Indira stumbling groggily behind the ghost of a girl. Indira wasn't exactly *tall,* but she felt like a giant compared to her new acquaintance.

Indira realized that the little girl hadn't said what the ninth hearth was for. It loomed behind them now, and Indira paused at the exit to Hearth Hall. "What's the last one do?"

The little girl shivered, as if the hallway's chill had sucked the courage right out of her.

"I don't know," she said. "The words above that hearth are in another language."

Indira nodded before following the girl through the halls. Protagonist Preparatory bustled with life now. Characters of all shapes and sizes walked the wide hallways and disappeared down winding staircases. A handful of characters were waiting in line before the secretary, each of them glancing nervously at the other characters who had already secured their school jackets. Indira noticed a handful of navy jackets like her own, but some characters wore golden ones instead. She admired them at first, but eventually found them a little too bright and showy.

The girl led her through the hustle and bustle to the end of the hallway. A corner room had silver letters stamped on its wooden frame: 1001. "Want to sit together?" Indira asked.

"I'm Margaret Faye," the girl said suddenly.

"Indira Story."

They exchanged smiles before entering a room full of students. Indira walked down the center aisle of the classroom. Desks had been pushed into rows of four and were split down the center so the teacher could walk from front to back without any obstacles. Indira walked them down the aisle and spotted Maxi.

Maxi had her hair up and was smiling so brightly that she made her own golden jacket look dull by comparison. Indira led Margaret—or Little Margaret, as Indira found herself thinking of the girl—in that direction. She plunked down next to Maxi and gestured for a terrified-looking Margaret to sit next to her. Maxi snapped around and looked ready to say something before realizing it was Indira. Her face swung through fifteen different emotions.

Surprise, excitement, surprise again, worry, and then ultimately she settled on a strange mixture of eleven other expressions. Indira wasn't sure what was wrong.

"We have class together!" Maxi said in surprise. "You never told me about your auditions. We spent yesterday together and didn't even like talk about it all."

Indira really didn't want to talk about it. She did her best to change the subject. "How about you? How'd your auditions go? You have to tell me about them."

Maxi leaned back, brushed some lint from her golden uniform, and began. Little Margaret listened quietly, and Indira noticed her fidgeting every now and again, as if she wanted to add something to the conversation but just couldn't gather the courage to do so.

Indira listened first to a description of a greasy-looking skater dude who could have been cute if he even knew what a shower was. Each illusion Maxi described was a painful echo of Indira's own sequence. She tried not to think about it as she listened to her friend explain just how clever she had been. Unsurprisingly, Maxi had won all three of her scenes.

"And so I got approved for the protagonist track," Maxi finished. Her eyes fell on Indira and little Margaret, as if she had just remembered they were there. "Which is like whatever."

The word *protagonist* still hit Indira like a punch to the stomach. She was saved from responding, however, by the entrance of their teacher, Mr. Threepwood. A current of hushes snuffed out every conversation. Indira startled a little. She recognized him.

The same man who had made her a white mocha at the Talespin just the day before took a seat on top of his teacher's desk. She hadn't guessed that the man serving her coffee had actually been the owner. He set a leather bag to one side. He wore tan suspenders, dark khakis, and a white, three-button shirt. His long hair was pulled back in a loose ponytail. Indira thought he looked kind of like a hipster.

"Good morning, class! Welcome to Sympathetic Characters. We designed this course to build upon your connection with the readers. Our research shows that readers today have more options than ever. So about fifteen years ago, the sympathetic course sequence was initiated to make every character more loveable and appealing to their audiences."

His eyes settled on Indira and Little Margaret for the first time. He let out an embarrassed cough and did his best to smile at them. A horrible blush flooded Indira's cheeks.

"My sincere apologies. I thought the signs would do the trick. For today, I'd love for the side characters to sit on this side of the room." He indicated the opposite section of the class. "And all my protagonists should be on this side."

Indira expected a number of people to shuffle back and forth, but she was the only one to stand. Sweat broke out in a bright sheen across her forehead. She was so nervous that she barely noticed little Margaret duck after her across the aisle. When she had taken her seat on the proper side of the class, Mr. Threepwood clapped his hands together.

"Very good. Now, the whole goal for any character should be to connect with the reader. You want them to identify with you, care about you, and, if possible, admire you. We will go over the everyman-versus-superman theory, discuss proactivity, formulate strategies for becoming an underdog, and even go over how to ally yourself with other characters to improve your stock. Even the most talented Authors can't force a connection between a character and a reader. Most of that responsibility falls on your shoulders. This class should help make the task easier."

Indira used the sleeve of her jacket to wipe sweat from her forehead. She couldn't help but glance over at Maxi. What would Maxi think of her now? Had she *known* Indira was a side character? Every time Indira looked over, though, Maxi looked focused on the lecture.

Mr. Threepwood kept teaching, but Indira was distracted. She realized now that every side character had been given a navy-blue jacket. On the opposite side of the room, protagonist students wore golden jackets. *To help identify our students,* Brainstorm Ketty had said. Her own jacket no longer felt so majestic. The gold version looked so much more promising, didn't it?

"Frankly," Mr. Threepwood continued, "there are a number of things you *can* do. We will start with the most basic rules of being a character: having a similarity to the reader. I'll begin by passing out a survey. You will answer questions about your interests and try to discover connections that could link you to potential readers. And remember, every character has a story!"

He walked the rows, passing out surveys, and the class fell to working silently. Indira pulled out her pen and started scribbling down answers. But she felt as lifeless as she had after auditions. Not only was she *not* a protagonist, but now she had a living and colorful reminder of her place at the school. One by one, students turned in their classwork and returned to their seats. Indira was still working on her sheet when Mr. Threepwood clapped his hands together.

"I will end with this," he announced happily. "Fable is a mysterious place. There are thousands of anecdotes and stories that demonstrate all the different paths toward becoming a successful character. There is only one thing we know for certain. Some of the people on this side of the room will become protagonists." He pointed to the side characters. A few gasps sounded in response. "You will work tirelessly and blossom into a character that your brainstorms and judges could not have predicted."

He turned to the golden-jacketed students. "And some of *you* won't be protagonists. You will find the course load too rigorous, the pressure too challenging, and you'll settle for other roles. I say this to remind every one of you that your fate has *not* yet been determined. It would be foolish to act otherwise. Let's take this week a page at a time, all right? Class dismissed!"

As some of the others stood, Indira found herself staring at Mr. Threepwood. He had said exactly what Mrs. Pennington had said that morning. Why hadn't Brainstorm Ketty mentioned *any* of this to her? *Every cage has a key,* she thought confidently. *If I'm stuck in the cage of being a side character, then working hard is the key to getting out. All I have to do is be better, work harder, and impress my teachers. I can still be a protagonist. I can still save David.*

Indira was lost in thought as she walked to the end of the row. Little Margaret hovered like a shadow at her shoulder. Indira and Maxi arrived at the middle aisle simultaneously.

"Want to grab lunch later and compare schedules?" Indira asked.

Her stomach sank when one of the passing protagonists scoffed at the question. Maxi tilted her chin and seemed to be considering her response carefully. She darted a few looks at the other protagonists who were funneling out of the room, several walking arm in arm.

Eventually she leaned in and whispered, "I'm sorry. Things are just different now. I'm a protagonist. I have to get used to that, you know?"

Indira shook her head. "So you can't have lunch with me?"

Maxi made an annoyed noise. "It's not like that, Indira."

"Then what is it like?"

"We're just different, okay?" Maxi tried to look apologetic, but Indira thought she just looked and sounded like a jerk. "Sorry, but I have to go."

Indira watched Maxi sweep out of the room in a sea of golden jackets. All the side characters, it seemed, were still turning in their assignments or simply waiting for their supposed superiors to exit first. Indira refused to cry, but she felt as if someone had stolen the joy right from her chest. Mr. Threepwood's words had been so hopeful, but Maxi's abandonment overshadowed them.

The worst part was that she could see Maxi's point. They *were* different now. Set apart. It shouldn't have mattered, but the color of their jackets and some of the classes they would take and even the name of the school made it plain as day: Indira wasn't like Maxi. It was possible that she never would be. Indira walked up and turned her survey in. Margaret followed her out of the room like a shadow. All Indira could think about were the words of prophecy Dexter DuBrow had shared as she entered the Adoption Agency: *Owner of three unfortunate grudges.*

There was Peeve Meadows.

There was the dog-ear.

And now there was Maxi.

Good, she thought angrily. *At least I know who my enemies are.*

21

Escaping Alice

Indira and Margaret moved toward Hearth Hall, silently agreeing that a few minutes of courage or energy or even rest might do them some good. They had passed through several hallways when Indira stepped on a tile and her foot stuck to it. Her hands scraped painfully against the stone wall as she came to a jolting stop. Margaret looked back, a little wide-eyed.

"Are you all right?" she asked. "What happened?"

Indira yanked at her foot but couldn't get it to budge. "I'm stuck."

Margaret set down her knapsack and examined the situation like a scientist would. She had walked around to one side and was about to offer a suggestion when the floor and wall gave a sickening lurch. The very stones groaned and the room revolved. Indira caught a final glimpse of a terrified Margaret before being whisked away into a hidden room. Her foot freed itself, but the wall sealed at the same time. There was no way out.

Hearing a creak behind her, Indira wheeled. Almost the entire room was filled with rabbits. All with white fur and glassy, pinkish eyes. And they were watching her. Stone seats circled a stone table. More surprising, every seat but one had a student sitting in it.

A snowy girl with blond curls stood. "Oh good. You're all here now." She waved Indira forward. Seeing no other choice, Indira navigated slowly through the camp of rabbits and was forced to climb over the back of the empty chair. The blond girl smiled approvingly.

"My name is Alice. This is How to Get Captured and Narrowly Escape. It's not a normal class, but then, I'm not a normal girl."

She sat down and her bright blue dress billowed out. She snapped her fingers and one of the bunnies came scuttling forward. They all watched the little creature approach a rather large chest that sat in the very center of the table. Indira had been so distracted by everything else that she hadn't noticed it. The bunny used its little paws to spin the dials of a combination lock attached to the chest's front before shooting back to join the others.

"We'll start with simple escapes," Alice explained. "Then we'll work our way into more drastic and daring encounters. You'll have to use all the clues to get yourselves out of the room in thirty minutes. Today's challenge is a classic rescuer-and-captives scenario!"

Alice clapped her hands together twice. The sound of stone sliding against stone echoed. Indira flinched as a pair of sturdy bracelets slid up from the arms of her chair and closed over her wrists. A quick glance showed the rest of the table similarly bound. Only one girl, off to Indira's right, could still move.

"All you have to do is say the answer to the following question and the challenge will come to an end: Apple plus cinnamon plus orange equals . . . ?"

Alice grabbed the base of the nearest candlestick.

"Best of luck! We'll discuss your results tomorrow!"

She gave the candlestick a tug, and the stone floor beneath her opened up. They all watched as the golden hair tossed and the robin's-egg dress billowed out. The stones turned and the chair vanished into the floor, leaving them alone with hundreds of rabbits and each other.

"Why are all the teachers so *weird*?" a boy to her right asked.

The only girl who remained free stood. Indira couldn't help noting that she wore a golden protagonist jacket. "Right. My name is Chem. I guess I'm your rescuer?" She circled the table with a thoughtful expression. "We should start by looking for clues. Let's think about that equation, too. Apple, cinnamon, and orange."

Indira's eyes flicked around the room. The rabbits were

all moving around, hopping here or there. It was almost as if a little village of rabbits had decided to hold a secret meeting. The walls, though, were stone and bare. She did not see any inscriptions or letters or anything.

"There are nineteen total letters in those words," Chem announced suddenly. "That has to be it. *Nineteen!*"

Her words echoed. Indira and the others waited, but their wrist braces didn't release.

"Maybe not," the boy next to Indira said. "It's gotta be something else."

Indira scanned the room again, and this time something *did* catch her eye. The rabbits were impossible to keep apart, moving and hopping constantly. Except for one. In the corner of her vision, there was one rabbit that looked just like the rest, but it wasn't moving.

"I think I've got something," Indira said.

Some of the others looked her way, but Chem was running back through the numbers, still trying to figure out how to add the three words together.

"Hey," Indira said. "I found a clue! There's a statue over there. That rabbit on the far end isn't moving like the rest of them are."

Chem gave her a disbelieving look before crossing the room. Rabbits scattered left and right, but the one Indira had pointed out didn't even budge. Chem bent down and hefted the statue up. "It has numbers," she announced. "For a combination lock."

A sense of accomplishment nestled into Indira's chest. She had found the first clue.

"Seventy-three, forty-eight, twenty-two," Chem read aloud.

The boy sitting nearest the chest adjusted his shackles and leaned forward. He spun the dials until there was a satisfying click. The chest yawned open, but at the same time, the overhead lights flickered out. There were a few seconds of creeping darkness before the candles staggered around the table all lit up at once. A soft glow circled the face of every student.

Chem plucked up the nearest candles and held their light out over the chest. There were books inside. One for each of them. She passed them around the circular table.

"All right. You're looking for anything connecting to the words *apple, cinnamon,* or *orange.* If you come across *anything* connected to those, let me know immediately."

Indira's own book was a tattered thing with a blue cover. She pulled a candle closer, adjusted her shackles, and started to flip through. It was a recipe book. A glance over her neighbor's shoulder showed his was the same thing.

"Got one reference here!" a boy called out.

"Me too," another voice echoed.

"They're all recipes," Indira said. "Of course they have those ingredients."

In the first few pages, she flipped through cobbler after

133

cobbler. Her eyes fell on the words *apple* and *cinnamon* and *orange*, but without any apparent pattern at all.

"Maybe it's the total number of times they're mentioned," Chem explained. "Let's start to keep a count. Whatever the total is for each of them . . ."

"Seven now for me!"

"I've had eight apples!"

"All the recipes in my book seem to be for . . . zombies."

Indira obeyed Chem's instruction. She was counting the references on page 38 when the boy next to her closed his book. She watched him lean forward and inhale deeply. She thought maybe he was doing some kind of meditation until he leaned back with a grin on his face.

"Y'all don't smell that?" he asked. "Go ahead. What do you smell?"

Indira leaned forward a little and gave a sniff. The sharp scent of mint flooded her nostrils. She leaned back, fighting off a sneeze, as the rest of the room did the same.

"Strawberries over here."

"Mint," Indira answered.

"Well, mine smells like cinnamon," the boy replied.

Carefully he lifted the candle out of its holder. Indira tilted her own light his way, and there, on the bottom of the wax, the number 2 had been carved.

"Who has apple?" Indira asked. "And who has orange?"

It didn't take long to figure it out from there. The recipes had all been a distraction. If the boy hadn't noticed cinnamon wafting in his direction, they might never have solved it. He kept on grinning as they looked. On the bottom of the apple candle, the number 5 had been carefully carved. An elegant 1 was waiting on the bottom of the orange candle. Indira smiled over at the boy as they totaled the numbers up.

"Eight," Chem said. "Our answer is eight."

All the lights clicked back on. The rabbits had disappeared. Alice was crossing the room toward them, face full of pride. "You've done wonderfully! Take a seat, Chem!"

The girl circled to find her empty seat and sat back down.

"Now, remember to finish your homework," Alice said. "Class dismissed!"

Alice clapped her hands again. Without any more warning than that, all their chairs dropped straight down. They landed on the floor below, in a sort of dining room, set perfectly around a table that had fortunately been empty. Indira and the other students stared at each other in confusion. She couldn't remember Alice mentioning anything about homework.

The group stood up one by one and headed off to their next classes. Indira couldn't help wondering if *all* her classes would be this strange.

At least I got one of the clues, she thought as she walked on to her next class.

22

Professor Darcy

Indira found herself at the edge of a stormy courtyard. A small group of students stood in the rain, getting quite soaked as they stood there. A man leaned against an eroded pillar, eyes fixed on the valley below. Indira stood with the other students. It was hard to not notice that they all wore side-character navy jackets. The teacher, Professor Darcy, wore a water-darkened coat of a similar color, with a series of white neckties pressed nearly up to his chin. His wet hair clung to his forehead, and Indira thought his side-burns looked a bit out of style.

The class watched for nearly two minutes. The rain continued to fall. Professor Darcy continued to stare into the distance. Indira's clothing had almost soaked all the way through before their teacher turned around.

"*That* is how you look longingly off into the distance,"

he announced. His bright blue eyes were filled with passion. "Now, if each of you would choose a pillar to lean against. You cannot hope to improve if you don't take what I do and give it your own style. So choose your pillar and look longingly off into the distance."

Indira and the other students spread out at his command. She leaned against a pillar as the rain continued to drench her clothes and prune her fingers. Professor Darcy whirled in circles, shouting advice as they practiced.

"I want my students to be confident. The purpose of this class, Love by Page Twelve, is just that: to fall in love by page twelve. But you must also consider what will happen on page thirteen and beyond." He clapped his hands together excitedly. "All right. As you look into the distance, elevate your chin slightly. Too high and you look filled with pride. Too low and you look like a person without hope. If you have a cloth or a token to press tightly between your hands, that helps. Nor am I against crying! It's evocative and a part of life. Let the tears flow!"

Professor Darcy thundered about, correcting postures and praising one boy's willingness to unbutton his collar dramatically. (He missed the boy muttering, "It was just too tight.") After that, he took them through a number of other "exciting" techniques: the wistful sigh, the proper method for breaking eye contact, and the first-arrival smile. ("Remember, you're not just happy—you're complete!")

After Professor Darcy gave his final speech to the class,

the boy with the dramatic collar put his hand in the air. "Is there a reason we had to practice all this out in the rain?"

Professor Darcy gave a most romantic smile.

"Well, everything is more dramatic in the rain. Is it not?"

And with that he led them back inside and through the halls of Protagonist Preparatory, offering final pieces of advice to individual students. Indira was very thankful *not* to be one of the ones pulled aside. So far her character education seemed bizarre. She had learned to be more likeable, had escaped from a room full of rabbits, and had learned vague romantic techniques in the rain. There was one more mandatory class on her schedule.

Next stop: the Sepulcher.

23

Dr. Montague

You might not know, my dear reader, exactly what a sepulcher is. In the Real World, it is a burial vault for the dead. Sepulchers have been used for centuries to house our lost loved ones. The Sepulcher in Protagonist Preparatory acts as a burial vault for stories. Every Author who has ever begun a story and abandoned it has left their mark in the strange and endless catacombs of the Sepulcher. It should not surprise you that these vaults are quite extensive. I have added a few headstones to this burial ground myself.

Nor should it surprise you that most characters consider it a haunted and frightening place. Every unfinished story has created unfinished characters — destined to exist in the first handful of chapters, but who never find out how their story would have ended. Many unfinished characters go on to work normal jobs in the world of Imagination, but many also wander around without purpose. Authors rarely revisit those stories and characters, and even more rarely decide to pick them back up. It is considered the most haunting fate any character can suffer.

Dr. Romeo Montague's reasons for conducting his class in the Sepulcher were many. His own story had succeeded because of climactic events in an actual sepulcher. More importantly, the location provided a creepy and tragic atmosphere in which to conduct his I Thought You Were Dead class.

Indira descended more staircases than she bothered to count. Deeper and deeper underground she went until the air around her felt oppressive and chilly. She shivered to imagine a ghost setting a hand on her shoulder and leading her ever downward.

She wasn't sure what to expect, but she was greeted by a narrow, black-painted hallway. On each side, canvases hung along the walls. Bright covers and twisted fonts, all exclaiming the titles of incomplete books. Their Authors' names were so faded that they could scarcely be read. The black hall led to a wide, columned chamber. Chains extended down from the ceiling and held little bowls of golden light. Ten other hallways led away from the room, slanting slightly downhill into deeper recesses of the Sepulcher.

Indira's eyes fixed, however, on a boy waiting at the far end of the room. He sat just beyond the swinging circles of light. His skin was olive, and his hair fell in perfect dark curls. Indira was about to ask if he knew where Dr. Montague's class was when he spotted her and pushed up to his feet. "It's about time," he said. "You're the last to arrive."

Indira frowned. "I came straight from my other class."

"I came straight from my other class, *sir.*"

Indira almost laughed. "Sir? I'm pretty sure we're the same age, kid."

"Oh, I highly doubt that."

The boy stepped forward into better lighting. Indira barely stifled a gasp. His hair and height and expression all looked youthful, but his skin looked like the bark of an old tree. She'd never seen someone so *ancient* before. He offered her a smug look before saying, "Welcome to I Thought You Were Dead. I am Dr. Romeo Montague."

Indira swallowed. "I—uh—where's the rest of the class?"

"Waiting for you," he replied. "Come along."

He led Indira down a secondary hallway. More book covers appeared along the walls, each a sad ode to some half-finished tale. Indira kept glancing sideways, feeling she had completely blown her introductions. She had called him *kid.* Intending to redeem herself, she decided to play the part of a curious student.

"What are all these books?" Indira asked.

"Failures," Dr. Montague replied. "They are the ghosts of good and bad ideas both."

The hallway didn't seem like it would ever end. They passed cover after sad cover.

"How deep does the Sepulcher go?" Indira asked. "It's depressing to think there are this many failed stories."

Dr. Montague let out a laugh. "No one's ever mapped out the entire labyrinth. If you ask me, it'd be an impossible task. Take Harry Potter, for example. His story was such a smashing success in the Real World that it filled up an entire floor of unfinished stories down here. The Wizard Union celebrated his success, of course. One of their own becoming one of the most famous characters in history? Sounds good on the resume, until you realize how many other 'chosen one' wizards ended up in shelved novels that would never see the light of day."

Indira frowned. She'd never really thought of those kinds of consequences. She was also starting to realize that Dr. Montague was a glass-half-empty sort of person.

The two of them rounded a final corner and came to a smaller chamber, identical to the first one. On one wall stood a line of oddly shaped vials filled with liquids that bubbled and winked. Indira gasped, however, at the sight of her classmates arranged in a circle. Each of them lay in complete silence upon a bed of stone. She heard the light and steady breathing of a collective group of sleepers.

"As the last to arrive, today's task falls to you."

"Today's task?" Indira asked, eyes still wide.

"Every *good* tragedy begins with someone trying to do the *right* thing. Tragedy is when a character tries to do the right thing but fails. Your task is simple. Six students. Six antidotes. Revive them by giving them the correct ones. You may begin." When Indira didn't move from the doorway, Dr. Montague tapped his foot impatiently. "I've never had a side character complete this task successfully. It would be a fine addition to the auditions." He glanced at his leather wristwatch. "You have thirty minutes. Begin."

Indira couldn't help feeling like Dr. Montague had taken a shot at her just for being a side character. That it came from someone so prim and proper just made it more annoying. She slid past him and began examining the vials. She noted the shapes and colors and even temperatures, setting her hand above them. The first nearly scorched her palm. Others sent shivering goose bumps down her arm. Not knowing what else to do, she snatched up a curving green bottle that smelled like freshly mowed grass.

The idea took root . . .

. . . so . . .

. . . someone who worked with their hands?

Maybe someone who loved to play and be outside?

She walked from character to character, turning over their hands, until she found a muscled boy with thick calluses and dirt under his nails. Indira looked back at Dr. Montague, but he had taken a seat in one corner and appeared to be reading a newspaper. Uncertain, Indira sat the boy up as best she could and tipped the antidote through his open lips. The liquid caught a little in his throat, but after a few seconds he coughed, swallowed, and blinked to life.

"He poisoned me!" The boy pointed in their professor's direction.

Dr. Montague huffed. "Oh *please*. You agreed to participate."

"You told me it was apple juice!"

"Side characters. Always gullible. Don't be so daft next time," Dr. Montague responded unkindly. "And you're fine now! If anything, your color looks improved."

Indira snapped a finger to get the boy's attention.

"Did you see any of the others put to sleep?"

The boy shook his head. "They were already sleeping when I got here. Well, three of them were."

"Which three?" Indira asked. The boy pointed to a pair of twin girls and a frail-looking boy. She nodded toward the vials. "Do you remember which three glasses were there?"

"I'm not sure." His eyes looked a little red and hazy. "That big yellow glass was there. I'm not sure about the other ones. They all look the same."

They didn't look the same at all, but Indira couldn't blame him for not remembering. She left his side and snatched up the glass the boy had indicated. She smiled, wondering to herself if little Patch would have said it was a dandelion or a yellow-brick road. She didn't see a set of vials that could possibly go together, so she eliminated the twins and moved toward the frail-looking boy. Before sitting him up, though, she had the nagging sense that something wasn't right.

She glanced back at the vials. There were, she realized, only four remaining. But there were five students. It took her a moment of thinking before she had it.

The twins had likely arrived together. Dr. Montague wouldn't have offered them *different* drinks. The yellow glass was double the size of all the other vials. Following her hunch, Indira tilted a drop of the sunshine liquid onto each of their tongues. The two woke up at the same time, sat up with perfectly straight posture, and laughed about something.

"Excuse me," Indira said. "Did any of these people arrive before you did?"

Both girls pointed at the frail-looking boy.

"And do you remember which glass he used?"

The right twin said, "Blue."

The left twin said, "Red."

They each glared at the other and began to argue. Each insisted that she was thinking of the right color. Indira went back to the table. There *was* a blue vial and there *was* a red vial. She glanced over at Dr. Montague, who tapped his watch and said, "Twenty minutes left."

"What happens if I give them the wrong antidote?" Indira asked.

"Well"—Dr. Montague offered a malicious smile—"this is a tragedy class, isn't it?"

On that ominous note, Indira returned her attention to the vials. Three potions for three sleepers. She turned back to the still-arguing twins.

"*You're* sure that it was blue, and *you're* sure it was red?"

Both nodded. Indira snatched a purple liquid that sat between the blue and red vials. Without hesitation, she tipped the glass and let a few drops fall into the boy's mouth. His eyes snapped open, and he immediately started spitting out whatever she'd given him.

"All right," Indira said to herself. "Two more to go."

"It is appropriate at this point," interrupted Dr. Montague, "to provide you with clues. The person who drank the blue vial has never seen the moon. The person who drank the red vial likes the sound of thunder. Carry on!"

With that, Dr. Montague went back to reading his newspaper. One of the remaining sleepers was a girl, the other a boy. The girl had bright red hair and looked like a princess. The boy was lanky and dark-skinned, with a military-style buzz cut. The first classmate Indira had woken up pointed to the redhead.

"Her name's Rose," he said helpfully. "She told me the other day she was a night owl. So she probably has seen the moon? I don't know."

The twins crossed their arms, standing beside the buzz-cut boy. "But Gavin's scared of storms. So he can't be the one who likes the sound of thunder!"

A new outburst of arguments. Indira lifted the vials experimentally, sniffed them again, and then circled the room in search of clues. She was getting frustrated when she noticed a little sun carved into one of the stone tables. Looking around, she realized that each table had its own emblem: stars or hearts or clovers. She whipped around and ordered, "Sit them up."

Her classmates obeyed, pulling at shoulders and sitting their unconscious peers upright. Indira smiled, seeing a beautiful moon carved beneath the redheaded girl and a lightning bolt beneath the boy. She snatched the red vial and tipped it into the boy's mouth. She felt a surge of pride (especially considering Dr. Montague's clear doubt in her abilities) as the boy blinked to life. But a sigh sounded from the corner. Everyone looked back at Dr. Montague.

"Side characters. You *never* get it right."

Without warning, the boy convulsed. He looked briefly as if someone were choking him, and then his eyes guttered out and his mouth hung slackly and his fingers twitched.

"What's happening?" Indira shouted. "Help him!"

She crossed the room and snatched up the blue vial.

"Too late, I'm afraid." Dr. Montague came forward. He leaned over the boy and folded his stiff arms in a regal pose. "A lesson for all. This is how tragedy *works*. What's your name?"

This he directed to Indira, who was doing her best not to cry. Had she *really* killed someone? Her hands trembled. "Indira," she whispered. "Indira Story."

"Ms. Story has illuminated *every* foundational principle of a proper tragedy. Even a side character should learn these rules, and I plan to have you muttering them in your sleep. First, every tragedy should have someone who is working to do the *right thing*. Ms. Story wanted to succeed. She had no ill intentions. Second, every tragedy should involve an important *choice*. Ms. Story made several, none more important than her final decision. Third, every proper tragedy involves a miscommunication. The messenger is delayed. Or if not delayed, then his message is misheard or misinterpreted."

Anger snapped to life inside Indira. "*You* said that the one who liked the sound of thunder needed the red vial! I gave him the red one."

"Indeed you did, but that is *not* what I said. I told you that the one who *drank* the red vial liked the sound of thunder. *Drank*. Past tense. The red and blue vials act as antidotes for one another. If you had stopped to consider my words and followed the other clues I had set out for you, you might have seen that. As I said, *miscommunication*."

"Finally, of course, every tragedy must involve loss." He gestured to the boy on the table. "If we do not see the weight and consequence of our misdeeds, of our pride, then we are not true tragedians. Consider this before next class, for you will all face a task like the one Ms. Story faced today, and you will all learn these valuable lessons by your own hands. Class dismissed."

The other students slowly and awkwardly filed out of the room. Indira had fallen to her knees beside the boy. Behind her, Dr. Montague plucked the red vial from the table and poured the redheaded girl a drop. She gasped to life, and he quietly instructed her to come to his office later so he could explain the first day's lesson. The girl nodded and left.

Indira couldn't tell if she felt angry or sad. She'd never been responsible for something so awful. She couldn't believe that something like this would be allowed to happen at Protagonist Preparatory. And she was even angrier with herself than she was with Montague.

In a way, he was right. She should have listened. If this had been a real story, she would have lost a friend. But here in Fable she had killed a fellow character. What would happen now? Would she be arrested by the Grammar Police? Thrown out of school?

The terrifying possibilities loomed overhead.

"That wasn't horrible for a side character," Dr. Montague said. She rounded on him, ready to curse and yell and accuse, but he held up his hands peaceably. "The point of the task was not for you to succeed."

"But what about him? He's dead now!" And the tears really did come, streaking to her chin. "And it's my fault."

"Well, yes," the professor replied harshly. "He's dead. But I don't see why that's something to cry about."

Indira looked up in horror. "You're heartless."

Dr. Montague frowned. "Who's your mentor?"

She tried to wipe the tears from her face, but they kept rolling down her cheeks.

"Deus," she finally said.

Dr. Montague actually started laughing. Forgetting he was a professor and forgetting that there were rules about hitting your teachers, she stood and removed the hammer from her hip. Dr. Montague noticed it and quickly sobered. "I'm sorry, but that explains every-thing."

"How?" she asked.

"Deus isn't the most thorough mentor. Don't take offense — he's a *powerful* mentor, but he doesn't often bother with little details."

"Like what?"

"Like the fact that characters do not die in this world. Not in the way you'd imagine."

"I . . . what?"

Dr. Montague continued. "A character can die, but it is nearly always a matter of the spirit, not of the body. You received a more intense lesson than I intended. Good. Per-haps the consequences of your actions will invoke a more permanent change. The boy isn't dead."

"He isn't?"

"You've been to Hearth Hall?" he asked.

Indira nodded.

"And you've seen the Ninth Hearth?"

She nodded again.

"Some of us like to call it the Nine-Lives Hearth. It is one of Fable's more charming functions. If a person dies, they regenerate before the fire." He set the vials back on their shelves and shrugged. "You may want to apologize still. After all, it isn't ever *fun* to die, and it takes a few days to regenerate fully. He'll be behind in his classes because of you."

Indira was so relieved that she didn't bother to remind

her professor that he was also to blame for how things had unfolded. "Is he up there now?"

Dr. Montague shook the boy's boot. "He will be in a few more minutes. All right, get out of here. I have to prepare for my next class. I've been looking forward to it all day."

Indira took a final look at the dark-skinned boy with the buzz-cut hair. She didn't tell Dr. Montague this, but she wanted a solid image of what her mistake had cost. Even if the boy was regenerating upstairs and the consequences weren't permanent, she wanted to remember how much there was to lose from simple mistakes. With a quick nod, she exited the room.

Winding her way back up through the Sepulcher, she saw a new group gathered downstairs. Her stomach lurched at seeing Maxi among the golden-jacketed protagonists. Indira ducked back upstairs before being noticed, but as she climbed staircase after staircase, she remembered Dr. Montague's words about this particular group.

I have to prepare for my next class. I've been looking forward to it all day.

She wanted to believe the words Mr. Threepwood had spoken that morning, the idea that a side character could become a protagonist with some hard work and dedicated study, but the rest of the day had been its own lesson on the subject. The status jackets, Dr. Montague, everything seemed to point to one truth: every character had a story, but some characters were treated better than others.

Keeping Ghosts Company

Before her tragedy class, Indira had wanted nothing more than to go home to the Penningtons' and fall asleep. She would have even welcomed the pep talk she knew Mrs. Pennington must have been preparing for her. Now, though, she felt obligated to redeem recent mistakes. She planned to start by apologizing to the boy she'd accidentally poisoned.

Indira strode into the vast Hearth Hall. Students sat in front of various fires, recovering their courage or enjoying some rest or snagging a little more energy before their next class. It was the one room she'd seen at Protagonist Preparatory that didn't suffer from a separation of gold and blue. The different-colored jackets mingled here without much complaint. That made sense to Indira. Courage and rest and energy were things that everyone needed, regardless of status.

Indira made her way to the Ninth Hearth. It stood at the far end of the hall, a towering framework of twisted stone. It was just as Margaret had described. Indira didn't recognize the words, or even the language, that had been carved above the fireplace. She did, however, recognize the boy seated before the roaring flames.

He didn't look up as she sat down beside him. Indira thought her heart might break as she watched him stare into the fire as though it were the only thing that existed.

"Hey there," she said softly.

He glanced over, and for the first time Indira realized just how insubstantial he was. Light angled through him and around him as if he were a ghost.

"Hello." His voice was hardly more than a croak.

"I wanted to apologize," Indira said. "It's my fault you're stuck here. Well, I was tricked, but it's mostly my fault still. I should have been more careful."

The boy let out a ghostly sigh.

"Can you . . . do you know if you're allowed to leave the fire?" she asked.

He shook his head. He pointed to the spot where they were sitting and shook his head again.

"Dr. Montague said it might be a few days," Indira explained. "I'm sorry again. I'll keep you company, and if there's anything you need . . ." She wasn't quite sure what to offer a ghost, though. Did they eat food? Did they like to read books? How would he use the bathroom? "Well, I'll come back and share notes with you from class. What's your name?"

He glanced her way again. Either the magic of the Ninth Hearth or Indira's kind questions had sketched a little more of him back into reality. He whispered, "Gavin Grant."

"Indira Story," she said. "I'll be sure to visit you tomorrow."

He grunted appreciatively and she left him there.

It had been a *very* long day. She was ready to go home.

By the entrance of Protagonist Preparatory she saw another familiar face. Phoenix was walking down the hallway toward her, his golden jacket pulled awkwardly over his wizard robes. He didn't notice her at first, and Indira considered walking right past him, but he glanced up when they were just a few feet apart. A smile lit up his face. "Indira! How are you?"

Horrible, awful, and rotten. "I'm okay."

He gave her sleeve a tug and smiled wider. "I like your jacket."

Indira's heart clenched. Maxi was the kind of girl who cared about status. The family she'd adopted proved that much. But Phoenix? How could he say something like that? When he knew what it meant to wear gold and what it meant to wear blue, how could he of all people make fun of her? She raised her chin, slow and cold.

"I thought you were better than that," she said.

Confusion clouded his face, but Indira didn't give him a chance to explain. She stalked through the front entrance and ignored the sudden bloom of heat behind her. She walked all the way home without even looking where she was going. Maxi had abandoned her. Phoenix had made fun of her. Even if she *could* get promoted to protagonist, she felt that those wounds would still sting. She arrived home well after Patch had gone to bed, but Mrs. Pennington was still awake.

"Indira!" She swung to her feet. "How was—"

Something about Indira's expression or posture cut Mrs. Pennington's question off. Instinctively, her foster mother came forward and spread her arms. Indira disappeared into the offered hug. She stood there for a minute, wrapped up in what felt like the last welcoming place in Fable. Every other corner of the city felt like betrayal or failure. Here, at least, she was safe.

"Do you want to talk about it?" Mrs. Pennington asked.

"No," Indira said. "Not tonight."

With a final squeeze, Mrs. Pennington released her.

"I've left some food out for you. Go have a bite to eat. Tomorrow is a new day."

Indira nodded once, and Mrs. Pennington started upstairs. Beneath the glow of one of the kitchen lights, Indira saw a plate with a note taped to it. She tripped over Patch's toys and into the kitchen. The note read:

*Courage doesn't always roar. Sometimes courage is
the quiet voice at the end of the day saying, I will try
again tomorrow.*
—Mary Anne (something with an R . . . It's late and I
can't remember!)

Love, Mom

Indira unfolded the tinfoil and found two slices of cold
pizza. They tasted like a brand-new day.

25

Misunderstanding

Indira began her day as an enemy pirate who Patch had—according to his own personal narration—been hunting across all seven seas. The two managed to come to a peace agreement over waffles. After breakfast, Indira accepted a much-needed hug from Mrs. Pennington and headed out for her second day of school. She was still feeling a little nervous, but Mrs. Pennington's advice from the night before was fresh in her mind.

Courage meant trying again. Indira wasn't about to give up yet.

The day's first test came just two hundred yards down the street. A familiar figure with familiar red hair was waiting for her, leaning against a street sign like he'd been there for hours. Phoenix offered a hesitant smile as she approached. "Indira! I've been waiting here all morning."

She took one look at him and marched right past.

"Hey. Wait! Indira, there was a misunderstanding yesterday."

"'Misunderstanding'?" she shot back. "You told me you liked my jacket. No misunderstanding there. I got the joke loud and clear."

Indira didn't slow her pace. In the corner of her vision, she could see Phoenix struggling to keep up, nearly tripping over his robe with each step. Wizards weren't exactly track stars, she supposed. "But that's my point," he said. "It wasn't a joke!"

"So, what, you just like the color blue?"

He finally managed to catch up. "On you, yes."

Indira glared at him. "Still being funny, I see."

"But I'm not trying to be funny," he insisted. "Indira, I didn't know what the colors meant. Brainstorm Underglass is really thorough in her first meeting with students. She didn't even get close to finishing that first day. My appointment got rescheduled late because the wizarding school tutorials were all morning. So when you saw me, Brainstorm Underglass had literally just given me my gold jacket. I thought gold was for boys and blue was for girls. I didn't know there was a whole system for the colors."

Indira finally stopped walking, and Phoenix nearly barreled into her. She stared at him, feeling both annoyed and a little guilty. "So you were just . . ."

"Complimenting you."

He hadn't been making fun of her at all. He was just trying to be nice. Indira stood there for a moment in stunned silence. It took a second to realize that an apology was in order.

"I'm sorry," she finally said. "Yesterday Maxi ditched me because I'm a side character. I guess I assumed you were doing the same thing. I just couldn't believe she would hang out with me one day and ignore me the next."

He nodded. "I'm not sure that's a protagonist thing. She gave me the cold shoulder too."

"It didn't help that some of the teachers reacted the same way," Indira went on. "It's like they think side characters are useless."

Phoenix's eyes flashed with fire. "They're wrong about you."

Something about the way he said that had her stomach feeling like a gymnasium full of butterflies. Not sure what to say or what to do, Indira started walking again. This time she stuck to a pace that was a little easier for a robed wizard to keep up with.

"I'm really sorry. I shouldn't have assumed the worst. Forgive me?"

Phoenix nodded quickly. "Of course. You're one of my only friends. I was so worried that you were going to stop hanging out with me that I accidentally set one of my textbooks on fire last night. Mr. Randle had to buy an extra extinguisher for the hallway."

Indira couldn't help smiling at that mental image. "Friends again?"

"Friends." Phoenix sighed with relief. "Now, can we please talk about how weird our professors are? Yesterday the guy from *The Lord of the Rings* kept pointing at the syllabus for our Spellbinding class and shouting, 'You shall not pass!' No one really got the joke, though."

It didn't take long for Indira's second day to start outshining her first one. The long walk with Phoenix took her mind off all the disappointment from the day before. The two of them discussed their favorite classes and marveled at how cool the brainstorms were. She was so deep into the conversation that she barely noticed that they'd arrived at Mr. Threepwood's room.

Phoenix bumped her shoulder. "See you at lunch?"

"Count me in."

Indira was still smiling as she took a seat next to Margaret. The classroom was divided the same way it had been the day before: blue jackets on one side, gold jackets on the other. But this time Indira felt like she had a shield to ward off the bad vibes. The morning had been one giant step in the right direction, and she wasn't planning on going backward now.

Courage was trying again.

Courage meant taking the next step, and the next.

26

Practice Makes Perfect

"If you don't pick up your clothes, you're grounded!"

Indira frowned. "Try being a little tougher."

Mrs. Pennington huffed a sigh and disappeared back into the hall. A second later, she pushed through the door. "If you don't pick up your clothes, I will end you!"

"A little too far that time. You sound like a professional wrestler."

Mrs. Pennington threw her hands in the air. "It's no use. I'm not cut out for being mean."

Indira shrugged. "Maybe that's a good thing. Let's try it again."

Practice. That was the theme of Indira's next few weeks. She practiced being a good daughter to Mrs. Pennington, who needed to practice her own mothering techniques. Indira hadn't realized it at first, but the adoption process was the Penningtons' audition. If Mrs. Pennington and Patch wanted to get into a story of their own, they would do so by proving their talents while taking care of Indira. Mrs. Pennington even confided in Indira that there would be an unannounced test scenario at some point.

So they went through dating advice (awkward), grounding procedures (not fun), and how to handle eye rolling and sarcasm (kind of fun). One benefit was that Mrs. Pennington also started giving Indira a standard allowance for helping around the house. It didn't hurt to have a little spending money whenever she visited Fable. Indira thought Mrs. Pennington was already a pretty great mom, but like every character, she still had work to do.

Indira also practiced being a good older sister to Patch. It wasn't hard to remember the way David had cared for her. She took those memories and tried her best to be the kind of older sibling he had been. She read bedtime stories, played pirates, and corrected his spellings of words like *insect* and *telescope*. Indira was starting to realize that the magic of Fable operated in the background of everything. The world or fate or some other invisible force had tugged her into relationships that, if she chose to really learn from them, would sharpen parts of herself that she didn't even know were in need of sharpening.

She didn't forget her First Words, either. *Every cage has a key.* Whenever the day threw frustrations her way, she would breathe deeply and remember that the key to *this* cage was working harder than everyone else. If she could do that, she might just become a protagonist.

Every week or so, she'd write up a quick letter to David, too. A few updates and funny moments. She missed her older brother and knew it must be hard for him without their weekly morning visits. He never wrote her back, but Indira didn't blame him. It couldn't be easy to think about Indira pursuing her dreams in the one place he'd always wanted to go.

It wasn't difficult to avoid Maxi at school. Sometimes the girl even skipped out on their morning class with Mr. Threepwood. Indira found herself very thankful that she didn't have to avoid Phoenix too. They spent a good amount of time between classes together. She'd learned that if she could get him to laugh hard enough, he'd actually cough smoke out like a dragon. From then on, she made it her personal mission to get him to belly laugh at least once a day.

Instead of holding a grudge against Maxi, Indira spent time being a good friend to the other people she met. Margaret shadowed her through the halls, and before long the shy girl felt comfortable enough to add her own opinions to their discussions. Indira kept visiting Gavin Grant at the Ninth Hearth until he recovered fully and rejoined their classes.

Gavin loved soccer and telling stories. He also had a knack for making crude jokes, which he practiced during each visit. She loved watching him practice juggling tricks with his worn soccer ball. He had the widest smile she'd ever seen and never took things too seriously (even his own death).

The rest of Indira's time and energy went into becoming a better character. She took things "a page at a time" in Mr. Threepwood's class, learning first how to be a character who always took action and then learning the power of being misunderstood. He had even taught them a new favorite saying: "Loyalty leads to bravery. Bravery plants the seed of self-sacrifice. And self-sacrifice is the highest call of every character in every story."

After making them recite the mantra each morning, he would boom his lectures with passion. He reminded them every day that *every* character had a story. He reminded them that if they could have an impact on even one reader, they'd be doing their job. Indira loved the advice, but she also started noticing his tendency to spend more time working with his protagonist students. He continued to talk about potential and possibilities, but Indira began to feel that his eyes, like most eyes, were for the bright, shining students in their golden jackets.

And each day Alice's class on narrow escapes was, well, inescapable. Indira would turn a corner and find herself sliding down into some random basement or being escorted by odd cats that spoke only in riddles. Alice would give them some brief instructions before vanishing from the room, encouraging them to attempt more and more daring escapes. Usually, their exits were as strange as their entrances.

Her most effective teacher turned out to be Professor Darcy. He did not seem prejudiced against his class of side characters. Each day he took them through exercises in the Rainy Courtyard with all the enthusiasm of a schoolboy. Indira learned to flutter her lashes and look disinterested (for the sake of gaining still more interest!) and proved quite proficient in improvised one-liners.

Her *least* effective teacher, though, was definitely Dr. Montague.

He had seemed disinterested in teaching side characters that first day, but now he wore his annoyance on both sleeves. Often, he dismissed the class early or posted cancellations. Indira and the rest of the students were made fun of as side characters without much of a purpose. At one point Dr. Montague even reflected, "After today's performance, it would be an insult to side characters for me to call you side characters."

Her favorite class of all turned out to be Weaponry. It was an independent study, which meant she could go by herself whenever she had the time to go. Brainstorm Ketty had written in a request for a minimum of two hours of practice each week. The first time Indira set eyes on the Arena, she knew it would be one of her favorite places.

The massive room was about the size of a football field. Thick ropes sectioned off different challenges and practice areas. That first day, a hulking protagonist with spiked blond hair performed lunges with a spear in one corner.

Opposite him, a boxing class was in progress. Indira spied a rather tan-looking man at the center of the Arena and went over to report.

"Hello," she said. "I'm Indira Story."

Up close, the man looked *too* tan. He had combined natural processes with unnatural ones that left his skin looking bright orange. Indira could smell the tanning oil from ten feet away. She noticed a massive, unstrung bow set on a table behind him. His eyes were trained on a pair of sword fighters. "I am Odysseus," he said without looking at her. "What's your weapon?"

Indira slipped hers from its belt loop. "A one-handed hammer."

He spared it a glance, grunted, and gave a nod. "First time here?"

"Yes, sir."

"Tutorial first," he explained. "Stand on the black square over there."

Indira obeyed. The square reminded her of the dragon-eye they'd used to travel from Origin to Fable. She took her place on the square and tightened her grip on the hammer. Odysseus twisted his bronze bracelet and punched a button. Something beneath their feet thundered with power. Indira could feel the floor vibrating.

"Fight first. We'll make some decisions after that."

"Fight who?" Indira called back.

But the answer appeared in a blink. The Arena vanished, and Indira was facing two angry humanoids. They were a little taller than her, and each wielded a wooden club. Indira tightened the grip on her hammer as they came toward her, fanning out.

I have no idea what I'm doing, she realized.

One of them let out a little chirp, and both lashed forward. Indira caught the overhead blow of the one on the right and kept her feet moving away from the one on the left. Another swing, another block, and she brought her own hammer curling low. It nailed the creature in the hip but left her vulnerable. The second one brought its club down on her shoulder, and she crumpled into a roll. Pain seared through her side, and she came stumbling to her feet.

The creature pressed. She fended off a rain of blows, her arm growing more tired with each one. It pushed her farther and farther back until the other had recovered. Now both creatures grinned as they advanced, struck, and pushed past her defenses. Indira blocked a final swing before the hammer slipped out of her trembling fingers. One of the creatures slid forward and cracked her on the side of the head . . .

. . . and she blinked back to reality. She was on all fours, gasping into the dirt of the Arena. Odysseus stood beside her. "Not bad," he said. "You're all arms, though. Feel that sting in your biceps?"

Indira nodded. She felt a lot of stings in a lot of places.

"You were letting your arms do the work. A good fighter uses every muscle. A good fighter throws her hips into blows and moves her feet on defense. It saves energy."

"It wasn't fair," Indira gasped. "There were two of them."

Odysseus smiled. "In time there will be five, then ten, then twenty."

Indira spat on the ground. Her mouth was dry and her muscles were sore. She couldn't have been fighting for more than thirty seconds, though.

"Tired?" Odysseus asked.

"Do it again," Indira said, putting herself back on the square.

Odysseus laughed. "That's the spirit. With your weapon and your size, I will teach you Bartitsu. Rule number one: disturb the equilibrium of your assailant."

"Equilibrium?" she asked. "Assailant?"

"Balance. Make your goal to get the *attackers* imbalanced. Use momentum. Nudge. Trip. Sweep legs. Whatever it takes. See if that makes a difference. We'll add rules from there."

She earned a series of new bruises, but in her third fight she managed to knock one of the creatures out cold with an undercut. She left the Arena grinning.

Practice became Indira's new mantra. She visited the Arena whenever time permitted. All the frustrations of being a side character vanished when she was sweaty and sore. She liked that. As the weeks ticked by, she became a better character, a better sister, a better daughter, and a better friend. She wasn't too bad with her hammer, either. All that practice and growth turned out to be really important. It's one of the few ways to prepare for life's challenges.

Especially when a bad day comes along.

27

A Bad Day

The tricky part about bad days, my dear reader, is that they so often start off just like the good ones. Indira ate granola in her yogurt for breakfast and taught little Patch how to butter his own toast and even had a chance to go on a morning walk with Mrs. Pennington. Fable still existed as two separate cities, with one half hanging upside down in the sky, but Indira thought it looked on the verge of a change. Like fall leaves just before they start to turn, Fable seemed ready to search her wardrobe for something dramatic and different.

The first bad sign came after she'd parted ways with Mrs. Pennington and was walking the city streets toward school. She passed a wall of posters and graffiti, halting at the sight of a new addition. A missing-person poster.

The boy had golden curls, wide eyes, and a smile that

was all sorts of crooked. He looked vaguely familiar, but Indira couldn't place the name. "'Allen Squalls,'" she read aloud. "'A second-year wizard, Allen had recently been demoted to the cameo track at Protagonist Preparatory. Allen was last seen outside the Cliffhanger Hotel. If you have any information . . .'"

Indira shivered as she read. She'd forgotten that in a place like Fable there was still a chance that *bad* things could happen. She found herself glancing suspiciously down every alleyway as she headed to school.

Her morning habit was to visit Hearth Hall. She'd tested out all the different hearths now. Comfort had become her personal favorite. If she felt cold, the fire warmed her up. If she was sweating and hot, the fire blew a fine breeze. She arrived this morning and took her customary seat at the Courage Hearth next to little Margaret, who had grown comfortable around Indira but was still working up her courage in facing the rest of the world.

"Good morning, Margaret," Indira said. Her friend looked up, smiled in her shy way, and returned her gaze to the fire.

"Good morning," she whispered back.

They sat in mutual quiet, soaking up not warmth, but quiet encouragements and reminders of their good qualities. As Indira stared at the flames—her thoughts drifting briefly to Phoenix—a pair of heels clicked to life behind them.

She turned to see Brainstorm Ketty strolling away

from the Luck Hearth. The brainstorm's dress was a scarlet trail, and those dual-colored eyes stood out in the firelight. Feeling more courageous than normal, Indira stood and called out, "Brainstorm Ketty!"

The woman paused, glanced at a silver wristwatch, and smiled. "Indira Story."

Indira glowed at being remembered. "I didn't know brainstorms used the hearths!"

Ketty nodded back at the fireplace. "Everyone needs courage or rest or energy. I come in for luck every time I'm planning on making a trip to the Real World."

Indira's eyes widened. "You're going to the Real World? Right now?"

"I am," Brainstorm Ketty replied, glancing once more at her watch. "Most of our observations take place in the off-season. But if a hot new Author suddenly appears on our radar, we have to follow up and try to find a part for our characters to play!"

"Well, I know you have to get going," Indira said. "But I wanted you to know that everything's been going really well lately. I think I'm getting better every single day."

Ketty faltered for a moment and then smiled. "Everything is going well? Isn't that a fine surprise! I've started scheduling meetings with my students. Why don't you come by this afternoon? We can discuss your progress."

Indira nodded excitedly. "Have a good day, Brainstorm Ketty."

She returned to the hearth, and Margaret stood, ready to go to class.

"I kind of like her," Indira said, watching the scarlet dress vanish around a corner.

"She's nice enough," Margaret agreed.

"Is she your assigned brainstorm?"

Margaret nodded. "She took on a *lot* of side characters this year."

"What do you mean?" Indira asked.

"The brainstorms all watch the auditions; then they select characters. Sort of like a draft."

"So why would she choose so many side characters?"

Little Margaret shrugged. "Maybe she likes underdogs?"

Indira nodded as the two of them began their normal route to class. After everything she'd experienced at Protagonist Preparatory, it was a big surprise to her that *anyone* did something just because they liked side characters. The two of them ducked into Mr. Threepwood's class and headed for their normal seats. Before she could sit, though, Mr. Threepwood called her to the front. Indira blushed a little, making her way down the row as her classmates talked among themselves. The teacher flipped open a folder as she arrived.

"Indira!" he said. "I've enjoyed having you in class, but I did have a little question about some of the homework you've been turning in."

She nodded, nervous she'd done something wrong. She'd been careful to do her best on everything. On some of the assignments, she'd spent hours researching different strategies before writing up her answers. Homework was less interesting than the scenes they sometimes ran in class, but Indira had been determined to get *all* of it right. The harder she worked, the more likely she could be promoted. And getting promoted was the only way to help David.

"The last assignment was tough," Indira replied. "But I thought my answers were okay. . . ."

Mr. Threepwood looked really confused now. She watched as he spread out all of her assignments. Indira blinked in surprise. Three of the worksheets were filled to the brim with her handwriting, but the other pages looked completely blank.

"This is your name at the top, isn't it?"

She squinted. He was right. The sheets that she'd assumed were blank actually had her name in the top corner. Only the premade worksheets Mr. Threepwood had printed for her still had writing on them. "I don't get it," Indira said. "I turned them all in. . . ."

Mr. Threepwood frowned. "I thought maybe it was a joke? Why turn the assignments in blank? I have plenty of students who forget an assignment here and there, but I've never had someone turn in a sheet with a name without writing anything else."

Indira shook her head. "But they weren't blank. . . ."

Mr. Threepwood raised an eyebrow. "Surely you can see my dilemma? I have several sheets with your name on them and no answers. These are strong evidence *against* what you're saying, Indira. I certainly can't give you full marks for something like this."

"I promise, Mr. Threepwood," she said. "I completed these assignments. I can even go through the answers with you. Just ask me the questions again."

Behind her, the door to the classroom had closed. It looked like most of the class had arrived, and the clock had ticked its way past the normal starting time. Mr. Threepwood arranged the papers and carefully closed the folder. "For now, your grades have suffered," he whispered. "But how about you come visit me at some point and we'll figure out what's going on. You can do better than this, Indira. I believe in you. Every character has a story!"

He gestured for her to return to her seat before turning to the board and writing out the instructions for the day's lesson. Indira started back, still blushing. It wasn't possible. Why were so many of the homework assignments she'd turned in blank now? She *knew* she had answered every question. What was happening?

She was walking back to her seat when Chem stepped in front of her. The two of them had been partners a few times. Chem always bragged about her photographic memory, but as far as Indira could tell, the girl wasn't all that great at actually using what she knew to do anything useful. Most of the time, Indira ended up doing the assigned work for both of them.

"Hey, Indira," Chem said. "This coffee is for you."

Indira blinked. "Uhh . . . I'm not sure . . ."

"Sorry, let me explain. Maxi wanted to apologize and just didn't know what to say. So she bought you this iced white mocha to patch things up."

Indira glanced over Chem's shoulder. Maxi was watching the exchange nervously.

"Really?" Indira asked.

She took the offered cup, and the world vanished. Two hundred feet straight down, pebbles tumbled into the ravine, and Indira came to the frightening realization that she was about to tumble with them. Her feet were sliding as she scrambled backward. A panicked scream escaped her lips as she backpedaled . . .

. . . only to reappear in the room. Lights flashed overhead as she tripped over the desk behind her. She lost her grip on the iced coffee, and everything happened in slow motion.

The coffee landed on her shoulder and the lid popped off. The brown liquid rushed down the collar of her jacket and flooded the floor. Indira was breathing heavily as she looked up at a smirking Chem. "Oh, I'm sorry! Did I say *white* mocha? I meant to say *fright* mocha. Silly me."

And then the other students were laughing. As Indira stood and the coffee dripped from her sleeve, half the class laughed at her. Most of the protagonists had turned to watch, and some of the side characters even joined in, hoping to be liked. Maxi had an odd look on her face, and even though a few of the protagonists stood, trying to quiet the others, Indira decided to run.

Their laughter followed her out of the room.

A Really Bad Day

She could feel blood pulsing up into her cheeks. The coffee had already sunk into her jacket, leaving a great dark stain down one sleeve and across most of her collar. She whipped it from her shoulders angrily and stormed down the hallway. Characters standing in her way changed course abruptly, muttering as she shoved past them. She ignored their stares.

Why had Maxi done that? Why had everyone laughed? What was funny about being mean to someone? Weren't these supposed to be the protagonists? The *good* guys? She shouldered through the bathroom, startling Gavin Grant as he washed his hands.

"What are you doing in here?" she spat angrily.

He sputtered, "It's . . . it's . . ."

"It's what? What *is* it, Gavin?"

"The boys' room," he said, pointing back at the door.

If her cheeks could have turned a deeper shade of red, they did. "Just great!"

She stormed across the hall into the correct bathroom and burst into tears. She wasn't normally one to cry, but even the toughest people can't help crying when they feel as if the world has turned its back on them. Indira ignored the warm, angry tears as she filled up the sink and dipped her stained jacket into the water. She set to scrubbing it and was so fixed on the task that she didn't notice the little bird until it landed on her shoulder.

"Oh, not now," she muttered. The bird was clearly one of Alice's messengers. It hopped on her shoulder, fluttering baby-blue wings. Indira continued to scrub until the bird started pecking her neck. "Hey!"

Turning, she held out her hand, and the bird dropped a little note into it.

You are excused from Alice's class for an appointment in the Rainy Courtyard. Professor Darcy has prepared an extracurricular activity for your class. For homework: ESCAPE from something.

Indira frowned. She had been enjoying Professor Darcy's class, but she didn't like the idea of an extracurricular activity. Not with how today had already gone. She crumpled the note and returned to her stained jacket. She was starting to think she was just making the stain spread, but she scrubbed it for a few more minutes before heading out.

She arrived at the back of the school and found some of her classmates already waiting in the misty rain of the courtyard. Professor Darcy stood, his coat soaked as always and his hair romantically pushed to one side. Gavin Grant waited near the back of the crowd. He offered Indira a warm smile. She walked over and elbowed him as playfully as she could manage.

"Sorry for yelling at you."

"It's fine," he said quickly. "I heard about the coffee thing. I'd have been mad too."

Indira looked around. Her other classmates cast careful glances in her direction. Word apparently traveled fast. "Wonderful," Indira said. Hoping to change the topic, she whispered to Gavin again. "What's this about an extracurricular activity?"

Gavin shook his head. "Professor Darcy figured out our crushes in the school and had the *genius* idea to bring them here for practice. We have to . . . you know . . . talk to them."

Gavin said it like it was the worst possible thing in the world. Indira would have agreed with him, but she thought it ridiculous that Professor Darcy could possibly know who they had crushes on. She craned her neck and saw a group of students waiting across the opposite end of the courtyard, under the cover of the leaning pillars. Her heart stopped when she saw Phoenix.

Could this day get *any* worse?

"Did Professor Darcy say how he figured out our crushes?" she asked.

"Something about asking the dragons to perform a survey spell? I don't really know." Gavin eyed the waiting group of students. "Whatever he did, it worked."

"Your crush is really over there?"

He nodded. "Isn't yours?"

"I don't have a crush."

"Right. Then you have nothing to freak out about." He scratched nervously at his collar. "I think I'm going to pass out. If I'm lucky, I'll just pass out."

Indira could see Phoenix's eyes in the shadowy courtyard, a bright and present pair of flames. Maybe she *did* have a little crush on him, but Phoenix's friendship had been the main reason she'd turned everything around at school. She swallowed at the thought of him finding out about her crush and not feeling the same way. What if it ruined the best thing she had going?

Indira watched as her other classmates tried to treat this like a normal exercise, but most of them fumbled forward into a rainy conversation that looked like the most painful experience that Indira could ever imagine. It was far easier to run away.

Before Professor Darcy could call her name, Indira slipped back inside Protagonist Preparatory. She cut through hallways and down staircases and got as far away as she possibly could. Indira found herself in the deep basements of the school. Muscle memory led her straight to the Sepulcher. Even the company of Dr. Montague would be less painful than being forced to flirt with her best friend in front of everyone else. She was walking the familiar hallway with its recognizable collection of unfinished books when she heard raised voices.

"Then get rid of me!" one shouted. "Go ahead and pull the plug. I have another version of my story coming out in the summer. I don't need to waste my time here."

"You're under contract," answered a deeper voice. Both the voices belonged to men. "Break that contract and we'll take everything."

Indira was caught between emotions. The first was the dreadful curiosity people have when driving by accidents on the side of the road. It's natural to slow down, crane our necks, and take in the damage. The second was the natural shying away we feel when it comes to angry, raised voices. No one enjoys playing witness to a heated argument.

Feeling the warring desires to know *and* to retreat, Indira finally decided to peek into the main room of the Sepulcher. Dr. Montague stood in the distance. He had his hands on his hips and a little briefcase by his feet. Opposite him was Brainstorm Vesulias. Both their faces looked as dangerous and as dark as thunderclouds.

"You already broke the contract!" Dr. Montague was yelling. "Broke it when you ignored my requests for *only* protagonists. I'm not going to waste away down here training up friars and nurses who have a few petty lines. I'm Romeo Montague, in case you've forgotten."

"You're *Dr.* Montague, in case *you've* forgotten. Trained to teach and sworn to do your best by *every* character who comes into your classroom." Brainstorm Vesulias poked Dr. Montague in the chest, and the touch almost looked like a strike of lightning. "Do not forsake your vows."

Dr. Montague launched into another verbal attack, and Indira found herself backing away. She had satisfied her curiosity, and now she felt it would be better to just wait out the storm. She didn't want to be caught. And it was uncomfortable listening to Dr. Montague speak that way about her and the other side characters. She retreated down the hallway, far enough that the voices were distant and muddled, and decided to flip through the pages of one of the unfinished books hanging on the wall.

The book only made it through seventy-two pages. The cover showed a delicate string of pearls. The string had been snipped with scissors or a knife, and the outmost pearl looked ready to fall to the floor. The story featured a protagonist named T. Kettle. The first chapter definitely grabbed the reader's attention. The girl came from a poor family and was forced to steal in order to survive. Indira read to the part where T. Kettle slipped past the museum's guards before realizing that the halls around her had gone silent. The voices had stopped.

She closed the cover of the book and walked quietly

toward the main room of the Sepulcher. It was quiet, but not empty. Dr. Montague lay facedown in a crumpled pile to her left. It was a strange sight, but Indira knew he liked to use strange teaching techniques.

Brainstorm Vesulias was gone. Indira crossed the room and stood over Montague for a second, but he didn't move. She reached down and tapped his shoulder lightly. When he still didn't move, Indira almost rolled her eyes. He'd played dead for one of their classes. These techniques were getting old. So she set a firmer hand on his shoulder and rolled him onto his back.

A horrified scream echoed through the catacombs.

The entire room went black. A lightning bolt illuminated a desolate plain.

Where are you taking me? Unhand me! What are you doing? What is *this place?*

Those questions echoed as Indira stumbled backward and nearly tripped. She could've sworn it was the voice of Dr. Montague. The lights had returned to normal and she was standing back in the Sepulcher, but Dr. Montague still wasn't awake.

Instead his twisted face stared up at her. His eyes had been replaced by a pair of plain brown buttons. A gold string looped through each one, forming a delicate *x*. More horrifying was the blood-red thread that sealed his lips. She could see that he was still breathing through his nostrils. *Oh, thank heavens, he's alive.* But his eyes had been taken and his lips had been sealed. Indira whipped around, searching for the person who had screamed.

It took her a moment to realize she was alone in the Sepulcher.

The scream had come from her.

29

A Really, Really Bad Day

People heard. The twins, her classmates, arrived first. Indira yelled for them to get the brainstorms and to get them now. That command was followed by a dangerous thought. *The attacker might be one of the brainstorms. Vesulias was down here right before it happened, and the two of them were arguing.*

Indira shivered. Could he really have done this? And if not him, then who?

She heard footsteps thundering overhead. People were coming. She stood beside Dr. Montague, unable to bear looking at his puppet eyes and stitched lips. As she waited, hands trembling and mind racing, she noticed the first clue. Sitting on the second step was a black stone. It shimmered in the golden light of the Sepulcher. Indira leaned down and plucked it up. It was bone hard and oddly warm. She held it up to eye level and nearly gasped.

It wasn't a stone. It was a dragon scale.

She pocketed the scale as a herd of people poured into the room. Indira recognized Brainstorm Underglass at the front. She glided forward, her collar high and dominating, her hair in a perfect bun. Behind her, Brainstorm Vesulias had a look of utter shock written across his dark features. If he was pretending to be surprised, he was a very good actor. Brainstorm Ketty came next, and Indira's stomach gave a twist. She was wearing her black dragon-scale jacket.

"I found him like this," Indira said. "I don't know what happened."

A doctor pressed through the gathered crowd and knelt. Indira stepped aside so the man could check Dr. Montague's vitals and listen for things that, she supposed, non-doctors couldn't hear. The man announced that he was still alive but marked by dark sorcery, and the doctor didn't know the proper counterspells. Indira was about to explain what had happened when a raised voice echoed from the entrance.

"Everybody out of my crime scheme!" A fresh-off-the-page detective pushed through the crowd. He had an actual magnifying glass and a patterned cap, all set off by an ankle-length trench coat. "I need a ten-foot perimeter around the decreased."

"We sent for Sherlock Holmes," Brainstorm Underglass said crisply.

"Mr. Holmes wanted to be here, ma'am, but he's on

holiday in the Iron Lakes. A well-deserved vaccination after how hard he's worked lately. Luckily, I got your call." The detective slung an identification card out for her to see and whipped it back up just as quickly. Underglass started to complain, but the detective slid past and hovered over Dr. Montague. "Detective Malaprop, at your service. Time of death?"

"He's not dead," Brainstorm Vesulias answered. "His hands are moving."

The detective leaned closer and examined Dr. Montague's hand with his magnifying glass. After a few seconds he pulled out a spiral notepad.

"Time of death: in the future. Possible attacker could be a seamstress. Buttons were employed, as well as some expert stinching. Note to self: investigate all local haberdasheries." Detective Malaprop was so engrossed with his investigation that he missed the incredulous stares of the brainstorms behind him. "Witnesses?"

"The girl found him," Brainstorm Ketty supplied. "Her name is Indira Story."

Every eye turned to Indira, including a magnified one. Detective Malaprop regarded her through his glass with suspicion.

"What did you see when you arrived on the scheme, ma'am?"

"The scheme?" Indira asked in confusion.

Detective Malaprop gestured around the room. "The setting, the location — the *crime scheme*. Describe it to me."

Indira felt nervous in front of so many people, but she swallowed once and spoke. "Well, I was down here earlier than normal and heard an argument. I can't remember what was said." And she really couldn't, in that moment. All the added stress was pressing the words exchanged between Vesulias and Montague beyond her mental reach. "But I waited until they were done talking. I didn't think it'd be polite to listen or interrupt. When I couldn't hear them anymore, I came into the Sepulcher and found Dr. Montague on the floor."

"Was the victim facedown when you found him?"

"Yes."

"And what's your representation to the victim?"

"My what?"

"How do you know this man?"

"He teaches my I Thought You Were Dead class."

"Quite an ironic class title, given the circumcisions." Detective Malaprop clicked his pen and turned to the waiting crowd. "We have a clear-cut case of revenge. Aggression. Passion. I would be on the lookout for an ex-lover, a seamstress, or a ghost. Perhaps all three of them working together."

Brainstorm Ketty took a step forward. Light shivered down her dragon-scale jacket.

"Indira said someone was arguing with him. Shouldn't you ask her who it was?"

Detective Malaprop eyed the brainstorm doubtfully, flipped through his notes, and gave a surprised look. "Not sure how I missed that." He turned to Indira. "Can you identify the person to whom our victim was speaking?"

Indira avoided making eye contact. The dragon scale was pulsing with heat inside her pocket. Her voice shook a little. "I heard Dr. Montague arguing with Brainstorm Vesulias."

The crowd gasped. A few edged away from the man, as if he might attack them next.

"Is that true?" Underglass asked.

Even Detective Malaprop shivered at the short woman's dangerous tone. Indira had never understood what powers the brainstorms possessed. She knew they traveled between worlds, but she hadn't ever thought of them as dangerous. Now, as she watched the sparks form around Underglass, she felt there was nothing in the world that was *more* dangerous.

"Yes," Vesulias finally said. "I was down here. And yes, we were arguing. As the three of us discussed at our last meeting, many students have had complaints about Dr. Montague. He has been neglecting his duties to our side characters. I came here to inform him of our position."

Detective Malaprop huffed. "Was your position 'do what we want or become a puppet'?"

Brainstorm Vesulias scowled. Indira didn't think he was helping his case by looking and sounding so angry. "Of course not. I wanted to fire him."

"You wanted to set the victim on fire?" Malaprop stormed across the room, removing a pair of handcuffs as he approached. "With the power vested in me by the laws of Fable, the justice system of Imagination, and permission from my mother, you're under arrest for the assault of Dr. Montague."

"I didn't do anything!" Brainstorm Vesulias shouted.

Malaprop clinked the handcuffs over Vesulias's wrists anyway. Ignoring the patient protests of Brainstorm Underglass, the detective led his culprit through the crowd.

A ruckus ensued. Underglass and the rest of the crowd followed, shouting their approval or disapproval accordingly. Only the doctor remained with Montague, muttering counterspells that had no visible effects Indira could see. Indira quietly watched him work for a few minutes before an arm wrapped around her shoulder.

It was Brainstorm Ketty. "We agreed to meet this afternoon. Would you like to meet now? I can understand if you need to go home after what's happened. It's all quite shocking."

Indira definitely felt shaken, and she wasn't sure what to make of the little dragon scale in her pocket. Was it from some other visit to the Sepulcher? Or had Brainstorm Ketty been down here with Dr. Montague before the incident? Indira knew a single little scale wouldn't be enough to prove anything, but she wasn't convinced that Vesulias was guilty, either.

He *had* raised his voice and threatened Dr. Montague, but he had also looked surprised by what had happened. She remembered that all of them were quite familiar with the art of acting. Maybe Vesulias had simply been putting on a good show.

With a steadying breath, she nodded to Brainstorm Ketty. "I would like that."

"Are you sure?" Brainstorm Ketty asked, giving Indira's shoulder a squeeze.

"I want to know how I'm doing in my classes," she said.

Until today, everything had been going so well. She had been practicing and improving and working so hard. At the start of the semester Mr. Threepwood had reminded all the characters that the line between protagonist and side character was a thin one. Maybe it wouldn't matter if her navy jacket had coffee stains. Maybe, just maybe, she would be given a golden replacement if her professors noticed her improvement.

Every cage has a key, she thought.

It was time to find out if she had succeeded in unlocking hers.

30

But Seriously ... It Gets Worse

They backtracked up the stairs, and Brainstorm Ketty opened the door to her office. The chalkboard wall swirled with the same wild activity Indira had seen on her first visit. Once more, her eyes snatched at little bits of information:

> ~~Librarian Hall of Fame~~
> New Author in Maine, writing a horror that needs a strong female protagonist
> Potential leads? 5/8

Ketty reached behind her desk and pressed a button. Indira was expecting her name to appear in the place of the other swirling activity, but instead the name DARBY MARTIN etched itself on the center of the board. A web of notes sprang in every direction. There were so many, in fact, that Indira couldn't make her mind focus on just one. She wondered if Ketty had this kind of information on *every* student she taught. The brainstorm made an annoyed noise and pressed the button again.

This time, Indira's name did whisper onto the board. All around the printed words, little thought bubbles appeared. The ideas were scribbled in several different fonts.

"Our goal as brainstorms is twofold. First, we're always on the search for a proper Author for every student." Brainstorm Ketty pressed another button beneath her desk, and a massive list of names filled the chalkboard. She set a perfectly manicured finger on the board and scrolled down. The list appeared endless. "With so many Authors and so many characters, you can imagine that this isn't the easiest task in the worlds."

Indira nodded. "It looks kind of intimidating."

"And completely out of your control," Brainstorm Ketty added. "The best thing we can do is focus on what you *can* control."

"Which is what?"

"The type of character you're becoming. You see, Indira, there are four different classifications we have for our students. *Graduates* get placed in a story and click with their Author. *Returning students* don't catch the eye of an Author on the first go-around. They sign up for more classes, keep training, and try again next year. We've had students here for as long as a decade before they finally find the right story, and by then you can imagine they are very well-rounded characters. Some do very well for themselves that way."

Indira hoped she wouldn't be there for a decade. That was a long time to be anywhere.

"Lastly, we have *miscast* and *unfinished*." Brainstorm Ketty uttered the words as if they were curses, things that should be discussed in dark corners. "Miscast characters are characters that the Author *adjusts*. We have no control over it, you know. Once you're in the Author's hands, anything can happen. They might change your hair color or your personality. Sometimes they might even cast you as an antagonist. A difficult fate, but at least you're in a story."

"And what about unfinished?" Indira asked, dreading the answer.

Brainstorm Ketty shivered visibly. "You've obviously been down to the Sepulcher."

"Yes, ma'am."

"So you've seen the . . . unfinished books?"

"There are a lot of them."

"Yes, there are," Brainstorm Ketty said crisply. "And every character from those books is *stuck*. They never find their way into the hearts and minds of readers. Everyone thinks Fable is one big fairy tale, but even fairy tales don't end well for everyone. Most of our unfinished characters live in Fable. Many end up in neighborhoods like Plot Hole or the Flats. A handful do well for themselves—

Mr. Threepwood being a fine example—but most take up meager jobs. They play an important role in our society, but certainly not the role they once wished to have. The roles they always dreamed of playing in stories. Not at all."

Indira couldn't help but say, "I don't want to be unfinished."

"Of course not, dear," Ketty replied. "So let's take an honest look at how you're *really* doing. Taking a realistic approach will help you *avoid* those sorts of endings."

The board blinked back to Indira's portrait and the bubbled comments from her professors. "I'm afraid to say that we overshot your potential. The reports from your professors are a little distressing. Your grades in every class are well below average. In fact, it seems you have a serious problem turning in completed homework. . . ."

"I just talked to Mr. Threepwood," Indira said. "He said I'd have a chance to redo them. I really don't know what happened! I've been completing all my assignments."

"Let me finish," Ketty interrupted. "Aside from the missing homework, Mr. Threepwood also pointed out that you don't always complement the protagonists as well as he would like."

Indira opened her mouth to protest, but Brainstorm Ketty went on, pointing to some of the highlighted quotes on the board. "Alice reports that you're a quiet girl with a knack for finding the most roundabout ways to escape from situations. Professor Darcy claims that you skipped his midterm without reason today, and Dr. Montague, may he recover swiftly, states a concern for your lack of dramatic suspense."

The feelings of horror and dread doubled. Indira couldn't *believe* her professors would say such things, but their words were etched on the board in front of her, undeniably real. She felt each new comment like a punch to the gut. All this time she'd thought she had been improving, but each and every one of her professors was suggesting the opposite.

They thought she was getting *worse*. All hope of a new, golden jacket evaporated.

"Is that all they said?" Indira asked.

Brainstorm Ketty frowned. "That's really the *best* I could find. I don't mean to be harsh, dear, but consider what we just discussed. If I package you as a side character with romantic interest, it's very possible you won't click with an Author. Given your current grades and feedback, that's a recipe that points dangerously toward unfinished. I don't mean to dash your hopes, but we may have to consider you for more of a cameo role."

"A—a what?" Indira asked.

"A cameo. It's a term for characters who appear briefly, perhaps for a scene or two, in a novel. There's no shame in it. A little boring, perhaps, to be stuck in the same scene for your entire career, but some cameos are loved by their fandoms. The gatekeeper in *Macbeth* is a great example.

Short scene, but unforgettable! At least you wouldn't be unfinished."

"Cameo," Indira repeated. *A cameo?* First she hadn't been good enough to be a protagonist. Now her brainstorm wasn't sure she could even perform well enough to be a side character? How had everything gone so wrong? "Isn't there anything I can do?"

Brainstorm Ketty shrugged. "Keep working hard, I suppose? At least we're not transferring you to Antagonist Academy. We've had a few students in the past who didn't really fit in. They were sent straight to Fester. Don't get me wrong, every story needs a bad guy, but it's a hard life over there compared to here."

"I could be an antagonist?" Indira asked hopefully. That sounded better than a cameo.

Brainstorm Ketty considered that. She eyed the papers in front of her again and shrugged. "It's not the *worst* idea. Here's what we'll do. You hang in there, work hard, and I'll try to talk to your professors. But if it keeps trending this direction, yes, it might be worth considering the other options in Fester. All right?"

Indira nodded, feeling numb. Brainstorm Ketty was watching her carefully. She looked ready to say more, but a knock sounded. Indira struggled to her feet.

"Are you all right, Indira? I know this is a lot to think about."

She shook herself. "I . . . I'm sorry. I have a headache."

Another knock sounded, and Indira almost jumped.

"Feeling a little pain at the temples?" Brainstorm Ketty asked.

Indira's eyes narrowed. "How did you know that?"

"It's a side effect of the Real World. I'd just gotten back from my trip to visit that Author—the one I mentioned earlier—when the report of Dr. Montague's attack worked its way up from the Sepulcher. I wasn't able to observe the normal cleanliness procedures. I'm sure some of the Real World is just brushing off on you. You'll feel fine in a few minutes."

A third knock came. Indira finally realized Brainstorm Ketty was waiting for her to leave.

"I'm sorry," she said. "Thanks for your time."

Ketty ordered the person to enter. It was Gavin Grant. He offered his bright smile and rubbed one hand over a new haircut. "Didn't mean to interrupt," he said. "Just here for my appointment."

"Not at all, dear." Brainstorm Ketty waved to Indira. "Ms. Story and I were just wrapping up. Take my advice to heart, all right, Indira?"

Indira made her way outside Protagonist Preparatory, stained jacket in hand, hoping some fresh air might help her figure out how *any* of this was even possible. The argument she'd overheard, the dragon scale sitting in her pocket, and now all of Brainstorm Ketty's thoughts about her future.

It was the last thing Indira had expected to happen, and somehow almost as bad as being witness to Dr. Montague's brutal attack. Lost in thought, Indira didn't see the dog-ear coming. It snatched the blue jacket right out of her hands. Indira caught a glimpse of pink thread dangling from the dog's collar. She watched helplessly as her first grudge kicked up dust, darting into the nearest alleyway.

Instead of giving chase, instead of fighting, Indira sank to her knees. The burdens of the day weighed too much, and she sat there, feeling tired and lost. Her stolen jacket was like a sour cherry on top of a melting sundae. After a few minutes, she picked herself up and started walking the streets of Fancy. She heard snatches of conversation — all about different stories — and couldn't help thinking she was losing her chance of ever making it into one.

Eventually, she made her way back to the Penningtons'. Indira was so tired and beaten down, in fact, that she forgot the family plans that evening. At breakfast, she had agreed to meet Mrs. Pennington at the local skating rink for a birthday party Patch was attending. But the dark and empty house felt like one more bad sign in a day full of them.

Indira went straight to bed, but that didn't mean she slept well or even at all. She rolled from one side to the other, with the word *unfinished* echoing in her head.

31

Cashing In a Favor

Ever had a bad day like Indira's, my dear reader? Then you know just how important it is to have someone to talk to about it. The advice of Mrs. Pennington might have saved the day.

If only Indira had woken up, gone downstairs, and had the chance to talk to her adopted mother. But Mrs. Pennington had rushed home from the party and found Indira asleep in her room. Having just worked a double shift *and* attended a birthday party, she'd gotten Patch to bed and fallen straight to sleep herself. Patch was so tired that he slept well into the morning. Given the chance to sleep in for once, Mrs. Pennington enjoyed the extra rest, and that meant Indira came down the next morning to an empty kitchen.

It was then that Indira made up her mind.

If Fable didn't want her, she didn't want it. She went back into her room and packed the few belongings she had. Feeling guilty about what she was about to do, Indira decided that Mrs. Pennington at least deserved a note, some kind of explanation. The last thing Indira wanted was for her and Patch to feel like it was something they did. She rifled through the kitchen drawers and found stationery in the shape of a flower. It was such a Mrs. Pennington style that Indira almost started to cry. She crumpled up her first few attempts and finally went with the truth. It was short and simple:

> *You were the best part of my time in Fable. I'm going to miss you both.*
>
> *Love, Indira*

Without saying goodbye (which made her feel *very* guilty), she walked out of the Pennington home, fully intending to leave for good. She felt guilty as she passed the spot where Phoenix sometimes waited for her. A little doubt whispered in the back of her mind that he'd probably figured out that she had a crush on him.

As she roamed through the city, she wondered if little Margaret was waiting for her. It was about that time of the morning when she would have normally sat before the Courage Hearth with her friend. Indira didn't need more courage, though. She'd already made up her mind. If she couldn't succeed as a character here, she would try to make things work elsewhere.

Every cage has a key.

She'd follow in Peeve Meadows's footsteps. Her only remaining key was to become an antagonist. All she had to do was find an escort to show her the way. Luckily, someone owed her a favor. Indira started her search in Reach-for-the-Sky, combing every street and courtyard. She walked right up to groups of Marks, interrupting their stories, before moving on when she didn't find the woman she was looking for. Indira might have lost her lucky penny during auditions, but she still had one more favor. All she had to do was track down the Mark who had lost her watch that day.

It was past noon when Indira heard a familiar drawl.

"With the guns firing and General Sherman just marching on through! Y'all would have thought the Four Horsemen of the Apocalypse were knocking at the door!"

The Mark in question fanned herself with a folded-up flyer and was confiding her story to a pair of women. Indira spotted the lovely freckles along the Mark's arms and those distinctive light-brown eyes. She didn't hesitate to march right up to her.

"I'd like to cash in my favor," she announced.

The woman lifted a curious eyebrow and smiled. "Oh, my stars, it's you."

Indira nodded. "It's me."

The Mark checked her watch. "You've caught me at a

wonderful time. Your wish is my command, sweetheart. What is it you need?"

Indira had been hoping she would say that. *Your wish is my command.* People always dug themselves in holes by using the old clichés. Now the woman couldn't refuse.

"I want you to escort me to Fester."

The group of Marks gasped. The woman who owed her the favor stopped fanning and knelt forward. "Are you out of your little mind, sweetie? Fester is where the bad people are."

"You said my wish was your command," Indira insisted. "No matter what."

"That's when I thought I was dealing with a rational sort of person. Do you have any idea what goes on in Fester? Demons and witches and football coaches who steal playbooks! It is the very center of vice and sin and ruin. What about a new dress?" The Mark smiled kindly. "Or how about I take you out to Fable's finest restaurant — my treat?"

Indira was determined, though. "You promised me."

The woman let out a sigh. "Dear, I don't know what happened to make you this desperate, but do you really want to stoop to that level? Do you *really* want to be the bad guy in the story? You were meant for more than that, honey."

For the first time, Indira was caught off guard. Something about those words echoed. She saw a flash of the last time she'd had breakfast with David. What had he said?

You're supposed to be a hero. I can feel it in my bones, baby sister. You're meant for more than this. Indira was remembering the look on her brother's face when the Mark leaned a little closer.

"Honey? Are you sure this is what you want?"

It wasn't. It really wasn't what she wanted at all. She'd made promises to David.

"One second," Indira said. "I'll be right back."

She jogged over to one of the nearby food stalls. A bored-looking character was selling sausages and biscuits. Indira bought a few of each before returning, clutching the warmly wrapped food to her chest. "Change of plans. Do you know how to get to Quiver?"

The woman tightened her shawl and smiled. "A much more sensible choice."

Indira looked around. "Great. How do we get there? Is there a train? A dragoneye?"

"Too slow," she replied. "The Marks have a better system."

The woman looped Indira's arm in hers. Indira was expecting her to lead both of them to some kind of underground transportation when reality stretched and shivered. They stepped through a curtain that Indira hadn't known was there. For the briefest of moments, they stumbled through the dark backstage of the world of Imagination. Indira heard an echoing noise in the pitch black, and then reality re-formed around them.

Quiver.

32

A Necessary Reminder

Indira blinked.

The streets of Quiver looked exactly the way she remembered them. It was already the afternoon. Some of the early-shift workers were making their way home from the mines, covered in that strange golden dust from the story nuggets they worked tirelessly to excavate. It was such a familiar sight that she almost forgot about the unfamiliar person standing beside her.

"Not exactly paradise," the Mark noted. "But your wish is my command. Has the favor been satisfied, sweetheart?"

"Yes," Indira replied. "Thank you. And thank you for convincing me not to go to Fester."

"It would have been a mistake," the Mark said. "Why come to this place instead?"

"I needed a reminder of why I went to Fable in the first place."

The Mark nodded in approval at that answer. There was a little shift in the air as the Mark stepped back through the invisible curtain. Indira found herself standing alone down by the docks. She picked her way through the narrow alleyways and headed for David's apartment.

Indira couldn't help noticing that the city was exactly the same. It was a little sad to imagine David waiting in his room after each exhausting day, always doing the same work and always wondering if his baby sister would visit the next morning. She imagined how wonderful—and how difficult—it must have been when she hadn't ever come. All he'd had of her over the past few months were the letters she sent.

A grin stole over her face as she strode up to his door and knocked. "Special delivery!"

There was a ringing clatter inside. She heard a little curse before the door cracked open. David glanced out. "I thought I told—" His eyes went wide. "Indira!"

He swung the door open so hard that it almost came off the hinges. Indira laughed as he scooped her into a massive hug. "Good heavens! You're *heavy*." He set her back down and smiled wide enough to fill the whole doorway. "Look at those muscles! You've been training!"

She blushed a little as she walked inside. It was a bit surprising to find it cleaner than ever. The only real mess was an abandoned frying pan on the center of the floor in the kitchen. Her brother hurried over to clean up the sauce that had splattered everywhere.

"You're *cooking*?" Indira asked. "Like . . . actual food?"

David glanced back at her. "It's a work in progress."

"Impressive," she said. "Since I ruined the meal, how about sausage and biscuits?"

She laughed at how quickly he abandoned the mess. The two of them took seats across from each other at his makeshift table. Her brother looked a little taller and a little more tired. Golden dust painted the backs of his hands and streaked his forearms—clear signs of the eight-hour shift he'd already worked that day excavating precious story nuggets.

"How are you doing, D?" Indira asked.

He set down his biscuit. "As if we're going to talk about *me*. It's been so long, Indira. I'm not going to sit here and bore you with mining rotations. You've been to *Fable*."

David said it the same way she had always said it. The same way that every kid who grew up in Origin did. Like it was this distant, fairy-tale dream. And in so many ways, Fable was beyond everything she'd ever imagined, but that didn't soften the sting of yesterday. Indira's experience hadn't been a fairy tale at all.

"It's . . . fine. It's fine."

David's eyes narrowed. "Something happened, yeah? I can see it written all over your face, baby sister. What's got you so down?"

No one else knew the whole story. She felt like no one

would *really* care to hear it except for David. So she started at the beginning, telling him everything that she'd left out of her letters. The mistakes she'd made with Peeve. How she had failed auditions. The whole ordeal of being abandoned by Maxi. She did her best to include the *good* parts as well. How the city changed outfits every now and again. The smell of Mrs. Pennington's pies. The steady friendships with Phoenix, Margaret, and Gavin. But that didn't stop the story from eventually spiraling back to *now*.

"I was going to quit," she said. "Kind of. I was going to Fester. It's another city . . ."

David nodded. "For the bad guys."

"You know about it?"

"They recruit here all the time."

Her eyes widened. "What? How have I never heard of them?"

"You were in Origin," he said. "Everyone there still has hope, Indira. Here? A lot of our crew feels angry about how things turned out. It's the perfect recipe for a bad guy, you know? They come looking for the characters who've had enough. It's pretty tempting. The recruiters call it a second chance. A way for us to play a significant role in the story."

Indira nodded. "And . . . you've never thought about going?"

"Of course I have." David glanced at the golden dust coating his hands. "But you and me, baby sister? We're not like them. We're not the bad guys. I know you too well. There's not a mean bone in your body. We both know you were meant to go to Fable, Indira."

She shook her head in frustration. "I thought that too! I was destined to go there and be a hero in a story. I had all these big plans for you and me, but I messed it all up, D. My brainstorm doesn't even think I can be a side character now. Nothing I do seems to work. I feel stuck."

"Every cage has a key," David replied. "All you have to do—"

Indira stared at him. "What did you just say?"

He shrugged. "Every cage has a key. Sorry if that sounds weird. A few weeks back I heard that phrase and I haven't been able to stop thinking about it. Sometimes I feel a little trapped here. But there's always a key to every situation. I've been able to step back and solve things now. It's helped so much."

Indira couldn't stop herself from lunging across the table. She wrapped David in an awkward hug that almost took the two of them to the floor. "You *really* heard those words? Exactly like that? *Every cage has a key?*"

David nodded, confused now. "Yeah. I thought maybe I'd read it somewhere?"

"Those are my Words, D!" Indira was almost shouting. "My mentor told me they're like a promise and a warning. Those are the words that are supposed to begin my story. If I make it into one, that's how it all begins! Don't you get it? If you heard them too . . ."

It took David a second to piece things together, but when he did, his eyes widened.

"I'll be in the story with you!"

"Exactly! All I have to do is get chosen."

The realization was still thundering inside Indira's chest. Her problems were far from solved. There was a *long* road ahead, but maybe her teachers had gotten it all wrong. Maybe Brainstorm Ketty just didn't see her potential. David had heard the same Words. There was a potential story out there that was big enough for both of them. Indira couldn't stop grinning.

"I have to get back to school," she said suddenly. "Is there a dragoneye?"

"A dragon-what? Never heard of it. There is a quest road, though," David answered. "Come on. The map is at the edge of town with directions to Fable. I'll walk you down there. You better grab your biscuit for the road. It's a pretty long hike."

It took a few minutes to navigate through the streets. Indira could feel the difference. Every single step she took had a *purpose* now. She was going to prove them all wrong.

33

A Clue in the Case

As David led Indira to the edge of town, he fished through a knapsack and produced a stack of familiar letters. Indira recognized the envelopes that Mrs. Pennington had given her to mail, and inside the stationery with her name. She frowned for a second, remembering that David had never written her back. She had started to assume that maybe he didn't care about her letters at all.

Which is why his next question surprised her. "Why'd you send all these?"

"I didn't want you to think I'd forgotten you."

He held them out for Indira's inspection. "But they're all blank. There's just your name. It would have been a little more helpful if you actually, you know, wrote something. Like updates on what was happening. These literally just have your name on there."

Indira snatched the first few letters and flipped through them. She was hit by a thunderous wave of déjà vu. None of these letters were *supposed* to be blank. She had sat down and written notes to David on each of them. No wonder he'd looked so surprised during her retelling of all that had happened. *None* of what she'd written had made it to him.

"This is what happened with my homework!" she realized, her mind racing. "The same thing. They're all blank."

And just like that a few pieces clicked together. All her homework had turned blank, even though she *knew* she'd written answers. Her name had been printed on the top, though, which ensured that she got credit for the incomplete assignment. Clearly, the same thing had happened with her letters. Just her name remained at the top of each one. The rest had vanished.

Her first thought in class had been that someone was messing with her. One of the protagonists—someone like Chem—was going in and erasing her work. But no one would have bothered to erase her letters to David. Which left only one possible explanation.

"It's the pen," she said, digging through her bag. "My pen is cursed!"

But that didn't make sense, either. She'd used the same pen on the premade worksheets Mr. Threepwood had provided, which *were* completed. It couldn't be the pen. Which left one option.

"The stationery." Indira dug through her own knapsack, removing a piece of the paper she'd been using in school. She took out a pen and carefully wrote the words *I am cursed*. Turning, she held out the materials to David. "Do me a favor. Write these words under mine."

He frowned. "Kind of dark, isn't it?"

"It's just a test. Trust me."

As David leaned over and scribbled the sentence, another thought slammed through Indira's head: *Brainstorm Ketty gave me this stationery*. Indira remembered that during that first meeting, the brainstorm had provided her with all the school materials she owned. Indira was tracing back through the connections and possibilities when David cleared his throat.

"Here." He handed her the sheet back. "The map I was talking about is over here."

Indira stuffed the paper back in her knapsack. She'd check it again in a few hours, and she had a hunch she was onto something big. David led her to a forest that curtained this side of town. There was a single wooden signpost ahead, and like Indira's letters, it was strangely blank.

"Not a very thorough map," she pointed out.

David laughed. "You have to tell it where you want to go. It's a quest map. Characters come through here for training every now and again."

Indira nodded before stepping forward. "Perfect. I'm on a quest to return to Fable."

Her eyes widened as the actual wooden sign groaned to life. It bent and twisted and carved inward, highlighting two separate paths Indira could take. David tapped one of them.

"See? This one is worth one hundred experience points," he explained. "But you might run into a dragon, and it suggests taking three people with you. This one . . ." He tapped the shortest and straightest route. "Looks like you'll have to complete one challenging task and have an uncomfortable reunion? It's definitely the easier quest, though. Just click that one."

Indira pressed her finger to the wood, and her desired quest clicked in. She stood there, memorizing the route, until she felt ready to get moving. David set both hands on her shoulders.

"I don't care how long it takes, baby sister. You were born for a story. You've got this, hear me?"

Indira looped in for a hug. "Keep safe. I'll come back for you."

"I know you will," he whispered.

Indira thought she might cry if she stayed any longer. She kissed him once on the cheek and headed straight into the forest. Talking with David was exactly what she had needed. It was a reminder that she still had a chance. She could do this, no matter what *anyone* thought.

The route led south. Forest loomed around her, but sunshine speckled through the trees, and it felt like a warm and welcoming place. The path wound over babbling creeks and moss-covered stones. Before long, she decided to remove her shoes. The dirt felt so good between her toes that it was hard not to skip her way back to Fable.

The creature appeared without warning.

One moment she had a stretch of empty path before her, and the next there was a *thing* in front of her. It sat cross-legged in the dirt, and it took Indira a few heartbeats to figure out what it even was. The creature's body was that of a man, and it wore a lovely blue business suit with a cream-colored tie and handkerchief. The head, however, was that of a lion. He had a majestic mane that framed his light gold face. His bright eyes sparkled mysteriously.

One challenging task, Indira remembered. Was this the task?

"Halt!" The voice was higher than you'd expect from a lion. "I am the unanswered question. I am the dark unknown. I am the missing word. I am the riddle keeper!"

She nodded. "I'm just Indira."

The lion thing smiled. "Pleasure."

"Same, but I have somewhere to be." Indira glanced past him, down the path.

"Not a chance!" the lion thing cried. "I come from a long line of guardians with malicious intentions. You shall answer a riddle to earn your way. But know the rules first! For if you answer this riddle correctly, I get to eat you."

Indira shivered a little before realizing what the lion thing had actually said.

"Wait. If I answer *correctly,* you'll eat me?"

"Yes, those are the rules."

"And if I get it wrong?"

The lion thing glanced down the path. "You get to go of course. Haven't you ever met a sphinx?"

Indira frowned. "I can't say that I have. It's just . . . I thought it worked differently."

"Well, now you know. It's good to learn new things. Are you ready for the riddle?"

"I think so."

"Are you sure you understand the rules?"

"Yes."

The sphinx rubbed his hands together in anticipation. It was rather odd to watch him speaking through the mouth of one animal and using the hands of another, but Indira listened intently as he spoke in a mysterious tone.

"Sometimes I'm a sphere, sometimes I'm a banana, and sometimes I'm not there at all. What am I?" He steepled his fingers quizzically. Indira wasn't really sure what the answer to the riddle was, but she focused on figuring out an answer that was *definitely* wrong. She thought carefully about each clue and decided on something that could never fit all three requirements, because it could never be a sphere.

"Are you a cube?" Indira asked.

The sphinx let out a heaving sigh. "No, I'm afraid that's not it at all." He moved aside from the path and gestured with one human hand. "The answer was the moon. Oh, bother. No one ever seems to get them right. Back to the drawing board."

Indira thought about suggesting that the sphinx rearrange the consequences of his riddle, but then realized she wasn't going to be doing any favors to the adventurers who came after her. She watched the creature slink off into the woods before setting off once more.

The map she'd seen must have been old, because she stumbled upon a town that hadn't been marked at all. She waited in the shadow of a sprawling tree and watched for several minutes, unsure how to proceed. The little town ahead could easily be a hideout for unscrupulous rebel antagonists. She pictured bandits with bandanas over their unshaved faces or notorious mobsters in pinstripe suits. She knew she could skip over the town, but that would require her to leave the path, and all of Alice's lessons drifted back to her. Leaving the path was one of those mistakes that always came back to haunt the character.

All right, then, she thought, *I'll just have to go through it.*

34

The Bookseller
Retirement Community

Her best strategy was to look confident. If they thought she was rough and tough, maybe they wouldn't mess with her. She began down the trail. The town consisted of a loose circle of weathered buildings, their sides brushed by desert and their colors made pale by the sun. Indira spotted a wooden sign that was nearly too faded to read.

THE BOOKSELLER RETIREMENT COMMUNITY

She had no idea what a bookseller was, but the word didn't sound quite as dangerous as *nemesis* or *pirate* or *rapscallion*. The windows of each building allowed a generous amount of sunlight inside. She saw figures moving within, but no one came out to greet her or challenge her. She could have just continued on to Fable, but curiosity had the better of her. She was about to knock on the door of the nearest building when a polite cough sounded behind her.

"Hello there, Indie."

It shouldn't have been a surprise to have Deus stumble upon her here. After all, he was her mentor *and* he was an unpredictable kind of person. She knew he was probably powerful enough to show up when he wanted and to summon forth whatever events he wanted to summon.

But so far? Deus hadn't really helped her. He hadn't really helped her through auditions at all, and none of his "convenient solutions" had saved her from the horrible day that had just happened. She wanted to be angry, maybe even shout at him, but he looked pretty tired and miserable himself.

"I'm busy," she said in an annoyed voice.

"Come now, Indie," Deus said. "We don't need to play this game."

"It isn't a game." She turned to face him and felt the anger seep back into her words. "My auditions? They weren't a game. My schooling? It's not a game. None of it is a game to me. But you haven't been much help so far, and I don't see how you can be much help now."

Deus sighed. "Lizzy lives there. She was a famous bookseller in the Real World. I believe she still has the record for setting up the most school visits in history." He pointed at the next building. "And Krista's in that house. She created one of the most celebrated reading programs in the world. Next to her is Ingrid, who invented 'book speed dating.' Our world rewards booksellers with a nice retirement among the very stories they dedicated their whole lives to sharing. It's the least we could do to thank them."

"I could have found all of that out by talking to them myself," Indira said stubbornly.

"Yes, and you would have also interrupted them during a well-earned vacation. The booksellers come here to relax and read and retire. They do not need characters coming in and bothering them while they're at it."

"And that's all I am?" Indira asked. "A bother?"

Deus looked ready to roll his eyes but stopped himself. "Of course not."

"It seems that way." When Deus merely looked at her, she went on. "Why didn't you tell me any of the rules? Why didn't you give me more lectures about the way things are here?"

"It is not in my nature to explain. It is in my nature to *make things happen*."

"So why didn't you make me a protagonist?"

"Why didn't *you* make you a protagonist?"

They glared at one another. Deus looked away first.

After a moment, he sighed again. "I've tried to be as helpful as I know how to be."

"So tell me what to do." Indira felt frustrated by everything. "I almost went to Fester. My brother, David, helped me see that would have been a mistake. But I still don't feel like a protagonist, either. According to my teachers, I'm barely a side character! I just don't feel like I belong."

He nodded. "That's normal. Everywhere you go, in the Real World or in Imagination, people feel that they don't belong. They think that their noses are shaped funny, or that their hair isn't the right color, or that they can never say the right thing when they should. It's one of the many attributes that humans and characters share."

"So what do I *do*?"

"You fight. So your auditions didn't go well? That happens! Some of my favorite characters failed their auditions. You think a *test* can decide the fate of Indira Story?"

"They said I'm going to be a side character. Maybe not even that!"

"Change their minds!" This last came as an exasperated shout. *"Prove them wrong."*

Indira thought about David. *Every cage has a key.*

"How?"

"There's a storm coming," Deus said. "There's a city out there that needs a hero."

Indira frowned. "And I'm supposed to be that hero? Right."

"You're already caught up in what's going on. I can't really say much else, but something big is about to happen. And when it does? Be the hero you were *born* to be."

"How do I do that?"

"I didn't escort a fool into Fable," he replied crisply.

"You're smart and brave, and you've been practicing with your hammer in Weaponry, right?"

She slid the weapon from her belt loop. "I've been practicing. I can fight five bad guys at once now, but it's just a hammer."

He laughed. "Just a hammer? You sure about that?"

Indira tried to hand it to him, but her grip tightened like iron around the weapon, and Deus struggled to take it from her. With a frown, he said, "Try putting it on the ground."

She did. He bent over the hammer and tugged. Nothing. He set his feet, trying to lift properly with his legs and put weight behind it, but the hammer wouldn't budge.

"That's not *just* a hammer," he grunted. "It's attuned to you. Pick it up."

Indira plucked it easily from the ground. For the first time, she felt its perfect balance.

"So what does that mean?" she asked.

Deus looked thoughtful. "Well, there have been plenty of magical hammers. Obviously, Thor's hammer, Mjölnir, is the most famous. It did this thing. . . ." Deus made a throw-and-catch gesture with his hand. "Like a boomerang. He'd throw the hammer and it would come flying back to him."

Indira hadn't ever used a boomerang, but she turned to the center of the village and took aim at the lowest branches of a pink-leaved plum tree. With a grunt, she

223

heaved the hammer end over end. She was frozen in that moment, watching it flash silver through the air.

And then she *blinked*.

Darkness dragged her through space. She opened her eyes barely in time to dodge her own thrown hammer. The weapon clanged to the ground. She heard a distant rattle, then appeared back at Deus's side. Confused, she crossed over and picked the hammer back up.

"Well, that's different," Deus said.

They both laughed. Indira asked, "What happened?"

"I've heard of this. There's something like it in the old folklore," Deus said. "They used to call it a way hammer. Try again." He lined her back up with the plum tree. "Only this time, catch the hammer."

Indira gritted her teeth and threw the weapon again. Her body was pulled from the ground and set down twenty feet away, in the hammer's path. With a fluid movement, she reached out and barely snatched it by the grip. She gasped and waited. But she wasn't pulled back to where she'd been standing a second before. Indira had actually *teleported*. She heard Deus laugh madly and clap.

"Well done, Indie." He strode across to meet her. "If your judges had known about your hammer, you'd have been selected as a protagonist even with botched auditions."

"I don't want to just be known for a hammer," Indira said quietly.

"Oh, I agree. It isn't the powers you possess; it's how

you wield them." Deus produced a rusty bucket from thin air. He set it upside down on the ground between them. "Have a whack."

Indira grinned. It was the first time she'd really had the opportunity to hit something outside training. She hefted the hammer and brought it down in an arc from above. The bucket split open like a pumpkin, with little wooden shards flying every which way. Indira found a satisfaction in the sound *and* in the result. Deus only smiled. "Try the other side."

"Of the bucket? It's destroyed, though."

"Of the hammer," Deus answered. "If it's a true way hammer, the two sides will do different things."

Indira searched for the biggest remaining piece of the bucket, then spun the hammer in her hand. The flat face of this side looked identical, but she swung it downward. The same sound of snapping wood and solid metal reverberated through the open space. But instead of it shattering into still-smaller pieces, Indira saw a thread of purple light split the air. Before either of them could blink, the bucket had re-formed itself. For once, Deus looked silent and stunned.

"Now what?" Indira finally asked.

"Practice, practice, practice," Deus muttered. "And when the time comes? Be a hero. Trust your instincts." Indira nodded. Her mentor's eyes darted to the western sky, as if he had heard someone call his name. "I am required elsewhere. Remember: every cage has a key."

The two of them shared a grin. She could already feel him misting away, so half of him was with her and half somewhere else. Before he could completely fade, she saw him nod in the opposite direction. Indira glanced that way and was hit by a wave of surprise. Phoenix was walking toward her. Excitement came first. That feeling was followed swiftly by anger.

Maxi was with him.

"What a coincidence," Deus whispered. "The three of you crossing paths out here."

Indira turned to say something sarcastic, but he was gone. A bright mist snuck over the village, framing the tops of the buildings and the pink leaves of the plum tree. Indira watched the mist scatter and stretch as Maxi and Phoenix closed the distance. Indira thought of a hundred rude things to say to Maxi, but decided to hold her tongue. She knew Deus had brought them together for a reason. So it was Maxi who broke the silence first.

"We need to talk about the mystery you've landed *right* in the middle of."

35

A Is for *Apologizing*

It was the last thing Indira had expected Maxi to say.

"I—you—what?"

Phoenix cleared his throat. "Maxi found me at school. She said she needed to talk to you as soon as possible. I think you'll be surprised by what she's been doing all this time."

Indira eyed Maxi uncertainly before nodding. "Go ahead."

"Look, I know I hurt your feelings," Maxi began. "I'm sorry about that. I didn't really expect to make friends so early on in the process. You're really cool, but I had a huge breakthrough in my investigation. I knew I'd be working on it day and night. It was going to be impossible to explain where I was going and what I was doing. And it was the only way to prove myself to the Editors. The whole spoiled-rich-girl thing was just a cover. Honestly, though, if I had known how involved you were going to be in what was happening, I wouldn't have ditched you. We could have helped each other out. A lot."

Indira felt like the world was spinning. She focused on a small, bite-size piece.

"The Editors? I remember you mentioning them. Outside the Grammar Police station."

Maxi nodded. "They're like secret agents. An underground organization that handles all the dark plots and global threats in our world. I've always wanted to be an Editor, but they're like really hard to join. I applied to their training program, but it's this whole process."

Indira felt as though her brain were melting. "But I'm not investigating any global threats."

"Of course you are," Maxi replied with excitement. "You just didn't realize it. My mentor was here at the start of the school year checking out a few fluctuations between Imagination and the Real World. Think major consequences. Realities can *literally* collapse if things between our world and the Real World go wrong. The Editors' cases are usually pretty open and shut. The Real World leaves *traces*. I helped my mentor with the first test, but after sweeping the whole city, we only found the normal traces. I mean, not even an *ounce* of suspicious activity. He said there was nothing to investigate and left me in Fable for alternative training. I knew I'd have to solve a big mystery if I wanted to make a name for myself."

Indira was nodding. "Okay. So there's no mystery?"

"As if!" Maxi looked frustrated. "I've been over the data a hundred times since my mentor left. The Editors aren't prioritizing this, but I think they should be. Those spikes in energy keep happening. They fade before I can follow any real trails, but someone's clearly messing with the connections between worlds. So that had me thinking: Who could mess with the Real World and not bring back any unexpected traces of it?"

Indira saw the connection now. "The brainstorms."

"Ding, ding, ding." Maxi offered her widest smile. "We have a winner. Or . . . three winners. Still, I knew it was kind of strange, because brainstorms *already* have access to the Real World. Why would they need to mess with the other connections and pathways when they already have a free pass to check out Authors whenever they want? But at least I had my suspects. Limited access, though. So I snagged their files from the police station and learned what I could in my sessions with Underglass, but for the most part I was working in the dark.

"I had my suspicions about Vesulias after the attack on Montague. I was even more suspicious when Underglass cleared him." Maxi raised her eyebrows. "You probably missed that little announcement—it happened this morning, when you weren't in school. He's already back, working and everything. So maybe the two of them are up to something? I was almost ready to dismiss my theory—maybe there was no tampering at all—but every time I

229

sweep the city for new data, I see the same thing. Someone is up to *something*. And if I can just find out what it is, I'll make a name for myself. The Editors will have to let me join them then."

"It wasn't Vesulias." Indira dug a hand into her pocket. She removed the dragon scale from her pocket and held it out for Maxi's inspection. "I found this in the Sepulcher."

"A *dragon*? An *actual* dragon? This is *so* above my pay grade."

"No, not a dragon." Indira replied. "It's from Brain-storm Ketty's jacket. I found it in the Sepulcher, just a few feet away from Dr. Montague. I found it *before* she walked in the room."

"Oh. *Oh*. That's genius. Why didn't you hand it over to the detective?"

"Honestly, I'm pretty sure he would have lost it."

"Good point," Maxi replied. "All right. So you really think it could be her?"

"I'm not sure. This is the only proof we have. Pretty thin if you ask me."

Maxi leaned in and smiled. "So we get more proof. Let's talk it all through. Everything you know about what's been happening. Every little detail. We've still got a long walk to get back to Fable, and these heels aren't getting any more comfortable."

Indira laughed. "You know, you didn't have to be *such* a jerk to me."

"Are you kidding? You're like the nicest, most loyal person *ever,* Indira. I hated how I made you feel, but if it had been something small, you would have just forgiven me. Besides, I couldn't just go halfway on my cover. I needed to look legit."

Indira nodded. She was probably right about that.

"Well, this is the way it should be," Indira said. "All of us together."

Phoenix grinned at her. "Couldn't agree more."

"Reunion tour!" Maxi shouted with delight. "The crew is back!"

The three of them began the long walk home, comparing clues as they went. Maxi offered some surprising expertise on the operating licenses brainstorms used to travel between worlds. Apparently, their investigations of the Real World could only be temporary. The brainstorms could float from Author to Author, analyzing their stories and trying to link potential students up with them. But they always had to return from their brief tours in the Real World or else risk serious harm to themselves.

Maxi listened intently as Indira relayed her own information. At first, Indira didn't feel like she had a whole lot to add, but Maxi homed in on the details that mattered most. "So Brainstorm Ketty has clearly been knocking you down a few pegs."

Indira nodded. "It's just weird. I thought I was doing *really* well in all my classes. And that's not all. I'm pretty sure she gave me bogus school supplies."

She reached into her knapsack and removed the piece

of test stationery. Unsurprisingly, the words that she'd written down had vanished. It made sense. All the worksheets that Mr. Threepwood had provided were complete. But any time she'd used her own paper—the paper that Brainstorm Ketty provided—the work had vanished.

It was a little surprising to see that David's handwriting was still there. Maybe the curse on the paper was intended specifically for her? Indira held out the sheet for them to inspect.

"Brainstorm Ketty gave me a whole pack of stationery at the start of the semester with my name printed on the top. I thought it was kind of nice. But I found out from Mr. Threepwood that I'd been turning in blank assignments. My answers erase after a few hours."

"But your name remains," Phoenix noted.

"Exactly. So I've been turning in the sheets and getting credit for doing none of the work. It's like she wanted me to fail."

Maxi shook her head. "What does someone in her position get from your failure? You'd think she'd want her chosen students to perform well. Maybe I can dig into the rest of Ketty's students and see what I turn up."

"I feel like we're missing a few dots," Indira replied. "It all has to connect, though."

Phoenix nodded. "Just let me know if you need me to set anything on fire."

As they approached Fable, none of them found the missing dots they needed. They agreed to talk the next day and examine the case with fresh minds and eyes. Indira wanted to dive fully into the mystery, but she knew another challenge would be waiting for her at home. It was possible she was in *really* big trouble. She had a few apologies to make herself.

First up: the Penningtons.

36

Family

Braced for the scolding she deserved, Indira knocked twice on the door. It whipped open with force. Indira met the furious gaze of Mrs. Pennington and could do nothing but dip her chin in shame. Instead of yelling, though, Mrs. Pennington swept forward and wrapped her arms around Indira. It was a tight, family-is-home kind of hug.

"I thought you were going to disown me," Indira said into Mrs. Pennington's shoulder.

"Your last name might be Story, but that doesn't make you any less a Pennington." The woman pulled away, cradling Indira's face in both hands. "Oh, come on in out of the cold."

It wasn't actually cold out, but Indira thought it sounded very motherly. Clearly, Mrs. Pennington had been practicing. She bustled Indira inside and sat her down in the kitchen. The flower-shaped letter Indira had written was still sitting on the table. Both of them did their best to ignore it. Mrs. Pennington wouldn't hear a word of an apology until dinner was set out. Indira dug in, far hungrier than she'd realized from the long journey. After a few big bites, Indira set down her fork and reached out for Mrs. Pennington's hand. She squeezed it.

"I'm sorry. Family doesn't leave without saying goodbye."

"No, they don't," Mrs. Pennington agreed. "So why *did* you leave, sweetheart?"

Indira sighed. "I felt special when I came to Fable. Like the world had chosen me."

"The way you made *us* feel special by choosing us. I understand that well enough."

"Well, classes haven't been that great. I thought I was doing well, but my professors think I'm no good. I met with Brainstorm Ketty, and she said we might have to consider a cameo role. I was so desperate after hearing that . . . I almost went to Fester to try out being a bad guy."

Mrs. Pennington nodded. "So you've forgotten."

"Forgotten what?"

"Who you are," Mrs. Pennington said quietly. "I did too, when Patch's father left us. A thing like that will make you feel all kinds of doubt. The worst part is that we all go through hard times that make us forget. Each and every one of us. I remember one night I felt sad about it all, and Patch climbed onto my lap. He just wanted to cheer me up. He told me he liked my pies. They were the best. He told me he thought my eyes were pretty, like marbles. He said my hair was nice and that I made him feel special. He reminded me who I was."

"You're not going to do that for me, are you?" Indira asked. She didn't think she'd like such honest things to be said about her, even if she needed to hear them.

"I won't sit on your lap," Mrs. Pennington said with a laugh, "but you do need to remember who you are. You're courageous. You are kind. I don't usually entrust Patch to other people, but if I dropped dead tomorrow, it would be all right so long as he had you. You're thoughtful, too. You picked us when you could have picked other, flashier families. Without you, we'd still be at the Adoption Agency. Oh, the list goes on, Indira. You just have to believe that an Author is going to see everything that we see."

"Thanks, Mom." It didn't feel like pretend. Mrs. Pennington was the real thing.

Patch chose that moment to stumble down the stairs. He had a massive map tucked under one arm and a handful of crayons. He smiled when he saw Indira.

"You're home! Good." He waved the map. "We attack at sunset!"

Indira exchanged a smile with Mrs. Pennington. "Not so fast!" she replied. "I told you to stop planning pirate raids for the neighbors. It's time for bed! Indira, you're grounded. Patch, back upstairs. Scoot, scoot, scoot. Let's get moving."

Before Indira could push up to her feet, though, the entire right wall of their house started to collapse. Instinct had her reaching for the hammer at her hip. Were they under attack? Another part of her brain thought maybe she was hallucinating. The wall landed with a *boom*, dust rising, and Indira squinted. Five people were sitting in directors' chairs, clipboards in hand, all of them taking notes. The five of them exchanged smiles before one of them stood.

"Bravo! What a *moving* scene. All the advice was just pristine, Mrs. Pennington!" The spectacled man was walking forward, hand outstretched. "Not to mention that comic relief Patch provided toward the end. Flawless delivery! You've got the highest marks this season."

Mrs. Pennington's cheeks bloomed red. She shook the man's outstretched hand and glanced over at Indira, clearly confused. "Was — I'm sorry. What's happening?"

"Auditions, of course!" the man exclaimed. "Surely you read the semester outline? We've started doing our randomly appointed observations. This scene was just brilliant. As I've said, highest marks all year. We'll get to work on your story placement right away. There's a formal exam that you'll still need to take, but you're clearly a natural!"

Mrs. Pennington blushed even more. "How long have you been behind the walls?"

"We set up this morning!" he said.

"Oh—oh!" Mrs. Pennington covered her mouth. "You didn't hear . . ."

"Your solo performance of the entire Adele collection?" He nodded. "Definitely heard all of that. For hours. Don't worry! That only counted in your favor. Potentially embarrassing singing! That's very in with our teenage characters at the moment."

Mrs. Pennington buried her face in her hands. "Oh dear."

"Anyway," the man said, "we'll get out of your hair. Great job! There's a story waiting for you out there, I'm sure of it. Good luck on the formal exam!"

It took a few minutes to get the wall put back up and for all five of the random board members to exit. Indira watched it all with curiosity. She'd known that the family auditions in Fable were different, but the idea that you could be auditioning without having any clue? It was a little terrifying. She was just glad that the Penningtons' audition had gone so well. Her performance and story placement depended on how she performed in school, but she still felt as if she was a part of the Pennington family, and the idea of them getting into a story made her heart leap with excitement too.

She went upstairs after the dust settled and helped Mrs. Pennington get Patch to bed. When the little guy finally fell asleep, Mrs. Pennington hurried Indira down for a celebratory ice cream. After that, she insisted that Indira was *still* grounded, even with all the good news.

That made Indira smile. She needed sleep about as much as she had needed a good talk. And the success of the Penningtons just made her feel more confident about her own chances. Upstairs, Indira closed the door to her room. Mrs. Pennington had made her bed and cleaned the whole place. It smelled like home.

37

Collision Course

Indira had the most vivid dream.

She found herself sitting in an open field. Children were playing in the distance. Someone had given them a bow-and-arrow set. Adults were sitting in a row of lawn chairs, watching them fire arrows at a target. Indira looked to her right and saw the Author she'd seen in the mirror during that first visit to the Talespin with Maxi. He shouted some advice about aiming. Indira could barely make out the words. She took a step closer, curious, when the same voice she'd heard that day *thundered* around her:

"Mine! Get away! Get out! Mine!"

She woke up to pain throbbing at both temples. Indira's headache wouldn't fade, but Mrs. Pennington's morning bustle was enough to keep the nightmarish voice from the forefront of her mind. Her foster mother saw her off before heading to work. Indira turned the corner and was thrilled to find that Fable had changed costumes yet again. The floating castles had vanished overnight.

Indira walked her familiar route and found herself in a dusty Wild West town. Horses swished their tails, tied to posts in front of saloons and general stores. Marks strode by her, tipping their cowboy hats and chewing straw. The city shone under a baked-red sun. Indira even saw a pair of wizards casting tumbleweeds from one of the rooftops. It felt like an appropriate setting. Indira had the feeling a showdown was on the horizon.

She found the school easily. Even in the chaos of carriage-filled streets, Protagonist Preparatory towered over the other buildings, still looking a little older and more stately. Its wooden doors were thrown open in welcome. Indira took a deep breath and made her way inside. She went straight to Hearth Hall in search of little Margaret.

Unfortunately, the room was empty. It was still early, but her friend wasn't in her normal spot in front of the Courage Hearth. She sat down to wait and listened to the fire's quiet reassurances. "I thought I'd find you here," a voice said behind her. Gavin Grant rocked her chair and smiled. "Decided to take the day off yesterday, huh?"

She smiled back. "Something like that."

"Well, you missed all the good stuff. Margaret was suspended."

Indira nearly fell out of her chair. "Our little Margaret?"

"I don't think the word *little* suits her now," he replied.

"She confronted Chem. Big-time shouting match, but Margaret totally won. It was all over school."

"I guess you're right. I need to stop thinking of her as little Margaret." Indira shook her head in disbelief. "I feel bad, though. I wasn't trying to get her in trouble."

Gavin shrugged. "Don't worry. She needed it. She wasn't crying or anything when she told me what happened. Looked kind of like she'd finally come out of her shell."

Indira tried to picture it and couldn't. "She really yelled at Chem?"

"Let's just say Margaret wasn't using her inside voice," Gavin replied. "She'll be back tomorrow, I think. Did you hear about Brainstorm Vesulias?"

Indira nodded. "Underglass cleared him."

"Off the hook. Guess Montague's attacker is out there somewhere. He's still in the infirmary."

Indira didn't know how to respond. She'd stopped suspecting Vesulias, but what would happen if they uncovered that Brainstorm Ketty had been behind the attack? She just hoped that Brainstorm Underglass would actually believe her. The warnings Deus had given echoed back to her: *You're already caught up in what's going on. . . . Be a hero. Trust your instincts.*

"Speaking of Montague," Indira said, "has he said anything yet?"

Gavin shook his head. "Apparently, it's a pretty complicated spell. And he can't exactly tell them anything, 'cause whoever did it took his voice."

Indira considered that detail for the first time. The attacker—Brainstorm Ketty, she felt sure of that now—had gone specifically after his voice and his eyes. There was no question about that.

"And you've heard about the dreams, right?" Gavin asked.

"The dreams?" Indira asked. Her dream had certainly been memorable. She still had a little lingering headache. "What dreams?"

Gavin gave her an uncertain look. "Well, everyone had dreams last night. At least, everyone I've talked to so far. The folks at the Talespin this morning said it was some kinda fluctuation between the Real World and ours? I don't know."

"Fluctuation?" Indira asked, heart pounding.

"Beats me." Gavin looked at her and frowned. "Hey, where's your jacket?"

Indira groaned. So much had happened over the past few days. She'd completely forgotten that the dog-ear had stolen her jacket. "Lost it."

"Rough week," he said. "Anyway. I'm late for Dorothy's Right Place at the Right Time class. How about we catch up in Darcy's?"

Indira headed to Mr. Threepwood's class. Wanted signs had been posted all over the school. They had a blank outline of a person and warned characters to be watchful for any suspicious activities. If they saw someone using illegal magic, they should report it immediately. Her class buzzed with conversation about the dreams. It was honestly nice to discover none of the conversation was about her and Chem. She heard students recounting what they had seen and how it had felt and what it could mean.

Mr. Threepwood spent five minutes calming everyone down before realizing it would be more fruitful to tackle the topic that had his class's attention. "All right, all right," the ponytailed teacher said. "Settle down. This is just one of those odd little things that sometimes happen when our world brushes shoulders with the Real World."

"But what does it mean?" one of the protagonists asked.

"Normally? Nothing. There have been characters who meddled with the connection between the two worlds before. Bad things always happen. Normally, though, it means that the two worlds are just growing."

"But isn't it weird that we all had the dreams at the *same* time?" Maxi asked.

Indira glanced sideways at her friend. The two of them hadn't had time to touch base yet today, but Maxi seemed to be keeping up normal spoiled-protagonist appearances with the other characters. Indira still couldn't process the idea that her friend was on a quest to be some kind of secret agent. It was pretty cool.

Mr. Threepwood answered, "That is a little strange, I suppose. There have definitely been times in history when

Imagination has reacted to what's happening in the Real World. It's not an exact science, though. It could be anything."

"So what will happen now?" Maxi asked.

"I'd guess things will return to normal."

After the class ended, Indira tried to get Maxi's attention, but her friend glided past her without a word. Before Indira could say something, their hands grazed. Indira barely held on to the note that Maxi managed to slide into her palm. She had to admit it was a pretty smooth move. Indira waited until she was alone in the hallway to read the glittered message:

Can't hang today! I have some "shopping" to do today.

Meet me in the Red Slippers Lounge tomorrow at 4:00 p.m.

I heard there's some really cool shops that you might like in the Librarian Hall of Fame.

I'm pretty sure you'd like their new Checkshire scarves!

Take a look and we can show each other our new "outfits" tomorrow!

Indira wasn't sure what Maxi had planned, but she doubted it had anything to do with actual shopping. Hopefully Maxi could use her skills to dig up more information.

It helped that her friend had been a little obvious in her directions for Indira.

There must have been someone or something in the Librarian Hall of Fame that Indira needed to find. The only clear clue she could see was the word *Checkshire*. She'd heard of cashmere scarves. She'd also heard of Cheshire cats. But what was a Checkshire? Indira tucked the note back into her pocket and headed down the hallway, eager to investigate.

38

More Pieces of the Puzzle

School continued as if things *were* normal, but outside, a storm was brewing—literally. In between classes, Indira could see the gray clouds gathering, the sky growing as dark as a whispered threat. Deus had predicted something, Indira just hadn't known it would be an actual storm.

Indira made it fifty yards before Alice summoned her to class in the usual way. Which is to say, Indira was convinced to climb into a dumbwaiter by a rather aggressive rabbit and lowered into an old, empty ballroom. For the first time, however, she was the first to arrive.

Alice wore her hair in a tight bun. She sat cross-legged on the floor and gestured for Indira to sit next to her. "I finally get to talk to you alone!" she said excitedly.

Indira glanced around the empty room and smiled. "Looks that way."

"You weren't in the building yesterday. Were you feeling sick?"

For some reason, Indira felt that Alice already knew the answer.

"No, ma'am. I had some . . . adventuring to do."

Alice smiled mischievously. "Naturally. Tell me the story?"

"I'm not sure where to start."

Alice gave her a grave and important look.

"Begin at the beginning. Go on till you come to the end. Then stop."

Indira wasn't certain why, but those words made her feel safe. She told the story about how she'd hunted down the Mark, and how at the last minute she had changed her mind about going to Antagonist Academy. Alice even cried a little when Indira described the visit to her brother. And she *really* loved the part about the backward sphinx.

"I've thought since the beginning that you have such a knack for adventure." Alice smiled kindly at Indira. "Of all my students, you have the best nose for it."

Unexpectedly, Alice reached out and plucked at Indira's nose. She pretended to have stolen it, laughed to herself, and waited. Indira could only frown in return.

"But I thought you didn't like me," she said.

"Didn't like you? Of course I like you. You're one of my best students."

"But Brainstorm Ketty . . . in her office there was a quote . . ."

Alarm bells rang inside Indira's head. Not only had Brainstorm Ketty given her cursed stationery, but she had *lied* to Indira. Why lie about how Alice felt? Had she lied about the other teachers too? There had to be a reason. This was the second piece of evidence that showed Ketty trying to make Indira feel like a bad character. It didn't make any sense.

"See what I mean?" Alice asked, laughing lightly. "You're doing it again. Seeking the adventure. Finding the clues. Solving the puzzles. You really are the *best.*"

"You mean the best of your side characters," Indira pointed out.

"No, not at all!" Alice replied firmly. "I have two classes that are only for protagonists. No one else has your instincts. Some of the best I've ever seen, honestly. Oh! The others will be here soon. Do you have any other questions?"

Indira stared. The compliment floored her. Only Mrs. Pennington had ever said something so nice. After a second, she remembered that Alice had asked if she had any questions. "Actually, I do have a question."

"Hurry, then. The rabbits are bringing the other students now."

"If you have a gut feeling about something, but that gut feeling could get you in trouble with some pretty powerful people, what would you do?"

"I'd take my gut feeling to someone just as powerful."
Alice shrugged. "Or find a way to make that person less
powerful? You should always trust your gut, though."

Indira gave Alice a tight nod. Doors at the other end
of the ballroom opened, and her classmates were coming,
escorted by the bizarre white rabbits. "Ms. Alice, I know
I missed your class yesterday, but I need to go follow my
gut. Is that okay?"

"Sounds like an adventure. Always an excused absence
in my book." Alice stood. "Take the dumbwaiter."

Maxi wanted to meet up tomorrow, but Indira needed
to follow her gut. She knew that, in all the classic stories,
characters were constantly miscommunicating. Alice was
right. She needed to go to someone who could *really* help
them stop Brainstorm Ketty. Indira hadn't forgotten the
crackle of power that had surrounded Brainstorm Underglass down in the Sepulcher. If anyone could match Ketty,
it would be the other two brainstorms. Awkwardly, they
all kept their offices in the same hallway. Indira headed
there, hoping not to run into Brainstorm Ketty along the
way. Just in case, she made a mental note that if she did
get spotted by her own brainstorm, she'd ask about what
school clubs she should join.

Walking down the hallway, she passed the front entrance to Protagonist Preparatory. The doors, as always,
stood wide open. Outside, Indira saw lightning strike.

It was a great purple slash across an iron sky. Rain
muddied the desert streets, and thunder shook overhead.

Indira bit her lip. She couldn't separate that dark sky from whatever dark plot was happening. Deus had warned her about the storm, but he had also warned her that the city needed a hero. She just needed to piece together the clues before things got worse. She passed Brainstorm Ketty's office and stopped in front of an identical door at the end of the hallway.

Before she could rethink her decision, she knocked twice.

39

The Girl Who Cried Wolf

"Enter," a voice called from within.

Brainstorm Underglass had molded the surroundings to her own style. The clean-cut precision of her office made it look nearly empty. She sat in a straight-backed chair, arms crossed in her lap, her desk meticulously clean. Like Ketty, Brainstorm Underglass had a blackboard wall behind her desk. Neat little lists were organized there like spreadsheets.

"It's Indira, isn't it?" Underglass asked.

Indira nodded. "Yes, ma'am. I'm sorry for interrupting."

"Not at all," Underglass replied. "I'm a bit surprised to see you, though. You're one of Brainstorm Ketty's students, aren't you?"

"I am, but it's not about my classes. Not exactly."

Underglass considered her. "Go ahead."

"Well, I heard that Brainstorm Vesulias was found innocent," Indira began.

"Correct. While we did confirm that Vesulias was with Dr. Montague before the attack, we also confirmed that he couldn't possibly have performed the magical spell that was used. His name has been fully cleared. We've even gone as far as suspending that fool of a detective."

Indira nodded. "I think I know who *is* responsible."

The brainstorm's eyes narrowed. "Your original testimony accused Vesulias."

"Not really. I only said that he was arguing with Dr. Montague." Indira fished into her pocket. She set the dragon scale on Underglass's desk. "Someone else was down there."

"What's this now?"

"A dragon scale. I'm pretty sure it matches Brainstorm Ketty's jacket."

Underglass made a thoughtful noise. "All this proves is that Brainstorm Ketty was in the Sepulcher. So was I. So were *you*, for that matter. Are we all suspects now?"

"I found it on the steps." Indira leaned closer. "Before everyone came into the room."

She expected a gasp or widening eyes. Underglass just shrugged.

"But you didn't see her in the Sepulcher?"

"No, but the dragon scale—"

"Did you happen to hear Brainstorm Ketty speaking with Dr. Montague? Or do you have some other reason to suspect foul play between the two?"

"Not really, but—"

"So your belief is that Dr. Montague and Brainstorm Vesulias had an argument. In the brief time span between when Vesulias left and when you returned to the room, you believe that Brainstorm Ketty performed a devastating magical spell and fled the scene." Indira opened her mouth to explain, but Underglass held up a single, silencing finger. "And *then* Brainstorm Ketty managed to get back into her office, where I found her before heading down to the Sepulcher? I appreciate your bringing this to my attention, but Protagonist Preparatory cannot suffer more false accusations against its administrative staff. The details just don't line up."

The brainstorm stood and gestured toward the door. "Good day, Indira. Oh. And please be sure to be in proper attire. We require the jackets be worn at all times."

Frustrated, Indira stood, pocketing the dragon scale and leaving. She hadn't even gotten to the part about the cursed stationery. It wasn't right. Indira didn't know how to explain her feeling to anyone other than Maxi and Phoenix, but she felt certain that Brainstorm Ketty was behind all of this. She was passing by her brainstorm's office when she noticed that the door had been left open a crack.

Indira glanced up and down the hallway. Empty.

She set a tentative hand on the door and pushed. She could see Brainstorm Ketty's desk and a glimpse of her disorganized chalkboard. She saw no sign of Brainstorm Ketty within. After taking another quick glance down the corridor, Indira slipped inside.

Her breath caught. Brainstorm Ketty's black dragon-scale jacket hung over her chair. She wasn't in the room, but Indira knew she might be back at any moment. In the stories, this was the point where suspicious girls and boys always got caught. Indira just had to play it smart and make sure that *didn't* happen to her. She crouched in the shadow of the doorway and scanned the blackboard for clues.

Dates and lists and ideas, but none of them looked connected. She kept her grip on the handle and combed the lists again. Her eyes fell on a familiar name: Darby Martin.

This time it had been scrawled in the topmost right-hand corner. She saw a series of lightning bolts around it and a phrase etched below: *Absence makes the heart grow FONDER.* She took a mental note of the name before glancing back down the hallway. Nothing.

Breathless, she made her way across the room. Every time she'd been inside, she had seen Brainstorm Ketty fiddling with the controls to her board. Maybe there were more lists, more clues. She found a series of buttons attached to the brainstorm's desk. After a few seconds of listening for footsteps, she pressed the second one.

The letters on the board cleared. Indira saw a much more organized list take their place. This time, Indira recognized the names of her classmates. These were Ketty's assigned students. She saw at least fifty listed.

Her own name and about twelve others were tucked into their own section. Indira saw that several of the characters had been crossed out. That was strange. She also noticed that she still had a massive star next to her name. A few lines down, another star had been scribbled beside the name ALLEN SQUALLS.

"The missing kid," Indira whispered. "That's the missing kid."

Indira's heart pounded as she found a third star etched in the top corner of the board. There was a legend there explaining each symbol. Beside the star, a description: IMMINENT THREAT. She took an involuntary step backward. What did *that* mean?

Indira didn't have time to puzzle out the meaning, because behind her the door handle started to turn, and her heart just about leaped through her chest. She shoved a finger back at the first button, and Ketty's random notes filled the screen again. The door started to push inward, but there was nowhere to hide. Only Ketty's looming desk and a little shelf of books.

Indira's breath stuck in her throat, and her eyes widened as the door opened.

Gavin Grant stood on the other side, peering in.

"Brainstorm Ketty?" he asked uncertainly.

Indira nearly knocked Gavin over trying to get back into the hallway. He let out a little surprised half shout. "I was waiting for her," Indira said. "But she's not here. Sorry, Gavin."

His eyes narrowed. "You were waiting *in* her office? Isn't that like her private space?"

Indira took a step closer. "Please don't say anything, Gavin."

There was a brief silence. Gavin's eyes darted between the room and Indira.

"Fine, but you owe me one."

She nodded. "Thanks, Gavin. I'll catch you in Darcy's class."

"It's canceled," he replied. "Thunderstorm."

She gave him a nod and took off down the hallway. A few turns and she was back among the other characters, passing from one class to another, in the clear. She breathed more easily as she made her way to the front of the building.

Outside the front doors of the school, dark clouds loomed overhead and the sky crackled with excited energy. The world had been reduced to gray and purple and black.

Indira didn't have many new clues. The names that kept showing up in Ketty's notes. The label of IMMINENT THREAT that made no sense whatsoever. And then there was the assignment that Maxi had given her: to visit the Librarian Hall of Fame.

She glanced outside and figured the building was about fifteen minutes away. She frowned, though, as a slow trickle began outside. Then steadier. The skies opened up.

The mystery would have to wait for now.

40

Hammer Time

Indira was still thinking about Brainstorm Underglass's reaction, and the clues she'd found on Brainstorm Ketty's board. And she couldn't help thinking about the other buttons on that desk. There had been at least four more. What was on those boards? Still more clues? Delayed by the storm, Indira decided to go to the one place she knew she could take out her frustration: the Arena. Odysseus waited at the center of the great room, as unnaturally tan as ever.

He didn't look up, but he grunted, "Back for more?"

"I want to hit something," she said, smiling.

Odysseus laughed. "Remind me, what's the first rule of Bartitsu?"

"Disturb the balance of your opponent."

"Close enough. We had you fighting five bads, right?"

Indira nodded. "I think I can handle more."

He considered her, shook his head. "Show me you can and I'll give you more."

Indira rolled her eyes and went to the black square. Odysseus fiddled with his bracelet, and the ground hummed with energy. Her vision distorted, and five creatures surrounded her in a blackened pit. Two were archers, Indira noted, and the other three had spears. A longer reach. Indira set her feet and waited as the archers strung their bows. She backed away a little, drawing the spearmen forward. As the archers strung and released, she smiled and threw her hammer.

It whipped across the narrow pit, and Indira felt the magic of it tugging her across the space in the blink of an eye. She caught her hammer on the opposite side and rained down blows on both archers before the spearmen could come to their defense. Seeing their fallen comrades, the spearmen hesitated. Indira pressed them: a flashing, aggressive charge on the one on the left. As expected, the one on the right came in overeager, and she spun, bringing her hammer up into its stomach. The other two fell quickly.

Indira's breathing was a little ragged, and she felt an ache in her forearms, but she received a round of applause from Odysseus as she appeared back in the Arena.

"How did you do that?" he asked. "I saw you blink across like magic."

She held up her hammer. "New tricks."

Odysseus laughed. "New tricks, new game. Try the blue square."

Indira nodded. She stood on the blue square and the world vanished again. She waited for the normal bad guys to appear. For a few seconds she thought it hadn't worked, but then a grunt announced something else. Something *bigger*. A shadow fell over her, and she rolled to the left as a war hammer crashed down where she'd been standing. It sent sparks flying from stone. Indira turned. A greenish monster growled with menace. It wore thick charcoal armor along its chest and upper thighs. Indira backpedaled. *How am I supposed to imbalance that?*

The creature let out a battle cry and came forward again. Indira let her feet do the work. She slid aside from the first few blows, gauging her enemy, analyzing weaknesses. She saw that the legs of its armor were more of a skirt and didn't protect the monster at the knees.

Indira baited the creature into another swing and then pressed forward, going low and striking at the exposed kneecap. A sweeping backhand turned the blow aside and sent her spinning. *Wow*, she thought, *it's fast, too.*

The two of them circled. Indira waited patiently and was rewarded; the creature stumbled into a wide stroke that left it imbalanced. She feinted at its knees, and when it repeated the same defense as before, Indira aimed a counterstrike at the soft spot beneath its shoulder padding. The beast roared, but Indira didn't have enough power to make the blow really count.

The fight lasted only a minute longer. The creature couldn't land a blow as Indira danced, but her hammer hung low at her side, and she couldn't even swing when Odysseus brought her back out of the illusion. "Not bad," Odysseus said. "When they're that big, you have to use their own weight against them. Play with their momentum if you can. That teleportation trick? That would have been useful. Time for the second rule of Bartitsu: subject the joints to strains that they are anatomically unable to resist."

"Anatomically?"

"The body," Odysseus replied. "Look at how they're built and strike the weak points."

"Easy for you to say," Indira muttered. "How many rules are there?"

"Three," Odysseus said.

"Can't you just tell me the third one?" she asked.

"Earn it first. Try fighting that last battle again. Try to imbalance the creature by striking at weaknesses, and try to use your strengths to limit its strengths." Odysseus grunted. "Or, if you happen to be a fire mage, you can just blast them out of your path."

"What?" Indira asked in confusion.

"Hey, Indira."

Phoenix stood behind her. Indira grinned at him. Seeing him still made her stomach dance a little, but at least now it wasn't dancing because she was afraid to lose his friendship.

"Here for the gauntlet?" Odysseus asked Phoenix.

He nodded, and Odysseus went over to make preparations at his table.

"The gauntlet?" Indira asked.

Phoenix shrugged. "Just training."

Indira lowered her voice to a whisper. "I've found a few more clues."

Phoenix was about to respond, but Odysseus returned. He nudged Phoenix with a shoulder. "Be careful! This one bites!"

Indira shot Odysseus a glare, and Phoenix blushed horribly. The bronzed warrior shrugged in return and began punching buttons for whatever sequence Phoenix was about to go through. "Ready?" he asked. Phoenix glanced at their instructor and nodded.

As the simulation rumbled beneath their feet, he locked eyes with Indira.

"Can we meet in Hearth Hall?"

Indira smiled. "Sure. Tomorrow morning. I'll see you there."

After a few more practice rounds, Indira doubled back to the front of the school. Outside, the storm had paused. Dark clouds were hanging overhead, waiting to unleash more damage, but Indira had the rain-free window she needed. Mrs. Pennington would probably scold her for being outside in this weather, but she had a mystery to unravel.

She left Protagonist Preparatory, one hand squeezed tightly around the dragon scale in her pocket. Maxi's clue led her onward. The word *Checkshire* was waiting in the Librarian Hall of Fame. All she had to do was find it.

41

Checkshire

A bookish-looking clerk stood at the entrance to the Librarian Hall of Fame. Indira's first visit had been incredibly brief, as Maxi had gotten bored rather quickly. Her chances of a more thorough search weren't looking promising now, either.

"I'm afraid we're closed," the clerk was saying. A small crowd had gathered, come to check out books or see the legendary librarians. "There have been some technical difficulties today. All the statues have come to life! Until we figure out why things are so wonky, we're not admitting anyone. We don't want there to be any accidents!"

Indira frowned. She couldn't afford to wait. Maxi was out there putting the pieces together. Indira needed to do the same. She was about to push forward and explain her situation to the clerk when she spotted a more promising option to her right.

There, along the first floor, a window had been left open. She glanced at the clerk, who was busy answering questions, and slipped away from the crowd. The window was ten feet up. Indira eyed the distance and knew it would be difficult to climb.

Luckily, she wouldn't need to climb at all.

She slipped the hammer from her belt and centered herself before the open window. She wasn't sure what she'd find inside the room, but she took aim and *threw*.

The world around her *shifted*. The open air was replaced by the stuffy interior of an office. Empty desks, scattered papers, half-open books. Indira almost forgot there was a hammer flying at her. She snatched the spinning metal from the air and ducked. Voices were echoing down the hall. As quietly as she could, Indira moved toward the doorway and glanced out. A pair of women were walking in the opposite direction. Indira waited until they rounded the corner to head the other way.

Indira passed by several offices and was just thinking there wasn't anything weird going on in the Librarian Hall of Fame when an open doorway fed into a vast, carpeted ballroom.

The clerk was right.

The Librarian Hall of Fame had come to life.

Thousands of golden statues waited in the polished hall. They were all evenly spaced around the room, their plaques boasting their names and favorite books and the number of patrons they'd helped in their lifetimes. Indira walked forward, overhearing conversations well outside the range of whispers. Her previous notions about librarians as keepers of quiet and stillness slowly vanished. Some were shouting animatedly to friends, some were discussing their favorite books, and others were laughing heartily at jokes.

When she could manage to get their attention, Indira asked if any knew of Checkshire. Most shook their heads and returned to their conversations. Some took a curious interest, wondering if it was the title of a new book. The truth was that Indira didn't know if she was looking for a book or a person. Indira climbed four staircases and examined four separate levels, all full of statues that had come to life. It was a long time before she finally found a hunch-backed little statue that had heard the word.

"Checkshire? That devil! He's up on the eighth floor, restricted section."

Indira thanked the statue and moved along. Even with directions, the search took a while. She walked nearly every row before finding an unlit wing in the darkest corner. Two statues stood at the entrance to the shadowy alcove. Indira could see a line of statues beyond them, tucked out of sight from the prying eyes of students such as herself. A great pool of melted gold glittered on the floor beside the two closest statues, who were speaking in low voices. One of them, she realized, was a cat. She watched it pace atop its golden pedestal, hissing occasionally.

The other statue looked old and stately. His hair was neat, and he wore an old-fashioned vest. He was saying, "Of course it's connected, old boy. We didn't all wake up by accident."

Indira saw that the name inscribed upon the cat's statue had been filed away. A gilded *C* was all that remained of it. She managed to get within a few feet of them before the older gentleman cleared his throat. The two looked up at her with suspicion.

"Restricted section," said the man in the vest. "These books are not for innocent eyes."

Indira ignored him and turned to the tabby cat. She could see the fine pattern of his coat and the lovely speckling in his eyes, even though he was wrought in gold. A pair of crooked glasses completed the look. "Are you Checkshire?"

The cat snorted and replied in an accent that sounded more like an old-timey gangster than a librarian, "No, I'm Christopher Columbus."

She pretended not to notice the sarcasm. "Indira Story."

"Congratulations, kid," Checkshire shot back. "But you heard Horace. Our books? They ain't for little girls and boys. They're all dark and dreary and, you know, adult."

Indira strode right up to the front of the statue. She looked at the spot on the plaque where his favorite book should have been. It had been filed away too. Someone was covering their tracks. "What happened to your plaque?" she asked.

The cat's eyes narrowed. "I don't know nothing about *nothing.*"

Indira glanced at the man in the vest, Horace.

"You don't think I'm going to actually believe that, do you?" she asked.

The cat snorted. "You're out of your *depth*, kiddo."

Indira decided to test him. "Was Brainstorm Ketty out of her depth, too?"

Beyond them, perpendicular panes of glass showed the outside world. Lightning struck, bathing the narrow hall with white light. The statues exchanged nervous glances in the darkness that followed. Checkshire hesitated, then said, "Brainstorm Ketty? Never heard of her."

"You sure she didn't come talk to you?" Indira traced a finger over his scratched-out title. "If I had to take a wild guess, I'd say she's the one responsible for this."

Checkshire's fur stood on end. He started pacing, and Horace looked around the room, as if the ceiling were now rather interesting. "You don't know *nothing*," the cat hissed.

"Look." Indira tried to make her voice calm. "I just want to help. She's up to something. Whatever she's doing, it can't be good."

"Oh, just tell her, Checkshire." Horace looked afraid now. "You can't get in trouble for being threatened and robbed, old boy."

Checkshire scowled at him. "Horace! You rat! You told me you'd take it to the grave."

"I'm already dead," Horace said primly.

"She's attacked one of my professors," Indira interrupted. "I'm pretty sure it will happen again if I don't do something. You have to help me!"

"All right, all right! I gave her the book."

Horace gasped at Checkshire's confession.

"What are you gasping for, Copernicus? You were there! Look, kid, you have to know it wasn't my fault. I did the best that I could. Told her to get lost."

"And?"

"She kept coming back and asking about the book. But you'd be proud of your uncle Checkshire. Didn't *budge*. I says, 'Restricted means restricted, miss.' She don't give up. Keeps trying to convince me that, since she's some big-shot brainstorm, she deserves to have the book. She makes me these offers and how do I react, Horace?"

"A vault," Horace said kindly. "Not a word."

Checkshire kept pacing, his thick tail waving through the air. "But it all changed when we figured out that, hey, she just happens to be a wizard!"

"Ketty? She's not a wizard."

"Tell that to Louie!" Checkshire pointed a paw toward the puddle of gold on the floor. "One day she comes up here and changes her tactics. She says if I don't give her the book, she's going to figure out at what temperature gold melts. You know, playing the tough guy.

"I call her bluff. But then, kapow, she melts Louie. I've never seen someone go so quick. Thank God she melted

Louie instead of Horace. I mean, may he rest in peace, but I couldn't have spent an eternity with Louie rattling on and on about how great this and that is. And so, you know, I didn't exactly need Horace here to tell me we should play ball. I gave her the book."

Another bolt of lightning lit the dusty windows.

"What book did she want?"

"My favorite," the cat replied sadly. *The Raven King's Recipes.*"

Indira frowned. "The Raven King? Never heard of him."

"One of the greatest wizards to ever live," Horace supplied. "In the Real World and in Imagination. Some of his spells are still used in Fable, you know. His recipes were extensive."

"Why did Brainstorm Ketty want them?"

Checkshire adjusted his glasses. "We weren't sure. At first."

"But you are now?" Indira asked.

"The signs are obvious, kid," Checkshire replied. "All these fluctuations. The storms kicking outside these windows. The statues all awake at the same time. She's messing with the connections between the worlds."

"Dreams," Indira said, thinking. "All the characters had dreams of the Real World."

Another exchanged glance. Horace shook his head, like it was all a pity.

"Dimensions," Checkshire said. "She's playing with the

borders. Maybe she's trying to get to the Real World? Or maybe she's trying to bring someone *from* the Real World here?"

"But why?" Indira asked. "She's a brainstorm. She can go there whenever she wants."

Horace answered, "There are limitations. Restrictions. Brainstorms can visit the Real World, but they aren't permitted permanent visas. They have to return to Imagination."

Indira nodded. She remembered Maxi saying the same thing. Checkshire pointed a golden paw in her direction. "And if she's messing with the king's spells, there could be *serious* cross-dimensional consequences."

"Like what?" Indira asked. "A few storms?"

"Storms? A little lightning will be the *least* of your worries. Let me make this clear. The Raven King was *unique*. He knew magic. He built most of the connections between the worlds in the first place. Called the King's Roads. But he was a *powerful, powerful* sorcerer. I'm not trying to speak ill of Brainstorm Ketty, but she's no Raven King. Clearly, she's messing around with his spells. Storms? That's just a side effect. If she actually succeeds in whatever she's got planned, though? You can kiss your school goodbye!"

Indira waited for the cat to say he was kidding or exaggerating, but he just shook his head sadly. "We're stuck in here, kid. It's not hard to put two and two together. You're the one that has to take this to the brainstorms if you want to put an end to it."

"I already went to the brainstorms," Indira said. "They don't believe me. I told them Brainstorm Ketty was behind the attack on my professor. They wanted more evidence."

"What happened to your professor?" Horace asked.

"Brainstorm Ketty took his eyes and his voice."

Checkshire's tail whipped back and forth in nervous fright. "Now that I give it a think, that's one of the king's spells. I don't even want to know what she would do *that* for. The book is the key, kid. If you get the book, that'd be enough evidence to put her away."

"Give me a copy, then," Indira said. "I'll take it to the brainstorms."

Checkshire shook his head. "Tough luck on that, kiddo. Most books have duplicates. *The Raven King's Recipes* is unique. I got no more copies to give."

"Can't you make it overdue or something?" Indira asked. "Recall it from her?"

The cat shivered. "Too risky. She'd come back for me! I'm not going like Louie."

"But we could put a stop to all of this," Indira said stubbornly.

"Even as a statue, I prefer to not be melted down to gold coins by evil wizards."

"Then what?" Indira asked helplessly.

"Get the book," Checkshire said. "Find her copy and turn her in. Piece of cake."

"So I have to risk my life when you won't risk yours?"

"Hey, you're the hero, kid. I'm just your average cat librarian from the city."

Indira slipped her hammer from her belt.

"And what if I threaten you? Recall the book or else."

Checkshire smiled sadly. "Nice try, kid. Evil is evil. And you ain't the type."

Indira flushed with frustration. "Fine, don't help me."

"Look," the cat whispered. "It's a red book, black letters; cover has a raven taking flight on it."

"Can't you tell me anything else?" Indira asked.

"Be careful?" Checkshire offered.

Horace nodded, as if that were indeed sound advice. Indira lifted her hammer and gave the cat a little poke on the shoulder. Checkshire let out a sharp protest that followed her back through the rows of golden statues. She had a lead, but it didn't look like help would be easy to come by. She just hoped Maxi was having more luck and that their meeting the next day would let them piece together the clues they both had gathered.

There was still the IMMINENT THREAT thread to unravel. Indira wasn't sure what the label meant. Outside, the dark clouds loomed ominously overhead once more. She made her way home and she finally knew for sure: Brainstorm Ketty was up to something *big*.

42

Breaking and Entering

At dinner, Indira tried to remain calm and play it cool.

Indira knew she could ask Mrs. Pennington anything, but now she had a better idea about the kind of person Brainstorm Ketty was. She couldn't risk the Penningtons getting hurt because of her. Especially when they were so close to getting in a story of their own. What if Ketty sabotaged them? The brainstorm had actually destroyed one of the statues to get her way. And now it was clear she had cast one of the Raven King's spells on Dr. Montague. The situation could get far more dangerous.

There were two places Indira thought the book could be. Brainstorm Ketty's office was one of them, but Indira felt that would be a risky place to keep it. The other possibility was in her private residence. Unfortunately, Indira had no idea where that was. She couldn't overlook either

275

option, but she was running out of time. Maxi wanted to meet the next afternoon. Indira already had the information she'd learned from Checkshire, but she was hoping to show up with hard evidence. They couldn't risk taking this to the other brainstorms with anything less than an airtight case.

Back at school, talk continued to center on the strange dreams. Curious interest, though, was slowly transforming into fear and concern. Indira's next step: Brainstorm Ketty's office. She could think of only one way of breaking into the office and making sure she wasn't caught. But she couldn't do it without help. As she walked into Hearth Hall, her eyes settled on the spot where she normally met Margaret. Indira frowned at her absence. Maybe she was still suspended?

Instead, she found Phoenix waiting for her. She wasn't surprised to find him waiting in front of the Luck Hearth. They were going to need all the luck they could get to take Ketty down.

"Hey," Indira said softly. She had planned to say more, but the words sort of sat on the tip of her tongue instead of coming out. Phoenix turned, a smile on his face.

"You mentioned something about new clues?"

She nodded. "And they all lead to the same place. Want to set something on fire?"

He grinned at that. "I thought you'd never ask."

Thirty minutes later they were in position. Both of them were nervous, but she kept telling herself that breaking a rule was okay if you could stop something completely terrible from happening. Checkshire had said that the spells Ketty had access to now had cross-dimensional consequences. What would happen if the school shut down? Or if the entire world of Imagination started to fall apart? Indira couldn't just sit by and let that happen.

The two of them stood at the center of an empty classroom. Indira held a desk steady as Phoenix climbed on top of it. Standing, he could almost reach the ceiling's sprinkler. Indira craned her neck. "Are you sure you want to do this?" she said. "You might get in trouble."

"Weird stuff is happening," Phoenix answered. "If what you and Maxi said is true, we have to do this. Doing nothing isn't an option."

Indira nodded. "I'm ready."

Phoenix coaxed a little flame into the palm of his hand. It started off like the flick of a lighter. He leaned forward and blew on it, shaped it, let it grow. The flame flickered into something bigger and rounder. He held it up to the sprinklers for a few seconds until they kicked on. A shrieking alarm sounded in the halls and throughout the school. Phoenix leaped down from the desk and sprinted for the door. His shoulders were dotted with water, but not suspiciously drenched. He flashed her a good-luck smile and slid into the masses of students exiting classrooms and making their way out of the building.

They had purposefully picked a room that was close to the brainstorms' offices. Indira waited as the alarms wailed. She jammed into a corner so as little of the water as possible was spraying her clothes. After a few minutes, she cracked the classroom door open. A flash of movement came left to right, and she darted back into shadow. Breathing heavily, she waited a few moments, then glanced back out. Brainstorm Vesulias was standing with his back to her, shouting for students to move in an orderly fashion toward the front entrance of the school.

Indira waited and waited, and it felt as if the brainstorm stood there for an eternity. She was about to give up when he followed after the last trail of students. Indira slipped down the hallway and headed straight for the offices. The alarms wailed overhead, and she checked both ways before slipping her hammer out. She spun it to the breaking side and hefted it back. She caught herself on the downswing, though, seeing Brainstorm Ketty's door handle twist. In a panic, she flattened herself to the wall. Ketty came out in a hurry. The woman closed the door behind herself, bustled into her dragon-scale jacket, and went down the hallway without looking back.

Chest heaving, Indira turned back to the door and tried the handle. Locked. She hefted her hammer again and knocked the handle away with a single swing. The metal snapped free of the wooden circle, and Indira wedged the door open with ease.

Inside, she took a deep breath and began searching for Checkshire's restricted book. Stacks of paper were scattered, and a variety of ornaments and keepsakes decorated the shelves. She saw a handful of books, but none with red spines or black letters. Carefully, she opened each drawer of Brainstorm Ketty's desk. Almost all of them were empty.

She was working her way through a cabinet when the alarms went silent. Her eyes scanned the room in panic. She had to get out. Now. People were going to be coming back into the building. If she didn't leave, she wouldn't have a chance. She pulled at the dangling knob, cracked the door open, and peeked down the hallway.

All three brainstorms were waiting. Their backs were turned as they spoke to passing students who were funneling through the entrance. The classroom she needed to get to was too far. She closed the door and twisted her hammer to the fixing side. With a solid strike, purple light sliced into the room. The doorknob shivered, blinked, and was as good as new.

"All right," Indira said to herself, remembering the backup plan she and Phoenix had discussed. "I'll pretend that I came here to see her about my grades and got confused when the alarms went off."

Indira realized that the blackboard was filled with Ketty's chaotic lists. She had a minute or two, tops, to check the other boards. She launched herself around the desk and fumbled for the buttons. She saw the name DARBY MARTIN again. Why did *that* student keep showing up? She'd never even heard of the kid. The next page listed Authors. Indira saw some highlighted names, but nothing suspicious.

Next: a random page of doodles.

Next: the board went blank.

Indira stared at it for a few seconds and was about to press the next button when she saw something appear. In a thin chalk outline, a white archway emerged. She watched an invisible hand color the arch with a light shading. Not an arch, she realized, but a door. Indira couldn't believe what she was seeing. She set her hand flat against where the handle was drawn and felt cold metal. She gave it a tug. White dust coughed into the air as the door groaned open on black hinges. A tunnel led into the waiting darkness.

It was a secret passageway.

Indira felt the need to see where it led, but doubts ran through her. If she left this way, the door would still be on the board when Brainstorm Ketty returned to her office. The brainstorm would know that someone *else* knew. She wouldn't know it was Indira, but she'd be alerted to the fact that someone was onto her. Indira couldn't leave by the normal doorway, either, not with the brainstorms hovering at the end of the hallway.

Taking a deep breath, Indira made up her mind. She squeezed past the chalk door and closed it firmly behind her. As she did, the latch on her side vanished. She patted the wall, but it was flattened stone now, without a place to grip or pull.

"Great," she muttered. "I hope I'm not stuck in here."

A kind of half darkness dominated the tunnel. She couldn't see her hands, but she could see a little glow in the distance. Carefully, she hugged the wall, tracing it with her hands, and it was only by sheer luck that she didn't go tumbling down a hole in the walkway. Her breath came in heaving gasps, and she leaned over, feeling for breaks in the stone.

Her hands found a colder, smoother kind of metal.

It was a ladder.

Below, a shaft of faint light. Indira began the descent. The bars were sticky and the darkness threatened to swallow her, but she kept climbing down until her feet couldn't find the next foothold. The light had grown just enough that she could see she had reached the bottom. She was forced to leap a short distance, landing with a roll. The shaft of light came from the end of a narrow hallway. She made her careful way forward until the tunnel dead-ended. Light leaked through the bottom.

Like light at the bottom of a door, Indira thought.

She gave the stone wall a little shove. It groaned open. Another secret door.

Wanting nothing more than to be out of the dark, Indira gave it a full-bodied shove. She came stumbling out into a quietly lit room that she recognized immediately. Her stomach twisted into knots as she pieced it all together. If she stood at the entrance to the secret room, she had a perfect view of the place where Dr. Montague and Brainstorm Vesulias had been arguing. The truth of *how* the attack had happened struck her right in the chest.

The Sepulcher. Brainstorm Ketty's secret passageway led to the Sepulcher.

43

Rendezvous

Phoenix met back up with Indira in the Rainy Courtyard. Since the heavy thunderstorms were expected to continue, Professor Darcy had been forced to move his classes to a safer (but sadly less romantic) location, so they didn't need to fear being overheard. "Did you find something?"

"I didn't find *exactly* what I was looking for," she answered. "But I did find something."

She explained the secret passageway and what she thought it meant.

"Well, that's all we need," Phoenix said. "If you can prove that Ketty had a way to get down there without anyone seeing her, Brainstorm Underglass will have to believe you."

Indira had thought the same thing. At first. "I don't think it'll be that easy."

"Why not?"

"I had to leave the door on the chalkboard to get out," Indira said. "As soon as Ketty goes back inside her office, she'll know someone figured out how she did it."

"So?" he asked. "The door's still there."

"It was a magical door, Phoenix." Indira could picture Brainstorm Ketty standing in front of her board, frowning at her own chalk-outline creation. "If she could make a secret passageway through the school with chalk, don't you think she's powerful enough to erase it? I'd lead Underglass to another bad clue. She'd never trust me. And Ketty would know I'm the one who's after her too."

Phoenix corrected her. "We. *We're* after her. Now what?"

"We go to our classes. Act like everything is normal," she said. "Then we talk to Maxi."

The two of them agreed to meet back at Hearth Hall a few minutes before Maxi's appointed time. Indira could barely focus in the classes she attended. It was hard to take Darcy's lecture on eyebrow use very seriously when danger felt like it was right around the corner. As soon as classes concluded—and the proposed hour finally arrived—Indira met back up with Phoenix, who led the way down to the Red Slipper Lounge.

It was mostly a protagonist hangout, but Indira guessed that Maxi had chosen the place for a reason. As always, Maxi was magnetic. Her laughter came pouring out into the hallway. Indira glanced in and frowned, seeing Maxi sitting cross-legged, flipping through a magazine and expressing her comedic disapproval of various styles, all while surrounded by other people.

Indira's stomach clenched when she saw Chem sitting with them. She hadn't forgotten about the fright mocha trick and her stained jacket, even if the dog-ear had stolen it days ago.

She took a deep breath. "Maxi?"

Maxi's eyes darted in their direction. Indira watched as Maxi took out what looked like lip gloss. She held it out for the other girls to see.

"I *love* this new flavor," she announced suddenly. "Check it out."

The girls leaned in, and a bright *flash* filled the room. Indira covered her eyes, blinking, until the light flickered back out. Maxi was already striding over to the two of them. Behind her, the scene had completely frozen. Chem and the other girls looked like perfect flesh-and-blood statues. Indira and Phoenix could only stare at the spell that Maxi had conjured.

"Let's talk," she said.

"What—are they—did you turn them into statues?" Phoenix asked.

Maxi waved her lip-gloss container. "A girl's gotta have tools. This one works on a five-minute timer. It's always nice to hit pause when you need time to figure things out, and let's be serious, we *really* need to figure things out."

Indira ignored Phoenix's bewildered look. "Tell us everything you know."

So they shared information. It became very clear that Maxi had done *a lot* of work since they'd parted. She'd checked into Ketty's financial records first. There had been a few red-flag purchases in prior years: she'd bought a black-magic kit or two, often through random aliases.

"But she also purchased a kidnapping kit," Maxi explained. "So, naturally, I cross-referenced all the data on kidnappings that have been reported in Fable."

Maxi slapped down three pictures.

"Allen Squalls, Leo Cafferty, and Margaret Faye."

Indira knew the first name, didn't recognize the second, and let out a *huge* gasp at the third. "Oh no. No, no, no! That's our Margaret."

Maxi squinted. "Your friend, right?"

Indira nodded frantically. "She was suspended from school. I just thought the suspension was still going or something. When was she reported missing?"

"Yesterday," Maxi answered. "And that's not all. I checked the records of each of the missing students. Take a wild guess which brainstorm they're all connected to. . . ."

"Brainstorm Ketty," Phoenix said. "Wow. How has no one caught on by now?"

"Still not all," Maxi said, holding up a finger. "I interviewed Ketty's current batch of students—well, only about eight of them, just anyone I could find, really. Know what they reported? Funny things happening to their home-work. Surprisingly negative reviews from their teachers. A bunch of them were getting bad grades, Indira. Ketty told every single one of them they weren't doing well enough in classes to qualify for a story. She's been demoting students left and right."

Anger pulsed inside Indira. It was bad enough that Ketty was doing something illegal and suspicious. But to take down other characters in the process? It was next-level cruel.

"So what do we do now?" Indira asked.

"You have a few minutes to tell me what *you* know," Maxi replied.

Indira traced back through the past twenty-four hours. Maxi was the perfect audience, gasping here and there, exclaiming ridiculous things. She even smacked Phoenix on the shoulder when she found out he had helped rig the fire alarms. When Indira finished, Maxi nodded.

"That explains the black-magic kits," Maxi said. "She started looking into the magic and realized the spells were too simple. She needed something with more firepower. But I still can't figure out *what* she's actually doing, you know?"

"The Raven King's magic definitely has firepower," Phoenix added. "He's legendary."

"Next step: find the book," Maxi said.

"It's not in her office," Indira replied. "And we don't know where she lives."

"Not yet." Maxi grinned. "Meet me in front of the school tomorrow morning."

Indira nodded. "What time? Sunrise?"

Maxi gasped. "People actually wake up at sunrise?"

"Seriously, Maxi?" Indira replied. "Protagonist Preparatory—maybe all of Fable—could be destroyed."

Maxi scowled. "Fine, but don't expect my best at *that* hour. I hope the Talespin is open. No way I'll even be able to function without coffee."

They watched Maxi return to where she'd been sitting in front of the other protagonists. She carefully positioned herself, and the lip gloss, in the exact position they'd been at the moment of the flash. She looked back one more time at Phoenix and Indira.

"Brainstorm Ketty has no idea what's coming for her."

There was another flash. The girls burst back into motion, all exclaiming over the lip gloss, as Indira and Phoenix slipped back down the hallway. He had a curious eyebrow raised.

"So Maxi . . . has some kind of magical tool kit?" he asked.

"And I have a magical hammer," Indira pointed out. "Combined with your fire spells, the three of us should be able to go up against anyone."

They had reached the main level of the school. It was almost dinnertime, but Indira felt as if they had so much more to do. What if Brainstorm Ketty finished whatever spell she was attempting while they slept? It felt wrong to go home and rest when so much was at stake.

"So do you want me to come with you tomorrow?" Phoenix asked.

"I do," Indira replied. "But someone should be at the school to keep an eye on Ketty."

Phoenix nodded. "You promise you'll be careful?"

"You mean as I break into the home of my brainstorm?"

"Good point."

The hallway forked, and Phoenix's wizard chess club was in the other direction. He paused at the split and shook red hair out of his eyes. "I'm really glad we're friends. Even if you made me set off the fire alarm. If anything happens, meet me at the Luck Hearth?"

With more courage than any hearth could summon, Indira crossed over to him and gave him a big hug. He was warm and smelled like bonfires and chocolate. His cheeks flushed as she pulled away, grinning. "See you there."

He waved before disappearing down the hall. Indira was ready to go home, but the passage led her past the hearths and right into a trio of adults. Mr. Threepwood stood talking with a man and a woman. They were short and stocky; both of them had a threadbare look. She noted that the man's jacket was missing a few buttons. As she passed, she heard Margaret's name.

"She's never run off like this," the man was saying. "We figured we should check with her professors. See if she'd been seen. The Grammar Police are already on the case, but we didn't feel right just sitting around."

Mr. Threepwood looked concerned. "Well, she did get in an argument with another student in my class. Very odd for her. She was sent home with a suspension."

"That's what I'm saying," the man, Margaret's father, replied. "She never came home with no suspension. At first we thought maybe she was here, studying late or something. . . ."

Indira had paused, and Mr. Threepwood saw her watching. He seemed to realize they were out in public, speaking of private matters. "Let's speak privately. Follow me."

They moved down the hallway.

I know who took her, Indira thought. *I'm coming to help you, Margaret.*

Dark clouds continued to hover over the city. Indira made her way back to the Penningtons', running through all the clues and conversations. She couldn't shake Checkshire's warning. *You can kiss your school goodbye.* The librarian had been a little dramatic during their conversation, but what if that really happened?

Brainstorm Ketty had already been willing to do other dark things to accomplish her goals. It wasn't hard to imagine even *worse* side effects if her spells actually succeeded.

They'd just have to stop her before any of that happened.

44

The Unreliable Detective

As she headed home, Indira noticed she had a tail. A shadow kept creeping up behind her, only to vanish when she glanced around. She picked up her pace, but continued to see a figure on the edge of her peripheral vision. Finally she broke into a sprint around one corner and hid next to a trash can. Her heart was pounding as she waited for footsteps, a shadow, anything.

A few minutes later, Detective Malaprop crept past her, eyes on the street he thought she had taken. Indira pulled the hammer from her belt and grabbed a fistful of his collar. He cried out in surprise as his legs folded beneath him.

"Why are you following me?" she demanded.

"Unhand me!"

She held up her hammer threateningly. Detective Malaprop was a good deal bigger than her, but he flinched at the sight of the little hammer.

"Just wait until the Grammar Police hear about this!" he shouted. "You're threatening a member of the justice department, little lady!"

Indira scowled down at him. "Brainstorm Underglass said you'd been suspended."

"You've got it all wrong." He scrambled to his feet and rolled his trench coat away from one shoulder. "*Suspendered!* I read the letter very carefully. I'm not to walk within one hundred yards of Protagonist Preparatory without a pair of suspenders."

Indira just stared at him. "Don't you think it's more likely that you've been suspended? That other thing isn't even a word!"

Detective Malaprop's eyes narrowed. "Hey! I'm asking the questions here!"

"That's what I don't get. Why are you following me? I'm not a suspect!"

"You most certainly are!" he cried out.

"That doesn't make any sense!"

"Admittedly, but I still have questions about what happened that day."

"Well, ask them while I walk home. I don't want to miss dinner."

Even though he didn't think it was proper protocol, Detective Malaprop agreed to walk and talk. They continued toward the Skirts. The detective scribbled down her answers as they went. Indira briefly considered telling him everything. About the secret passageway and the dragon scale and *The Raven King's Recipes*. But then he started asking her questions about a jewel heist, and she reconsidered. If he couldn't remember what case he was investigating, who knew what he would blab to others? The last thing she needed was for Brainstorm Ketty or the Grammar Police to get wind of what she and Maxi had discovered and ruin everything.

Indira was nearly home when Detective Malaprop discovered his error and flipped back to his questions about Dr. Montague. "This is my stop," Indira said, gesturing to the Penningtons' home. "Will you please quit following me?"

Malaprop looked desperate. "Can I ask you just one more question?"

"Just one," she replied seriously.

"Why Dr. Montague? What's so special about his voice and his eyes? Isn't it odd that the attacker collected those two items? Rather than his clavicle and his fingernails? Or perhaps his smile and his left eyebrow?"

Indira realized she didn't know. Dr. Montague was a character in some famous tragedy, but she had no idea if that played into the attack or not. She hadn't considered that Brainstorm Ketty might have been after *specific* things.

What was important about his voice? His eyes? Indira thought about the book Checkshire had described. *The*

Raven King's Recipes. She didn't know much about magic, but she knew that recipes required ingredients. The thought gained momentum.

"She's collecting the ingredients for something," Indira said to herself. It seemed so obvious now. "His eyes and voice, the missing characters, they're . . . they're *ingredients.*"

Of course. A dark spell would require dark things.

"Ingredients? I don't really like pizza, but thank you."

"Pizza?" Indira almost laughed. "Sorry, I have to go. Goodbye, Detective Malaprop."

"The game is affluent!" Detective Malaprop cried out excitedly. "We shall rendezvous later this week!"

Without another word, the detective left. Indira heard him dictating to himself as she slid out her key and unlocked the front door. She was glad she hadn't told him. Given the opportunity, he might have ruined the only thing she had on Brainstorm Ketty: the element of surprise.

For the second time in as many days, Indira considered telling Mrs. Pennington *everything.* There were stories in which children left adults out of the loop. That never went well. Even so, she couldn't risk her adopted mother's life. As they sat down to dinner that night, she decided that some things were worth protecting, even if it meant going against her instincts.

45

Breaking and Entering . . .
Again

Maxi was late.

Indira had been waiting outside the school for over thirty minutes now. It normally would have been fine, but Indira had no idea what kind of schedules the brainstorms operated on. She felt like they needed as much time as possible if they were going to break into Ketty's house. She had watched Brainstorm Ketty enter the school already. But did that mean she would be on the job for the rest of the day? Or did they take a long lunch outside school? Indira hoped that Brainstorm Ketty had no intention of heading home. If she got caught, there would be no way to explain why she'd been breaking into a brainstorm's house.

Indira's stomach turned a little. What if they expelled her? What if she never made it into a story? Somehow that fear seemed smaller when she thought of Margaret having gone missing.

When Maxi did show up, she was all apologies. "Sorry, the Talespin was closed for remodeling, and of course I couldn't find a white mocha anywhere else. All the cafés are trying to do a Western menu, and I just don't think the cowboy thing is for me, you know?"

"Did you figure out where she lives?"

Maxi unfolded the map and tapped a marked building. "223 Exposition Lane. Where's Phoenix?"

"Keeping an eye on Ketty," Indira said. "It's just us."

Ketty smiled. "Girl time! Hope you're ready to do some detective work."

The address was clear across the city. Indira led them back to one of the main thoroughfares. Even amid all the bustle, Indira kept her voice quiet as she explained her realization about the ingredients Ketty was collecting. Maxi whispered back her own theories. They were about halfway there when even speaking in whispers felt too loud.

Indira looked around. The streets were empty.

She grabbed hold of Maxi's elbow and pulled her into the shadow of the nearest building. They both eyed the deserted streets anxiously. "What's happening?" Maxi asked. It felt like the calm before a violent storm. In Westerns, empty streets meant a showdown looming. They waited for several uncomfortable minutes, but nothing and no one appeared.

"Come on," Indira whispered.

They tried to remain inconspicuous as they continued toward Brainstorm Ketty's house. As they went, Indira and Maxi spotted a strange trail of abandoned bronze watches. The Marks to which they belonged had all vanished. Indira bent over and snatched one from the dusty road. "The Marks," she said quietly. "Where'd they all go?"

Maxi shivered. "This is one of the telling signs. When the connections between the worlds are unstable, side effects like this occur. Ketty must be close to finishing her spell."

"We should run," Indira suggested. "We can't waste any more time."

"But these are new shoes!" Maxi said with real heartbreak.

Indira glanced down. "They're athletic shoes, Maxi. Aren't they made for running?"

"They'll be dirty, worn, sweaty athletic shoes if we run!"

Indira rolled her eyes and started jogging down the street. It was like running through a ghost town. Maxi huffed behind her, but the run wasn't a very long one. A few more turns and they found themselves standing in front of a series of tall cabins that looked like an old-fashioned apartment complex. Indira counted off houses until they found the two hundred building. A little engraved number showed them which unit was Brainstorm Ketty's.

Indira and Maxi went up the staircase and along the

railed walkway, then stopped in front of Ketty's door. "If anything happens," Indira said, "we meet up with Phoenix at the Luck Hearth."

Maxi nodded once before scrambling to get something out of her pocket.

"Put these on." She held out a pair of medical gloves. "No fingerprints."

Indira wiggled her fingers into the gloves. When Maxi had done the same, Indira signaled with her hammer. Maxi nodded again, and Indira brought it crashing down. The knob rattled off, and Indira kicked the door open. She'd taken a single step inside when a massive bird flushed from the darkness. Maxi let out a half scream as the creature fluttered out the door and dangerously overhead. It looked like a hawk as it spread its dark wings and fought its way into the sky.

"Well, there goes her pet bird," Maxi muttered. "Be careful."

Indira crept into the room. Brainstorm Ketty had left on a single corner lamp. It cast amber light into a snug living room. A dark leather couch sat across from a fireplace. The mantel showed pictures of Brainstorm Ketty with friends and former students.

The search began. She pulled at the drawers of an armoire in one corner, searched the cupboards of an empty china cabinet, and looked under cushions but found no sign of the red book. The living room led into a kitchen. Brainstorm Ketty hadn't been grocery shopping in a while.

The pantry sat empty, and the refrigerator was a collection of mostly expired foods.

Indira felt disorganized as she went. A few glances showed Maxi working in a more professional, efficient manner. The girl ran her fingers along bookshelves and behind cabinets, feeling for hidden compartments. Indira took note, trying to adapt the same thorough methods, checking beneath silver pots and pans. *If I were a secret red book, where would I be?*

Once they'd finished searching the kitchen, Indira and Maxi moved into the last room: the bedroom. It looked, oddly, like the room of a much younger girl. From the pattern of the quilts and the strange array of finger-paint drawings on the desk, Indira would not have guessed that a brainstorm lived here at all. The desk drawers were filled with old files and paperwork, but Indira saw nothing like a book anywhere. She checked the pillowcases, the bathroom mirror, even under the rugs.

She wondered if she'd have to knock on the walls and listen for the sound of false wood or something ridiculous. Indira sighed, combing the room again, before Maxi finally spotted something. It wasn't a book, but it was that oddly off detail that detectives always seemed to notice in stories. The top of the bedside table was empty, covered by a coating of dust. Right next to the lamp, however, a little brown rectangle shone, dust-free.

"The book was right here," Maxi said confidently.

Indira watched her friend fumble in a pocket. She

removed a bottle of what looked like hairspray, gave it a little shake, and triggered the release. A harsh rosemary scent poured out. They both watched as the fumes avoided the dustless spot on the desk.

"Correction," Maxi said. "The book *is* right here."

She set her hands around the spot and pulled a book out of thin air. Indira gasped. A red binding. Black letters. A raven taking flight on the cover. Maxi handed the book over to Indira for confirmation. "That's the one," Indira said. "This is the evidence we needed. All we have to do is take this to Underglass, and it's over."

Maxi nodded. "I'm totally calling in the Editors! This is my *big* break, Indira. A case like this? No way they turn down my application now! This is *amazing*."

Indira knew she needed to look through the book first. She wanted to pinpoint which spell Ketty had been gathering ingredients for so that she could walk into Underglass's office with airtight proof. As she was thinking of *exactly* what she would say, Maxi climbed up on the bed. She was raising some kind of handheld radio up to the ceiling.

"What are you doing?"

"I don't have a signal," Maxi answered, tiptoeing over pillows and extra blankets. Indira watched as she hopped down from the bed and nudged open the bathroom door. Her friend disappeared into the dark room and then made an "aha" noise.

"Of course the only signal is in the bathtub."

"Do you really have to call from her bathtub? Can't we just get out of here?"

Maxi made a distracted noise. "Call is patching through. Give me a few seconds."

As Indira stood there, waiting, one of the silver-framed pictures on Brainstorm Ketty's dresser caught her eye. She had skipped over it in search of the book, but now she couldn't help but study it. It was old. Much older than the pictures on display in the living room. Ketty kept it out, but not for visitors, only for herself. Indira lifted the picture frame off the shelf.

It was a picture of a young girl. Her hair had been braided over one shoulder. She wore a black smock and unassuming blue jeans. Indira wouldn't have known that it was Brainstorm Ketty if not for the mismatched eyes. One forest green, the other amber. The younger version of Brainstorm Ketty held a string of pearls in her hands, and she was looking down at them as if they were the most precious things in the world. Indira wiped dust away from the corner of the frame and read the words scribbled on the picture: *T. Kettle.*

Indira's brain hammered. She knew that name. She *knew* that she knew it. But how did she know it? Down in the Sepulcher. She'd been too embarrassed to keep listening to the argument between Dr. Montague and Brainstorm Vesulias. She'd backtracked down the halls of unfinished books and started reading one. Hadn't the cover featured a string of pearls too? There had been a young girl in the story named T. Kettle. A girl who stole things to support her family.

The truth thundered.

"T. Kettle. It's Ketty," she whispered to herself. "Ketty is an unfinished character."

Indira removed the picture from its frame and placed it safely between the pages of the book. Without her school jacket, she was forced to tuck the book into the waist of her pants, right up against her back. She carefully re-arranged her shirt so that it hid the book. In the bathroom, Maxi was reciting the numbers of a code. They needed to get out before . . .

CREAK.

A groan of floorboards was Indira's only warning. She reached for her hammer, but a man rounded the corner and flattened her to the floor. Indira tried to scramble away, but his grip was iron, and with a twisting move, he had Indira's hands behind her back. Handcuffs clapped over her wrists, and he shoved her back into the main room.

"Sit down, please."

Indira sat. The man was in uniform. A little badge on his chest indicated that he was a member of the Grammar Police. "My name is Officer Oxford. You're under arrest. Just because there are odd things happening in the city doesn't mean you can break into people's homes. Surely you noticed this house had a security system. The bird that flew out the door?"

Indira shook her head. "I didn't know."

She couldn't think of anything else to say. Indira kept quiet and secretly hoped Maxi would come to her rescue, but her friend's voice had gone silent. There was no movement in the bedroom at all. Officer Oxford snapped his fingers to get Indira's attention.

"I have to take you down to the station on account of breaking and entering. I'd read you your rights, but that's not really a thing here."

She was led outside. Indira had expected to be searched, but Oxford didn't seem particularly thorough. Indira could feel the Raven King's book pressed against her back. No matter what happened, she couldn't allow it to leave her possession. She'd have given anything to slip her handcuffs and drop the book somewhere for Maxi to find. But where was Maxi? Had her friend overheard the exchange? Was she trailing them now?

In the sky, clouds were gathering yet again. Another storm. Another dark sign that Brainstorm Ketty's spell was either under way or would be soon.

They were almost out in the street when they heard a loud pop. It sounded like a blown transformer. They saw a slash of electric blue cut through the sky. The bright light was followed by thousands of voices muttering in sudden confusion. Officer Oxford led her up a street filled with Marks. Far more than she'd ever seen in the city.

Nervous conversation surrounded them all the way to police headquarters.

Officer Oxford sat her down in a chair. "Wait right here while I fetch your paperwork."

Other police officers strode about the room. She heard them on phone calls or over the crackle of walkie-talkies. It seemed like everyone in the station was busy handling some emergency. No surprise there. Ketty's spell was clearly causing side-effect mayhem.

Indira squirmed in her handcuffs and caught sight of a familiar face. Detective Malaprop stood by the water cooler. He was reading a book upside down. Indira shot a glance to the far corner of the room. Officer Oxford was hunched over a computer, typing in her information. All the instincts Indira had gained in Alice's escape class came bubbling back to the surface.

"Detective Malaprop!" Indira didn't say it any louder than a whisper, but the detective fumbled his book in surprise. He looked around the room before his gaze settled on Indira. His eyes lit up. He marched over and sat down atop the desk in front of her.

"What are you doing here? And why are you in hamcuffs?"

"You told me to meet you here for our rendezvous," Indira lied. "Remember?"

Detective Malaprop frowned. "Of course. Yes, the rendezvous."

"Can you get me out of these?" Indira asked. "I got arrested so that they would bring me to you. It was the only way I could think to do it."

"Very clever," Malaprop praised her. He removed a ring of keys from his pocket, unlocked Indira's handcuffs, and slipped them off her wrists. "Now, I believe I have a list of suspects. All over the age of seventy and knee-deep in the illegal thimble business . . ."

Hands freed, Indira shot toward the entrance. She heard shouts behind her, from Detective Malaprop and from Officer Oxford, but she was already vaulting out into the busy streets. She was smaller than her pursuers and found it far easier to pick her way through the massive crowds of Marks now swarming the streets. Taking advantage of the foot traffic, Indira doubled back down another alley and watched as the Grammar Police forged a path in the wrong direction. She slipped farther down the alley and pulled the book out from where she'd safely tucked it away. With a finger, she traced the black letters.

It was about time she figured out what Brainstorm Ketty was *really* doing.

46

The Raven King's Recipe

Indira thought it would be foolish to go all the way back to the Penningtons'. Instead she made her way down the alley and found a secluded spot. She thought she was alone, but a scuffle broke out nearby. Indira heard a growl, and she glanced around the corner cautiously.

The sight startled her. Four big dog-ears had cornered a smaller one. The smaller dog was doing all the growling, trying to show teeth and look intimidating as the others circled and snapped. Indira noticed a familiar pink thread hanging from the collar of the trapped dog-ear.

Serves him right for stealing my jacket from me.

As she thought it, one of the dog-ears feinted forward, and the other three followed with an attack. The moment of satisfied revenge vanished as they brought her dog-ear to the ground. He snapped back at them, but the other dogs had him pinned, and whatever they were doing produced a miserable whimper. He might have been a pest, but he was Indira's pest.

"Hey," she shouted, slipping the hammer from her belt loop. "Leave him alone."

She ran forward, and the dog-ears scattered. Indira's eyes followed them until they were out of sight. She leaned over her dog-ear. He was still on his side, breathing heavily.

He had a huge gash in one side. Blood dripped from it into the dust. She gave her hammer a twist and set it against the wound. The dog-ear whimpered in fright.

"Trust me," she said. "I can fix it."

Her hammer strike flashed a dark purple into the air. Seconds later, the dog-ear scrambled to his feet, wound healed. The creature studied her suspiciously.

"Go on, now," Indira said. "Take care of yourself."

The dog-ear watched as she sat behind a pile of barrels. She opened *The Raven King's Recipes* and began turning the pages. When she looked up again, the pup had vanished. She returned her attention to the book. As Checkshire had implied, most of the spells were quite dark.

It was no surprise to her that this book had been placed in the restricted section. An entire section was devoted to "Making Enemies Suffer." It surprised Indira that this Raven King character had been a resident of Fable and not of Fester, the city of antagonists and bad guys.

She flipped through until she found a dog-eared page. Notes had been taken in the margins, and Indira recognized Ketty's handwriting. She found it a little sacrilegious that someone would write in a book as old and precious as this one. Not to mention it belonged to the library!

The recipe with Ketty's notes was titled "A Spell for an Unlikely Hero."

The ingredients and instructions made Indira's stomach turn uneasily:

Ingredients:

The voice of tragedy

$1/2$ cup of love at first sight

A token from the desired Author

Eight servings of dashed hope

$3/4$ cup of not-supposed-to-be-here

An extracted essence of fire (for power and purpose)

One permission to cross dimensions

Indira paused there. The first two ingredients sent a chill down her spine. An image of Dr. Montague's button eyes and stitched mouth floated into her mind. He definitely was the voice of tragedy, and Indira guessed he'd fallen in love at first sight in his story? So Brainstorm Ketty already had both those ingredients.

The phrase *dashed hope* set off even more alarm bells. "She was trying to dash my hopes," Indira said aloud.

The reason for the lies about her school performance seemed crystal clear now. "She wanted me to think that all my professors hated me because she needed *people* with dashed hope." That helped Indira stumble upon an even bigger revelation. "Margaret said most of Ketty's students were side characters. She didn't take us because she likes underdogs; she just thought we were the most likely ones to be disappointed."

Stunned, Indira rushed on through the other ingredients. She knew Ketty already had permission to cross dimensions. That came with the territory of being a brainstorm. She wasn't sure about the cup of not-supposed-to-be-here or the extracted essence of fire. Hoping to shed light on those, she read through the spell's directions:

Directions:

1. Gather the voice of tragedy and the love at first sight during the full moon. For the most potent effect, the two should be molded together and left out on a windowsill that was once used by victims of a wistful, forbidden romance.

2. Place the eight servings of dashed hope in a perfect circle (see page 34 for proper dimensions), arranged in order of severity.

3. Season each dashed-hope serving with the tragedy-sight mixture. When matured, it should look a lot like parmesan cheese.

4. Stir as needed.

5. After ten minutes, feel free to release the extracted essence of fire into the center of the circle. Your timing here is paramount, because you do not want to melt the servings prior to the arrival of the not-supposed-to-be-here.

6. Wait patiently. If you've done the spell correctly, someone or something should arrive unexpectedly. Capture him, her, or it and add the not-supposed-to-be-here.

7. Last, use the token of your target Author to *direct* your connection to them. It's always best to target the Author when they're actively involved in the creation of a story, as the pathways that connect them with possible characters become available during that time.

8. If you've properly attained your permission to cross dimensions, the final step will pull you through. Assuming you have all the ingredients and have followed every step successfully, this spell will put you *permanently* on the pages of a new story. Even an Author who doesn't initially desire your presence in the story will not be able to deny your entry.

Warning: This spell has adverse effects on all its ingredients. It is very likely to have consequences in the Real World and in Imagination. You will absolutely need a location that acts as a thin spot between both worlds. That should ease the disruption the spell causes for you and for others.

The ingredients had been haunting enough, but the directions were worse. The recipe sounded like a sacrifice. If Brainstorm Ketty's servings of dashed hope were *actual* students, then what she was doing was horrific. Indira remembered that Margaret was one of the students who had been kidnapped. Her stomach turned violently. Could Brainstorm Ketty really sacrifice her and the others?

She had to be stopped.

Indira read through the directions one more time. At first she wondered if Ketty might be a few ingredients short. Wasn't *Indira* supposed to be one of the dashed hopes? But Ketty had *plenty* of students to draw on for that one. Were even more students about to go missing? Indira guessed that the brainstorm had already checked that ingredient off.

She also stumbled over the not-supposed-to-be-here concept. It wasn't lost on Indira that this ingredient really *could* be in reference to her. She realized that if she was the person who confronted Brainstorm Ketty, the brainstorm would try to capture her. She would even be expecting Indira.

Well, she thought, *I'll just have to bring people Ketty can't capture. People who can fight back. I have Maxi and Phoenix. I'll have to convince the brainstorms, too.*

Indira stood up. In stories, impulsive boys and girls always rushed off to face the villain alone. She wasn't that foolish. If she acted quickly enough, it wouldn't have to come down to some final showdown between the two of them. She would go straight to Brainstorm Underglass, and they could all confront Brainstorm Ketty.

Together.

47

Moves and Countermoves

As she brushed the dirt from her clothes, Indira heard a scraping noise. She looked up to see the dog-ear. He had a playful ear raised into the air and her navy jacket in his mouth.

She smiled. "Returning stolen goods?"

Indira went down on one knee, and he trotted forward. The jacket was a little torn in places, and it still had the obvious coffee stain down one sleeve, but she would need it to look presentable to Brainstorm Underglass, who had remarked on Indira's appearance the last time she accused Ketty. Indira put it on and tucked the book into her inner pocket. She gave the dog-ear a scratch behind one ear, and its tongue tossed happily from side to side.

"Guess this means our grudge is over?" she asked.

He licked her palm in agreement. It was a relief to realize her unfortunate grudges were all behind her. She could only hope that Peeve didn't still hold a grudge against her. After all, the girl had beaten her pretty soundly. Maxi was working with Indira to solve the case, so that one was finished. And now the dog-ear had even apologized. The thought gave her hope as she returned to the main thoroughfare. She was unsurprised to find it full of concerned Marks. They spoke in whispered circles, discussing all the dark happenings.

Indira was halfway to the entrance of the school when her vision went black. She felt like she was falling, falling, falling . . .

. . . between worlds . . .

The Author sat in a dimly lit coffee shop. Trams trundled on their tracks outside the window. Indira saw him stooped over a glowing screen, fingers tracing a paragraph. . . .

Indira was on her knees. Dust from the Fable street clouded around her. Indira looked around at the other characters in the square. Chests were heaving; hands were at temples. They'd all experienced the same thing. Visions of the Real World and of the Authors who lived there. It seemed the effects of Ketty's spell were growing. If she completed the spell, Ketty could leave Imagination and force her way into a story. What would the consequences be? If she actually succeeded, what would happen to Indira and Fable and all the dashed hopes?

Not wanting to find out, Indira got herself up and ran down the main street toward school. She skidded across the entryway and turned down the hall. She passed Ketty's office and quickened her step. She knocked sharply on the door of Brainstorm Underglass's office. A few seconds of silence passed followed by a muffled call to enter.

Brainstorm Vesulias sat in the only available chair. His legs were crossed and he regarded Indira darkly. Brainstorm Underglass looked no more sympathetic. Her hands were folded, her collar high and dominating. Something like annoyance washed over her features.

"Can we help you, Ms. Story?" Brainstorm Underglass asked.

"I don't mean to interrupt," Indira replied. "But I've made some discoveries about what happened to Dr. Montague. And about the other disruptions happening in Fable."

Brainstorm Underglass sighed. "These problems are pressing and very important, but you have to understand that the *proper* authorities are investigating the matters. The Grammar Police have been working with us. You will have to trust that we are making progress in this."

"But I know who did it."

Underglass waved an impatient hand. "I know. It was Brainstorm Vesulias first, wasn't it? And then it was Brainstorm Ketty after that. No doubt you are now here to accuse me of these heinous crimes. We are very aware of your opinions, but you'll forgive me for doubting you at this point. We do not have time for this."

"But it *was* Brainstorm Ketty. I have proof this time."

Brainstorm Vesulias pointed a crooked finger at her. "I was wrongly imprisoned because of you! We will not waste any more time on the foolish whims of a fickle girl."

Frustrated, Indira dug into her jacket. She pulled the red book out and held it up.

"The proof is here. In this!" She stepped forward and slid the book across the desk to Underglass. "Just read the marked page."

The brainstorm looked ready to dismiss her before seeing the book. Vesulias leaned forward now too. "Where did you get this?" Underglass asked.

"I found it in Brainstorm Ketty's apartment," Indira admitted. "It's a restricted book."

Vesulias looked furious. "You broke into her home? The nerve of this girl . . ."

Underglass held up a finger. "I will give you *one* minute to explain yourself, Ms. Story."

"All right." Indira started in. "The other day you said that it wasn't possible that Brainstorm Ketty could have attacked Dr. Montague because you found her in her office right before the crime was discovered. I figured out how she did it. She used a setting on her blackboard. A door, drawn into a tunnel that led down to the Sepulcher."

Brainstorm Vesulias rolled his eyes. "This is preposterous."

"She needed Dr. Montague's voice and eyes for a spell

in that book," Indira said, pointing. "On the marked page. It's called A Spell for an Unlikely Hero. Brainstorm Ketty is trying to *force* her way into a new story."

Underglass gestured for Indira to continue before reaching for the book. She began thumbing through the pages. "My friend Maxi, she gave me a lead in the Librarian Hall of Fame. His name is Checkshire. Brainstorm Ketty threatened the librarian who had that book until he gave it to her. She even melted one of the statues to get it. The spell requires ingredients she's been collecting."

Indira explained the connection to the disappearances of Margaret and the others, as well as the cursed stationery Ketty had given her. Underglass half listened and half read the spell in the book. When she finished, she handed the book over to Vesulias.

"And Ketty has been telling all her students that they're doing poorly in classes, me included. Every single student. She's been demoting us, all so she could have people who fit the description of *dashed hope*."

As Indira sat there waiting for Brainstorm Vesulias to read through the spell, the picture of T. Kettle fluttered down onto the desk. Underglass held it up.

"And what's this?" she asked.

"Motive," Indira replied. "That's why Ketty would use a spell like this in the first place. She's an unfinished character. She never got to be the *hero*, because her Author never finished the story. I found that picture in her apartment. It's a picture of her as a young girl! The same name is down in the Sepulcher. She must have been really upset with how things turned out."

For the first time in several minutes, Underglass frowned. "That's not possible. We don't come into our powers that way. No unfinished character could possibly become a brainstorm."

Indira looked at her helplessly. "I can't prove everything, Brainstorm Underglass. But we have to act, don't we? Can't we just go and ask her?" Indira felt desperate. "Please?"

Vesulias looked up from the book. "The girl paints a rather fitting portrait."

Underglass nodded. "Very well. Have a spell ready."

The two brainstorms stood. Indira could feel the crackle of their energy rising with them. They strode out of the room, and Indira followed. Always professional, Brainstorm Underglass knocked sharply on Ketty's door. They waited a few moments, and she knocked again.

No response.

Brainstorm Underglass tried the handle, but it was locked. She looked over to Vesulias.

"Do you have a spell for this?"

In one smooth motion, Indira plucked her hammer from her belt and brought it crashing down on the knob. It smashed free of the wood, leaving a gaping hole and a loose frame.

"That will work too. Stand back, Ms. Story."

Brainstorms Underglass and Vesulias looked at one

another and then burst through the door at the same time. Indira stood a few feet back, waiting for the sound of an explosion or the loud voices of a confrontation. Nothing happened at first, and then a pulse of darkness flashed out. Indira watched it fill the frame of the doorway. It was so pitch-black that she couldn't see anything within the office. After a few seconds, light returned.

Indira turned the corner, shocked to find the room empty.

Brainstorm Ketty wasn't there. Neither were the other brainstorms. She scanned the room and finally saw movement. She gasped. On the blackboard at the back, a rough chalk outline of Underglass and Vesulias appeared. The two of them looked at one another, panicked, and then out at Indira. They cupped their hands and shouted, but their words made no sound. Ketty's spell had trapped them on the two-dimensional plane of the chalkboard.

Indira tried pressing the buttons on the desk. Nothing worked. The two brainstorms were trapped. Looks of terror spread over their faces. "What do I do?" Indira asked.

The two continued to shout uselessly. After a few minutes, she realized she was just wasting time. Ketty's trap had done its job. She must have set it after Indira had broken into her office the last time. Indira was sure that whoever had entered it unwelcomed would have suffered the same fate. A growing fear forced its way into her chest. She felt like she couldn't breathe. What was she supposed to do now? They were running out of time, and the two most powerful people on her side had been imprisoned. With one final apology, she rushed out of the room.

She needed to find Phoenix and Maxi.

Indira headed toward the Luck Hearth and found her path blocked by crowds that were all heading in the same direction. She fought her way through, but her progress was slow. It looked as if the entire school had entered Hearth Hall. She spotted some of her professors, hovering around the entrance, discussing the situation in quiet tones. Every hearth was crowded with characters, and Indira slipped through the gathered masses, eyes scanning the Luck Hearth. Phoenix wasn't there. Maxi was. Indira rushed forward.

"You got out of jail," Maxi whispered in excitement. "Sorry for not intervening. I thought it made more sense to stay hidden, keep at least one of us a mystery. I was trying to figure out how to spring you free."

"You did the right thing," Indira said. "I figured out the spell and took it to the brainstorms. But Ketty was prepared. She trapped the other brainstorms in her office."

"Is she in there now? How'd you escape?"

"No," Indira said, voice full of frustration. "I don't know where she is. Where's Phoenix? He's supposed to meet us here too."

Maxi shook her head. "Haven't seen him. What are we going to do?"

"Aren't the Editors coming? You called it in, right?"

Maxi nodded. "Yes, but they always wait twenty-four

hours before making a move. It's part of their contract with Imagination. They have to let characters try to solve things first. But when they get here, all we have to do is show them the book, and they'll take care of everything."

Indira patted her jacket for the book. It wasn't there. She slid a hand inside, found nothing, and wheeled back to the entrance. "I left the book!"

"Let's go back for it," Maxi said. She stood up and straightened her golden jacket.

"Wait, I didn't forget it. I gave it to Brainstorm Underglass." Indira gasped aloud. "She had it with her when she went into Ketty's office. So . . ."

"You've got to be kidding," Maxi concluded.

Great, Indira thought, *now we have nothing.*

Not to mention they were running out of time. Her brain was already working hard, and now she was mixing up the phrases she had read in the spell. It had said something about fire, and a token of some kind, and what else? She was thinking so hard that she almost didn't feel someone tapping her shoulder. "Hey, Indira."

Gavin Grant was grinning at her. His eyes were puffed up from a long snooze beside the Rest Hearth. Indira tried to smile, but she didn't have time to talk to him.

"Sorry, Gavin, kind of busy."

He held up his hands defensively. "Totally. I just have a message for you from Phoenix."

Maxi and Indira looked up sharply. "From Phoenix?"

"Yeah. I passed him in the hallway. Looked like he had

detention with Brainstorm Ketty or something? She was walking him down the hall. He said to come find him when you're free."

Gavin shrugged, like it wasn't the most important information in the world.

Indira steadied herself and said, "Thanks, Gavin. I'll do that."

Gavin smiled at Maxi before heading back over to the Rest Hearth. Indira whipped around to Maxi. "She has him. She has Phoenix."

Everything before had been bad enough, but now a furious rage trickled to life in place of fear. Ketty had Phoenix. The phrase from the spell echoed back: *An extracted essence of fire (for power and purpose)*. Phoenix was a fire mage. Indira winced, imagining what it would mean to *extract* that from him. Her hands balled into fists. If Ketty had hurt him . . .

"We have to find her," she said. "We have to figure out where she is. She has all the ingredients, everything she needs to complete the spell."

Not everything, Indira realized. The only ingredient she could remember that Ketty didn't have yet was the not-supposed-to-be-here. Indira shivered. That was either going to be her or Maxi. The spell was waiting for a rescuer to arrive.

"Wait," Indira said, thinking aloud. "If I don't go, she can't do the spell."

"What?" Maxi asked. "Are you sure?"

Indira was nodding. "One of the ingredients requires it. She needs someone to show up who isn't supposed to be there. The directions said that she had to wait for the person before completing the spell. So . . ." Indira's brain was whirling. "I just won't go. That happens in stories sometimes! Characters actually make things worse, you know. They go down into the dungeon, and it turns out *they're* the key that unlocks the cage for the bad guy. I'll . . . I'll just stay right here."

Indira crossed her arms, smiling at her own cleverness.

Maxi frowned. "What if someone else finds them, though?"

"Huh?"

"Well, you said *someone* who isn't supposed to be there. That doesn't have to be you. It could be anyone, right?"

Indira's heart raced again. Maxi was right.

"And if you think about it," Maxi continued softly, "whoever shows up won't know what's going on. They won't be able to stop her. But we know what she's up to, right? So we have the best shot at actually staying one step ahead of her."

Maxi was right again. If someone else stumbled upon Ketty's spell, everyone was doomed. But if Indira or Maxi showed up, at least one of them would know what they were up against. Everyone else would be walking right into the trap, helpless.

Indira paced. "So where is she? Where could she go?"

The instructions in the book had said something about the location, but Indira couldn't remember what it was. Maxi was frowning again.

"I sat by the Luck Hearth for like an hour. I don't feel lucky at all!"

"You already figured out two things," Indira replied distractedly. "You're doing great."

Indira was pretty sure the Raven King's spell had suggested performing the magic somewhere that connected to the Real World. A thin spot of some kind. Indira's mind flicked through all the significant places. Her first instinct was the Sepulcher. That was a dark place. Dark enough for casting a spell like this one, and definitely *where* all of this had begun.

"That's one possibility," Indira said aloud. "She could be down in the Sepulcher."

"That place is *gross.*"

"It's perfect for her," Indira said. "The Sepulcher is basically the home of all unfinished characters. If Ketty is forcing her way back into a story, she might do it there."

"So we go there first," Maxi said. "I wish I felt more prepared for a fight. I haven't had a white mocha all day. I can't solve crimes without caffeine, but with the Talespin closed, the closest coffee shop is, like, all the way on the other side of town. It's totally inconvenient."

Indira nodded absently. Then she grabbed hold of both of Maxi's shoulders. Realization thundered to life. "The

Talespin," she said. "The mirror at the Talespin shows the Real World."

Maxi was nodding. "So which one is it? The Sepulcher or the Talespin?"

Indira thought about that. The lives of their friends were on the line. She felt great about the Talespin. After all, why would a place in Fable be closed for renovations? Fable renovated everything itself. The shop being closed had to be connected to Ketty somehow. And the link to the Real World would make it a perfect location to attempt the spell. She didn't say any of this out loud, though, because she couldn't afford to be wrong. If both Maxi and Indira went to the same location *and* chose the wrong one, Brainstorm Ketty would win. She looked back at Maxi. Knowing her friend, she made a calculated guess.

"I think the Sepulcher is more likely," Indira said. "That's how Ketty's story ended."

"That's where I'm going, then," Maxi said, standing. "I've trained for these encounters my whole life. I'll go to the Sepulcher. You go to the Talespin."

Indira started toward the entrance before Maxi snagged her by the arm. "If she's there, be careful. Every character has a part to play. And this is our part. We get to be the heroes today."

She pulled Indira into a huge hug.

"I'm going to spread the word first. No one can start a rumor like me."

Indira gave her a firm nod and took off. Characters

scattered out of her way. She saw the professors staring as she ran through the doorway. Alice had a sly smile on her face.

Outside, the storm had arrived. Lightning flashed in the distance.

48

Unfinished

As rain began to fall, the Marks disappeared again. The sky swirled in an unnatural vortex that threatened to fling power down from the sky and devour whatever was below. Adrenaline pumped through Indira as she wound through the familiar streets. She didn't have the map—and she hadn't visited the Talespin since Maxi took her that first time—but she still remembered the section of town where it was located. She'd never forget seeing an Author—maybe her Author—and hearing the frightful voice echo, "Mine! Mine! Mine!"

If she couldn't stop Brainstorm Ketty, her friends would be in serious danger. And the city of Fable might not even exist by the time Ketty was finished. Indira had to stop her.

Rain came down and wind gusted and Indira was

drenched by the time she reached the Talespin. In its Western attire, the coffee shop looked like an old-time saloon. A pair of swinging doors had a taped sign over them that was slowly turning gray and flimsy in the rain. A rope bound the doors together, but Indira kept running and rolled under them without even stopping. She came up with her hammer in hand, eyes scanning the faint light of the main room.

It was empty.

Stools had been overturned in one corner, and it wasn't hard to figure out that there had been a struggle. A staircase led to the upper floor, but Indira knew that Ketty wasn't up there. She would be by the mirror. After all, that was the gateway into the other world.

Indira could feel something too. A pulsing magic that twisted her gut uncomfortably. She moved closer to a set of double doors that were a new addition to the coffee shop. Beneath the wooden panels she saw a slit of purple light. It even smelled dark and dank within.

She had come to the right place.

The spell's ready, Indira thought. *All she needs to do now is capture me.*

She gripped her hammer tightly and reached for the door's handle. With a deep breath, she pulled it open and took two steps into the room.

The scene was somehow more horrible than Indira had expected. The tables and chairs had been cleared away from the hardwood floors. Indira's classmates had been laid out on their backs in a neat circle. She saw Margaret — and to her great surprise, the twins — and even her teacher Mr. Threepwood among the victims. Thankfully, she also saw their chests rising ever so slightly. They were alive, but clearly unconscious. She realized that all their hopes had been dashed, just like the spell said.

In the odd purple light of the room, they looked somewhere between dead and dying.

She had no idea what would happen if Ketty's spell succeeded. Would they regenerate in the Ninth Hearth? Would her magic consume and use them as the ingredients to power her way to the next world? Indira didn't want to find out. At the center of the room, a huge iron cauldron bubbled in medieval gloom. Liquid crackled out of it, and steam hung in the air like fog.

Creepiest of all, a disembodied voice spoke in monotone. It sounded as if it was coming from the cauldron. After a few lines, she recognized the dark tones of Dr. Montague, the voice that Brainstorm Ketty had stolen.

". . . unsubstantial death . . . that the lean abhorred monster keeps thee here in dark to be his paramour . . ."

Indira searched for Brainstorm Ketty, but she wasn't in the room. Indira did spy Phoenix crumpled in one corner. His bright red hair had faded to brown. He looked shrunken, his magic forcefully taken. The thing that made him Phoenix had been stolen and used to fuel Ketty's destructive spell. Indira guessed that she must have already released the essence of fire, because the room was hot and growing hotter.

". . . and never from this palace of dim night depart again . . ."

Indira gripped her hammer and took two more steps into the room. She watched the shadows, waiting for Brainstorm Ketty to come storming out at her. But nothing happened. Indira waited impatiently at the edge of the circle, mind whirling, searching for some semblance of a plan. Her hammer could break or fix or fly, but it couldn't stop magical spells. In the corner, a familiar gilded mirror loomed. Its surface was the pitch black of a cave.

". . . and shake the yoke of inauspicious stars from this world-wearied flesh . . ."

Indira took another step forward, crouching low. Her eyes darted to the corners of the room before she leaned over Margaret and began working to untie the bindings around her thin wrists. In answer a voice boomed over Dr. Montague's depressing whispers, powerful and looming, both there and not.

"Come to be a part of the fun?" Laughter was in the voice. Deep and dark. "Indira Story on my trail. Indira Story, the final ingredient in the Raven King's spell. I half hoped Detective Malaprop would come stumbling along, but this is far more appropriate."

At first Indira couldn't find the source of the voice, but then the surface of the mirror boiled and bubbled like the cauldron. An image appeared in the smoke black. Brainstorm Ketty wore her familiar dragon-scale jacket over a charcoal dress and a pair of extravagant heels. Ketty was smiling down on Indira, and the mirror made her look bigger, more real, more frightening. She stood inside a massive stone tower with an onyx balcony in the background.

Indira struggled to find her voice as Dr. Montague continued to mutter darkly from the cauldron. "Why are you doing this?" It felt like the cliché question a protagonist would ask, but Indira couldn't figure it out. "Just because you were unfinished? Is that why?"

Ketty's eyes sparkled dangerously. "You have no idea what I've been through. You have no idea what it's like to be unfinished. And after all this time, he had the nerve to *actually* try it again! He had the nerve to *leave* me behind *again*."

Indira's mind was spinning. "Your story didn't turn out the way you wanted it to. I read it down in the Sepulcher, you know? Just because it didn't go the way you wanted doesn't give you the right to steal our chances at being in a story. Every character has a story. You told me that."

Ketty laughed. "Every character *does* have a story. And this one will be mine. I deserved to be finished. I deserved to be loved by readers. And now I'm going to be reunited with him. I'm going to carve my mark on a story that's all my own. Thanks to you and thanks to them. There's no one who can stop me now, not even you."

The brainstorm flicked her wrist, and the doors in the room all slammed shut. Black ivy wound over the knobs and slashed over the windows. Fire flashed up from the cauldron.

Sweat covered Indira's face. She was searching for something, anything she could do to stop this. With a sweaty hand on the grip of her hammer, she strode forward. She marched up to the mirror and took an arching swing at it. The glass shattered, falling to the floor in jagged pieces. The upper half clung to its frame, though, and Ketty's reflection laughed at her.

"You're too late, girl. You can't stop me that way." The laughter rang louder and darker, and strange purple light gathered above the cauldron. "The Raven King's spells are *thorough* and *strong*. I've been an admirer of his for a long time."

Indira flipped her hammer and hit the mirror again. The little pieces sucked back into place, and Ketty glanced down at her feet with a look of surprise.

"Now, there's a clever trick," the brainstorm said. "I was right about you. All those improvements you were making. You were fast-tracking your way to protagonist. Figuring out my riddles, figuring out my stationery trick, all that *hard work*. I knew from the beginning you were my biggest threat. But too late now, girl—*I'm* the hero of this story. He's not going to forget me this time."

Indira leaned over Margaret and patted her cheek.

The girl's mouth lolled open. She was breathing, but she wouldn't wake up. "Why are you doing this?" Indira shouted again.

She was angry now. Feeling helpless made her angrier than anything. *Every cage has a key.* Those were her Words, but she didn't know what the key to getting out of this was. She would die ironically, it seemed, failing her own story and her own Words.

"Because he left me. Not this time. He won't leave me behind again."

Indira's mind spun. That was the third time Ketty had referenced someone who wasn't there. It took Indira a few seconds to trace back through all the clues. Her mind landed on the *one* name that had never been mentioned by anyone else, the one name she'd only ever been able to connect back to Brainstorm Ketty.

"DM. Darby Martin."

Ketty gave her a nasty smile. "Clever girl. Figured it out, did you?"

The name had been on Ketty's board, more than once. Indira had assumed it was just another one of Ketty's students. Now she remembered the strange phrase—*absence makes the heart grow FONDER*—that was scribbled on Ketty's blackboard.

"Darby Martin," Indira repeated. "He's an Author."

"He's *my* Author." Brainstorm Ketty held up a delicate string of dirty pearls. "He left me unfinished all those years ago and . . . and . . . he *came back*. He had a *new* story to tell.

Can you imagine? The Author who abandoned me coming back to toy around with *new* characters. People like *you*. You were going to steal what was mine! Mine! *Mine!*"

All the pieces finally clicked into place. The way she screamed the word *mine*—the voice echoed from Indira's first visit to the Talespin. All the other characters Ketty had been so eager to sabotage. It all made so much sense.

"We were potential fits," Indira said. "For Darby Martin's story."

Ketty shot her another nasty smile. "Now she's catching on. As soon as I saw his name back on the radar, I tracked all his potential characters. It was easy, you know, to knock each of his potential protagonists down a few pegs. Just look at you, Indira. You actually *believed* me when I said your grades were tanking. You don't deserve him. You don't deserve to be a hero. You're not like me. I would *never* have taken no for an answer."

She'd been making room for herself. Not to mention gathering dashed hopes along the way. If there weren't any other protagonists who would be a good fit for the story, that would leave room for Ketty to force her way in. It was such a horrible thing to do.

Indira felt the bright anger fade. It was replaced with steel-cold determination. She was going to stop this from happening. She looked fruitlessly around the room again before her eyes settled once more on the mirror. Her hammer. It had always been able to take her from *here* to *there*.

That was how its magic worked.

Ketty's spell pushed its way free of the cauldron. Purple shadows thrashed like some great beast. Indira didn't know what would happen, or if it would work, but it was the last chance she had. She squinted one eye and threw her hammer at the top of the mirror. Brainstorm Ketty smirked as the silver turned end over end. It hit the mirror like a stone splashing into water. Ripples fled down the length of the mirror, and the hammer hung in midair. Indira felt her body being dragged forward by something immensely powerful.

She blinked to life behind Brainstorm Ketty, a silver swirl hurtling at her head. She went down on one knee and snatched the shaft of her weapon out of the air. Ketty staggered back in shock. Indira took a ragged breath. The air was thick, and wherever they were, Indira felt heavier and more substantial. The scent of the ocean flooded all around her. Indira wasn't sure if she was the Real World, but she was certain she had left Fable behind.

As Brainstorm Ketty stumbled away, Indira remembered the first rule of Bartitsu that Odysseus had taught her: *Disturb the equilibrium of your assailant.* She lowered her shoulder, using Ketty's momentum against her. The other woman was much bigger, but already half stumbling. Her foot caught on the cobblestones, and she collapsed backward.

"No!" Brainstorm Ketty shouted. On her back now, the brainstorm thrust a hand out to a nearby mirror. It was a match for the one from the Talespin, and Indira could see the coffee-shop room filled with the arcane coloring of the brainstorm's spell.

Rule number two: *Subject the joints to strains that they are anatomically unable to resist.* Indira leaped forward and brought her hammer down on the exposed hand. The hand, she realized, that was maintaining the magic of the Raven King's spell. Brainstorm Ketty howled as iron smashed her knuckles against the stones. The woman rolled over in pain, and Indira's eyes darted to the mirror. Some of the magic had stopped, even retreating back toward the cauldron.

If Indira could just keep Ketty distracted, the spell wouldn't advance. Indira squared her feet. Ketty held her injured hand out as she crawled away on the support of the other arm. Her face twisted in pain and rage. "You can't stop me," she hissed.

Indira advanced. The woman lashed out unexpectedly, but Indira ducked the blow and swung her hammer in an arc. The blow landed on Ketty's shoulder and was turned only slightly by the dragon-scale jacket. Ketty cried out in pain, but Indira's next blow was met with an armored forearm.

Before Indira could recover, Ketty pushed off her knees, and a heavy shoulder punched the air from Indira's stomach. She went flying backward and only narrowly avoided falling over. It was enough, though, to allow Brainstorm Ketty to climb back to her feet.

"You *fool.* I have worked *too* hard to get back in a story. I won't let you ruin this."

Dark magic sprang to life between Brainstorm Ketty's palms. She had a wicked grin on her face as the dragon-scale jacket shivered with movement. It looked like a living, breathing thing as it expanded. Up and out, the scales formed a shroud over the woman, a great swathing shadow that obscured her from view.

A sound like snapping bone echoed in the tower. Indira watched in terror as Brainstorm Ketty stepped forward, armed head to toe in smoke-black plated armor. The woman's different-colored eyes stared out from a jagged gladiator helmet. She didn't have a weapon, but Indira saw no weakness, either, no place for her hammer to strike. Brainstorm Ketty was laughing now. A gauntleted hand stretched out toward the mirror.

"Now do you see? Do you see the injustice of why *my* story went unfinished? How could Darby Martin ever give up on this?" Ketty cried. "All this power. All this magic. I could have been a god! And this time I will be!"

Magic snapped back to life in the Talespin. Purple tendrils lashed themselves to the dashed hopes. Indira knew that if she didn't do something, the spell would finish. She charged forward again, aiming her swing at the outstretched gauntlet. Ketty leaned forward, though, and caught the blow along her plated shoulder.

An answering backhand knocked Indira to the floor. She scrambled up and ducked the next blow, this time aiming for the brainstorm's knees. Three slashing blows caused Ketty to stumble but didn't bring her down. Indira

slid in a circle and forced Ketty to dip and adjust. ⅂.
stalled a little, and Ketty growled her frustration.

Indira finally landed a blow on the back of Ketty's knee
that caused her to fall.

Staggering, the brainstorm roared before turning on Indira. Indira had succeeded in stopping the magic, but now
Ketty gave Indira her full attention. The brainstorm rose
and advanced, using the jagged armor along her forearms
to block and strike, block and strike. Indira's footwork
was better, but she found herself being pushed toward the
ledge of the onyx balcony with each swing. Indira glanced
back at it, slid out of range, and steadied herself.

She launched her own attack, but the plate armor was
impenetrable. She struck forehand and backhand, catching Ketty's shoulder and hip and wrist, but nothing could
stop the answering blows. A kick from Ketty sent Indira
flying against the rail of the balcony. Indira gasped. Pain
shot down her back and through her hips.

Ketty planted herself in the entrance to the stone hall.

"The spell is nearly done," Ketty said. She shifted her
weight, one hand reaching back to continue the summon-
ing. She kept her mismatched eyes fixed on Indira, daring
her to move. Indira glanced over the ledge. They'd been
fighting inside a tower, and the fall from the balcony was
gut-twistingly far.

"This is your last chance," Ketty said. "I'll let you walk
through the mirror. You never know, the spell might
kill you. But if you attack me again, I'll throw you over.

Authors old and the Authors new. I mean
...st of my life in a story that's written *just* for
...on't keep me from my happy ending. You
...."

...*has a key.* Muscles tired and ideas used up,
Indi... ...the Words echo in her head. So this was how
it was going to end? She'd begun life in Fable hearing
those words, but now she was trapped in a cage without
a key. Facing a problem without a solution. Ketty was too
powerful to beat. No amount of hammering could stop
her magic. Already Indira was too exhausted to launch a
proper attack. Ketty could push her over the ledge easily.

Looking down at the jagged cliffs below, Indira shivered. She knew she wasn't in Fable anymore. Would death
here be permanent? She didn't think the Real World had a
Ninth Hearth to restore its dead.

But I'm not in the Real World. This is somewhere in between.

She didn't have a key, but she had an idea. If s'
couldn't unlock the cage, she could push it over the le
Cages could break as easily as they could be unlocke
dira tightened her grip on her hammer and straig
her shoulders.

"*Every* character has a story," Indira said qui
Pennington and Patch deserve one. Phoenix
ret. They should get a chance to meet their A
loved by readers. I can't let you take that a
because you're forcing your own way int
don't even belong in."

Ketty smiled grimly. "Spoken like a true herd

Indira remembered the words of Mr. Thr

"Loyalty leads to bravery. Bravery plants the see

sacrifice. And self-sacrifice is the highest call

character in every story. You might be a powerful

ter, but you could never be a hero."

"Words," Ketty spat. "Words won't save you nov

Before Ketty could make her first move, Indira s

forward. She knew what would happen next. The b

storm had been using her wounded right hand to mai

the magic. She'd been fighting—and clearly favorir

her left in combat. Different from and more difficult t

most fighters. But it meant that she would lead with

She would try to finish things, and that would give Ind

a single moment to do what needed to be done. She mov

close enough to bait Ketty. The brainstorm's smile faded

The dragon scales shimmered.

She swung.

Indira ducked, stepped in, and took a huge, two-handed

swing.

The hammer hit Ketty square in the stomach. The
armor was too strong to break or allow any real damage,
but the blow was still powerful enough to pull air from the
brainstorm's lungs. Ketty bent forward slightly, and Indira
used that moment to leap. She wrapped her arms around
the woman's neck and sealed her hold with a solid grip on
her hammer. Ketty stumbled forward, trying to shake herself free, but Indira held tight and kicked her legs out to

."

epwood.
d of self-
f every
charac-

v."

arted
rain-
tain
g —
han
it.
ra
d
.

Indira pushed off the wall with

d here, the stories of her friends

ng toward the edge. Brainstorm
nees collided with the stone rail-
ndira pulled closer and tighter as
t in a fruitless search for balance.
e on the stones.
them both over the railing.
cream. Her heart beat a furious dance,
tterly calm. She had figured it out. The
as her death. As the two of them spiraled
a chaos of limbs, Indira felt it had already
and adventure. When they hit, she knew
rm Ketty's magic would die and the spell

could ever take away that moment. No audi-
ever call her anything less than a hero, a friend,
rifice. The wind rushed all around them. Indira
about Phoenix and Maxi and the Penningtons.
ved them all so very much.
d then the ground caught her.

49

The Ninth Hearth

A strange thing happened.

The characters who were gathered by the windows of Protagonist Preparatory reported that the storms outside suddenly died away. The sun plunged through the gloom. Fable's buildings looked majestic and full of wonder once again. The population of Marks balanced out. No one reported strange visions of the Real World. Strangest of all, though, was the sight that greeted the characters waiting in Hearth Hall.

Every hearth blinked out at once.

Except for one.

The dark room and that looming fire drew the eyes of every waiting character. Hundreds of students looked up to find two ghostly outlines by that Ninth Hearth. The students crept forward as one, afraid of what they might find, of whose outlines would appear there.

Everyone recognized the first ghost. Brainstorm Ketty's scaled armor had transformed back into the more familiar jacket. She wore a black dress that might have been lovely if she hadn't been currently drawing glares from every single person in the crowd.

Maxi Maydragon's rumors had spread to the entire school. Every character and professor knew what the brainstorm had been plotting. Maxi had returned shortly after finding the Sepulcher empty. She'd rallied a team of heroes to the Talespin but found only the waking sleepers that Indira had saved. The rest of the school had been waiting inside the safety of Hearth Hall, hoping for news of their missing friends.

One can imagine the dark thoughts. Would their friends survive? Would Brainstorm Ketty succeed? If she did succeed, what would it mean for them? Would Protagonist Preparatory close its doors for good?

At first, most students didn't recognize the other person. She had dark, unruly hair that fell above narrowed eyes. A hammer sat along her hip, and she wore a handmade pink tunic beneath a navy-blue jacket. As a ghost, she looked even more quiet and reserved than she did normally. Both ghosts stared at the flames that even now were bringing them back to life.

Gavin Grant recognized her, though. He ran forward, did his best to wrap both arms around her ghostly form, and whispered something the other students couldn't hear. He eventually convinced her to turn toward the crowd.

"Everyone!" he shouted. "This is Indira Story, the girl who saved Protagonist Prep!"

The chorus of praise and applause echoed into the very stones of the school.

Less than an hour after Indira had rescued the school—and all of Imagination, for that matter—men and women with dark glasses and pristine suits began appearing around the building. Some wondered what had taken them so long. The Editors normally had tabs on everything and everyone. When necessary, they came in and did the dirty, behind-the-scenes work. They removed threats to the world of Imagination with crisp efficiency.

So it was no surprise that Maxi's future bosses stood vigil by the Ninth Hearth, waiting for Brainstorm Ketty to fully revive. Indira's discoveries had been brought to light. Ketty had broken enough laws that the Editors could put her away for good.

Members of the Wizard Union did eventually find the proper counterspell to release Brainstorm Underglass and Brainstorm Vesulias from their bizarre enchantment. The two suffered from mild coughs for a few days, and a fine chalky powder puffed into the air everywhere they walked. It was agreed that, when she was fully revived, Indira Story should be immediately promoted to the status of protagonist.

As for Indira, her days spent recovering from death

were never spent alone. As Mr. Threepwood had taught her, loyalty and devotion lead to bravery. Bravery sets a course for self-sacrifice. And self-sacrifice is the highest honor for every character. It also creates unbreakable bonds between us and the ones we love.

Mrs. Pennington and Patch visited in the evenings. Patch had given up piracy for paleontology. Even as a ghost, Indira couldn't help but smile every time he said the word *stegosaurus*. Gavin Grant loyally repaid Indira's own devotion by visiting between classes. When Margaret had recovered, she spent many an hour sitting quietly next to Indira. These visits were especially needed after long hours of Maxi sitting rather loudly in the same seat.

Brainstorms and professors visited, offering congratulations or apologies as was appropriate. Alice never arrived by the same route. Indira saw her lowered from the roof by some kind of harness system one day. The next she snuck out from behind a painting. Indira's favorite teacher sat cross-legged by the fire and told her stories about shrinking down to the size of a thimble and facing absurdly dressed queens. Indira could never remember the stories after she'd gone, but something about listening to them brought her back to life just a little more quickly.

In the early days of her recovery, Indira struggled to keep track of who came and went. It was nearly impossible. Her mind struggled to hold on to short-term memories. Always her attention drifted back to the flames. There *was* one person she knew hadn't visited. She had last seen Phoenix crumpled on the floor of the Talespin. His red hair—his fire—had been taken from him. Even in her ghostly state, Indira desperately wanted to check on him.

There was also one visitor she'd never forget.

She felt the slightest tickle down her arms and neck, as though a faint breeze had just blown through the hall. She dragged her eyes away from the fire long enough to see a man with a rather average, unrecognizable face.

"Who would have ever imagined such a wild ending?" Deus mused.

Indira's voice was still weak. "I think you did."

Her mentor came forward and snapped his fingers once. A wooden chair blinked into existence. He positioned it beside her and sat. It was the first time she'd ever seen him sit down.

"Oh, little old me?" Deus asked. "I'm just the grease that keeps the engine moving."

Indira held up one insubstantial finger. "You had me jump off the cliff that first day."

"Certainly a valuable experience in the end."

She lifted a second finger. "You taught me about my hammer's special powers."

"Well, it's hard to face the antagonist without those."

"*And* you let me fail my auditions."

He winced at that one. "A dark hour that led to a far brighter one."

Indira nodded. There had been so much time to sit and think about all the little details of what had happened. It hadn't taken long to figure out that Deus had likely given her a few nudges in the right direction, even though it certainly hadn't felt that way at the time.

Her mentor sat in silence at her side for a full minute. She realized that his stillness was a sign of respect. Deus never stood still for anyone. The moment ended, and he stood, his fingers once again dancing unpredictably. He paused long enough to wink down at her.

"I have a feeling this is just the beginning."

Indira smiled as her mentor snapped his fingers and vanished.

The recovery of the city's newest hero and the city's greatest threat took quite a while. The two of them had perished outside Fable's normal limits. Some local experts were unsure how they'd revived at all. After nearly a full month, the fire restored both of them. The only difference was in how they walked away. Brainstorm Ketty was immediately placed in handcuffs by the Editors. She was led off quietly, the recipient of sideways stares and barely heard whispers. Indira, on the other hand, walked through Hearth Hall arm in arm with friends. She couldn't make it more than a few steps without someone cheering her name.

Each little celebration was a good reminder.

Even without a gold jacket, she was every bit a hero.

50

Just the Beginning

The first thing Indira did was visit Phoenix.

She found out from Brainstorm Underglass that her friend was still living in the medical ward. Some of the wizarding doctors had been working hard to develop counterspells, but no one had ever encountered an essential element being stolen like this. There were historical examples of silenced wizards and wizards turned into sheep and all manner of strange happenings, but none in which someone's identity had been so thoroughly taken.

Indira found her friend sitting by a window. His hair was a faded brown color and his skin looked paler than normal. When he turned to look at Indira, his irises lacked their usual smoldering flames. Indira took a seat next to him.

"You did it," he said softly. She could tell he wasn't himself, but he still smiled at her. "People have been telling me all kinds of stories, but I was hoping to hear it from you."

Indira started—as Alice would have suggested—at the beginning. Even if she'd told it a hundred times already, it felt brand-new with Phoenix as an audience. He filled in a few of the blank pages of the story, explaining how Brainstorm Ketty had pulled him out of class and walked him right into a trap. "There are rules about wizard duels," Phoenix said. "She broke all of them! It was a total cheap shot. I almost melted the shackles with a pyro blast, but she just doubled the power of her snare spell. I didn't stand much of a chance after she got the drop on me."

Indira saw his chin dip down again. He looked out the window, and she knew he was thinking about the fact that he'd lost his fire. "Good news," she said. "I'm here to fix you."

That made him laugh. "Dr. Indira? None of the stories I heard involved medical degrees."

Indira laughed as she reached out and tried to sweep a playful hand through his hair. He recoiled a little bit, though, before looking out the window again. "You're still handsome," she said. It felt like a rather grown-up word to say. "But I prefer you the other way. Come on."

She stood up and walked over to the middle of the room. Phoenix stared at her helplessly. "Indira, no one can fix me. Even the doctors are stumped. I'm broken."

"If you stayed like this forever, you still wouldn't be broken. Not you, Phoenix."

His jaw clenched a little. "But I'm not . . . I'm not *me* anymore. I'm just a part of me."

"So let me fix you."

His eyes sparked with frustration. "This isn't funny."

"I'm not laughing," Indira said. "Do you trust me?"

"Of course I trust you, but —"

"Come here."

With a sigh, Phoenix crossed the room. Indira pulled the hammer from her belt. She frowned at the identical sides. "One second," she said. Reaching over, she smashed a bowl of mashed potatoes sitting on the bedside table. Chunks splattered out, and ceramic shards went with them. Satisfied that she'd found the breaking side, Indira gave her hammer a twist so that she was holding it the right way. She set a hand on his shoulder.

"Okay. I'm going to hit you in the chest."

Phoenix's eyes widened. "Are you crazy?"

"A little bit."

"Your plan is to hit me. With a hammer."

"Uh-huh."

Phoenix scowled. "Well, are you at least going to tell me how that will work?"

"Don't think so."

"You're being difficult."

Indira shrugged. "Ready?"

Phoenix just stared at her. After a second, he nodded. Indira wasn't one hundred percent confident it *would* work. So far in her experience her hammer only fixed things that it had been responsible for breaking, but she'd been thinking about Phoenix all day. The idea of him without his fire was too much to bear. What was the point of having a magical hammer if she couldn't use it to help the people she cared about the most? It had to work. It just *had* to.

With a deep breath, Indira pulled back the hammer and then socked him with it, right in the chest. Phoenix went flying across the room, and she could hear the wind suck out of his lungs. Indira let out a little gasp. He was clutching his chest, face twisted with pain, but then a different expression stretched across his face. The air swirled, and the light of the room took on funny angles and shapes. Phoenix sat up, coughing his lungs out and holding up a hand. "What kind of ridiculous plan was that?"

Indira snatched the handheld mirror from his hospital room dresser. She held it out so that Phoenix could see his own toss of bright red hair, the flicker of flame in each eye. Indira couldn't help smiling. She'd actually knocked the fire back into him. He sat there staring for a while before climbing to his feet to give her a huge hug.

A few days later, Dr. Montague was finally restored to full health. Indira was called in to confirm parts of his story. She shivered a little, hearing his voice and remembering the muttering darkness of the cauldron Ketty had used. Montague's restoration heralded the end of Brainstorm Ketty's secret plot. The Editors had been gathering testimony from all the victims. The tragedy professor confirmed her as his attacker as soon as his lungs synched back up with his lips. The Editors, with their dark sunglasses and even darker suits, escorted an enraged Brainstorm Ketty out of Fable for good.

Classes had already resumed, but before she could rejoin her classmates, Indira was called into the office of Brainstorm Underglass. She passed by Ketty's old office and shivered a little. She was just happy that all of that was behind her. She knocked twice, and Underglass commanded her to enter. The diminutive woman was smiling in a way Indira hadn't seen before.

Indira took two steps into the room before realizing they weren't alone.

"David!"

She lunged across the room to hug her brother. He was grinning at her, full of pride.

"Brainstorm Underglass came to Quiver," he said. "She told me about everything that happened with you and Ketty, but she had a second reason for visiting."

"We have news from the Real World," Underglass announced. "It involves you and David, so I wanted to make sure that you were both here for it."

The brainstorm reached under her desk and pressed

a button. The neat spreadsheets on her blackboard vanished, and the one thing she'd always wanted appeared:

Indira Story and the Thunder Brothers
by Darby Martin

Indira blinked. "Is that . . ."

David threw an arm around her shoulder. "*Your* story, baby sister."

Underglass nodded. "We'll get David caught up with some specialized tutoring. There's no mistaking it, though. The Author made his choice. I hope you're ready to be a protagonist."

Indira's hand drifted instinctually down to her hammer. "I was born ready."

51

Neat Little Bows

"Don't forget your jacket, Indira!" Mrs. Pennington bustled forward. "Ah! I just love that it's wintertime! Really, it's perfect practice for our story."

Indira couldn't help smiling. There had been so much good news lately. Gavin Grant had landed a side-character role in a big-time soccer novel, which thrilled him to no end. Margaret—it turned out—had protagonist potential. She'd caught the attention of a young Author and planned on continuing her classes the next semester to keep learning. But the best news of all was that the Penningtons had received their story placement. They would be featured in a short-story collection about life in Chicago. Mrs. Pennington had been buzzing ever since.

Indira accepted the offered jacket. "Thanks, Mom."

"Of course, dear. Now, will you be back for dinner? I'm

practicing some classic Chicago recipes, and all Patch will eat is the deep-dish pizza. I need a more refined palate."

Indira grinned. "Happy to participate in any of your cooking experiments."

Mrs. Pennington made a little shooing motion. "Lovely. Now go on! Have fun."

Outside, the sun was already making its descent. Indira had been enjoying a small break from school, which mostly meant that she slept in far too late for her own good. She pulled on her navy peacoat and made quick work of the buttons. The coat had appeared in her closet a few minutes after it started snowing outside. She knew she would miss Fable always knowing what she needed even before she did.

Down at the end of the street, Maxi and Phoenix waited for her. Indira saw a makeshift bonfire nestled between them. Phoenix was coaxing the flames as Maxi leaned down, rubbing both hands together dramatically. As always, the girl had chosen style over function. Her thick sunglasses warded off sunlight that wasn't there. She wore an adorable maroon vest with bright leggings, none of which seemed to be keeping her warm.

"I'm not made for this weather," Maxi called. "We've been waiting forever for you!"

Phoenix smiled at Indira. "It's been about two minutes."

"Sometimes forever is just one second," she replied.

Phoenix frowned. "What does that even mean?"

"Not sure. I think I read it on a bumper sticker."

Both of them laughed at that. A second later Maxi had positioned Phoenix between the two of them. She linked arms on one side and gestured for Indira to do the same.

"Sorry to invade your personal space," she said. "But you're basically a walking heater."

Phoenix offered his arm to Indira. She managed to only blush a little as she took it. The extra warmth came instantly. And just like the first day they met, the three of them set off together.

Snow billowed around them. Great clouds blanketed the sky. It was late in the afternoon but already felt like night because of the shorter winter days. Indira glanced over at Maxi and couldn't help asking the obvious question. "Do you really need those sunglasses?"

Maxi smiled. "Oh. You haven't heard? Someone's an Editor-in-training!"

Indira let out a whoop. She pulled around to hug Maxi, which forced Phoenix awkwardly into the hug as well. "Of course you are! That's amazing, Maxi."

"It's no big deal," Maxi replied, clearly still giddy. "I'm just going to, like, save the world and stuff. It's totally a piece. People like us? We do it all the time."

Indira grinned again. A cold gust swirled around them as they turned the corner into Fable proper. She loved the city's current costume. The whole place looked like something out of a Charles Dickens novel at Christmastime. Snow caught in the nooks and crannies of each huddled building, and everything was backlit by glowing lanterns and bright windows. Indira thought the buildings all looked like they were snuggling together for warmth. She held tighter to Phoenix's arm as they headed straight for a familiar building. The Talespin was waiting for them.

"Are you sure about this, Indira?" Maxi asked. "I don't want you to be weirded out."

Indira nodded firmly. "I want it to be *our* place. Not her place. You know?"

Phoenix squeezed her arm a little and smiled. The three of them made their way inside and joined the packed crowd. Mr. Threepwood had already had a grand reopening earlier that week. The mirror had been removed until the Wizard Union could be certain no one else might use it for nefarious purposes. Indira stood in line, laughing with her friends, waving at a few folks who swung by to say hello. They ordered white mochas and rounded the corner.

Mr. Threepwood was waiting there. "Indira! I'm glad you could come."

She frowned. "Huh?"

"Oh!" Maxi rushed forward. "She doesn't know yet. It's a surprise."

"Right!" Mr. Threepwood gestured. "Follow me."

Indira shot her friends a look, but they just shrugged, half laughing, as Threepwood led them through the crowded room. A back table had been cleared away. Indira was surprised no one was sitting there, considering how packed the place was. And then she finally saw the golden plaque that had been nailed to the wall above the booth:

PERMANENTLY RESERVED

FOR INDIRA STORY

"Sacrifice is the highest call

of every character

in every story."

Thank you for thinking we were

worthy of yours.

"I had it made for the grand reopening," Mr. Threepwood said. "Thank you, Indira."

She didn't trust herself to speak without crying. It was the kindest thing in the world. Before Indira could burst into tears, though, Maxi swept her into the booth. These were *their* seats now. A permanent place in the world she loved so much. Phoenix made a grand toast. The three of them tipped their mugs together and sipped their drinks and spent the evening laughing about everything and nothing. Indira knew they were sitting in the same room where Brainstorm Ketty had attempted her dark deed, but that wasn't the memory she'd take with her as she continued her journey. She felt as if the memory of Brainstorm Ketty was already fading.

Her friendships—and this place—were too bright for anything dark to last for long.

Indira spent her final few days in Fable with friends and family. Her Author had officially begun outlining a story that featured her and a whole cast of other fun characters she couldn't wait to meet. Brainstorm Underglass had explained that heroic actions—such as saving an entire school from imminent destruction—often echoed between the worlds. Her victory had swirled into the mind of Darby Martin and taken hold. She was going to be a protagonist in an *actual* story.

It was hard to say goodbye when the time came, but it helped to know that it was far from permanent. She hugged Phoenix so tight that he coughed out smoke. He was planning on continuing his studies at Protagonist Preparatory, but he promised they'd see each other soon, and the little glint in his eye had her stomach leaping. Maxi lowered her sunglasses, winked once, and promised to watch out for her whenever she could. Mrs. Pennington made her pancakes one last time, and Patch held a rather adorable ceremony to make her his "official" sister. Indira left feeling that she was the luckiest person, in any world.

I would tell you what happened next in Fable, my dear reader, but you know what they say. . . . That's a whole other story.

EPILOGUE

The Real World

Penny and her friends were at the mall. It was a Friday night.

The three girls roamed through the stores, trying on clothes and laughing at odd mall people as they went. They saw those boys with the cute hair from that other middle school. One of them even waved.

It wasn't a particularly eventful night, but at some point Penny's friend Emma forced the group into a bookstore attached to one wing of the mall. It had been a while since Penny had read a book just for fun. It wasn't that she disliked books. There was just so much homework most nights that she found herself trying to escape *from* reading instead of *into* a good book.

Penny was walking around the store, flipping through the Neverland app on her phone, as Emma picked up books she thought they might like. Penny had stopped to text someone when one of the employees accidentally bumped into her. He was carrying a huge cardboard box full of books.

"Sorry about that," he said.

He had an average face, unmemorable. Penny said not to worry about it and glanced back at her phone, but as the man turned the corner, she noticed that he had dropped one of his books. Penny leaned over to pick it up. The cover caught her eye. A great lightning bolt striking the portrait of a young girl. She liked how messy the girl's hair looked. Hers was always so neat and straight, and it was such a pain to curl it into something more fun.

She glanced at the title: *Indira Story and the Thunder Brothers.*

Indira Story. It was an odd name. She really liked it. Penny had always felt boring, safe. But Indira Story? Now that name sounded bold. She could feel an adventure waiting there.

She flipped to the first page and started to read. It felt a lot like being brought back to life. The first five pages hammered their way into her heart. This Indira was tough. Penny liked that. Characters who backed down or shied away weren't any fun. It was the tough ones, the fighters, that she had always liked reading about. She read five more pages in a blink, and before long she felt that she was actually there, in the story. She felt as if the author knew her.

It felt good. To be known like that. To see herself in this imaginary world.

"Penny?" She wasn't certain how long she'd been reading, but Emma and the girls stood by the store's entrance. "We're heading out. Ready?"

Their stares almost had her setting the book on the nearest shelf. She hesitated for just a moment and then clutched it breathlessly to her chest. She walked straight to the register. A kind man helped her with the purchase and even slid a bookmark into it, free of charge.

Penny flipped to the first page and nudged Emma.

"You'll love the start of this book."

Emma, being edgy and unpredictable, asked Penny to read it to her.

She started at the beginning.

"Every cage has a key. . . ."

Acknowledgments

One of the most valuable lessons I learned in high school was that I am the main character of my own story. Too often I was sitting on the sidelines and waiting for someone else to steal the show. It took me a long time to learn that the main character isn't necessarily the strongest or the smartest person in the room. To be a protagonist, you simply have to be active in the outcome of your story. That's a choice we get to make every day, and I would urge everyone — but especially my young readers — to start engaging with the world. Ask great questions. Take risks. Make friends. Dance a lot. You are a worthy main character, and we can't wait to see where your story goes.

The second most valuable lesson I learned is that it is an *honor* to be a side character in the stories of others. We get to play the part of the best friend and the comic relief and a thousand other roles. I wanted to make sure I thanked the people who played those roles in my life.

To Anne Dailey, Lynn Flood, Susan Letts, and so many other teachers: Every day you walk into school and become a side character in the stories of hundreds of students. You are a voice of reason, a whisper of encouragement, an invitation into more. Thank you for what you do.

To Catherynne Valente: I still remember reading *The Girl Who Circumnavigated Fairyland in a Ship of Her Own Making* for the first time. Every page felt so full of wonder and joy and whimsy. Thank you for extending an important invitation to a writer who was still finding his way. Your prose gave me permission to have fun in my own stories. I am quite sure that *Saving Fable* would not exist if I hadn't read your books.

To Emily Easton, Samantha Gentry, and the team at Random House: Most people have no idea how much time and energy you pour into the books they eventually read and love. I'll always imagine you as the editors in this very book, sporting your Men in Black sunglasses as you sweep in to clean up my latest manuscript. Thank you so much for all that you do. As always, I owe my own Deus Ex Machina—Josh Redlich—all the thanks in the world for snapping his fingers and making things happen for this book. Couldn't have done it without you.

A huge thank-you to Maike Plenzke. Knowing how difficult it can be to bring something imagined to life, I was so grateful for your dedicated approach to the cover of this book. Indira, Maxi, and Phoenix are perfect. It was amazing to see your vision for the characters I have come to love. Thank you so much.

To Kristin Nelson and the team at Nelson Literary Agency: Thank you for being the first ones to believe in this project. I went through the query process with this book. It didn't find a home, but a few years later, I set it in your hands. Your faith in this story and my voice never wavered.

To my wife and son: Any color or brightness in the worlds I create comes from knowing you.

I'll end with a reminder to boldly be both a protagonist *and* a side character. You can start right now. Jump right into life. You get to decide what happens next. And at the same time, find the people who need you—whether it's for a day or for a year—and boldly step into their lives too. Offer an encouraging word. Make someone laugh. You never know how one little moment might echo. We could all use a little more of Mrs. Pennington in our lives.

About the Author

SCOTT REINTGEN is a former public school teacher and still spends his summers teaching middle schoolers dark fiction and fantasy at Duke Young Writers' Camp. The birth of his son has convinced him that magic is actually real. He lives in North Carolina, surviving mostly on cookie dough and the love of his wife, Katie. Scott is the author of the Nyxia Triad, and *Saving Fable* is his middle-grade debut. You can follow him on Facebook, on Instagram, and on Twitter at @Scott_Thought.